Only one woman

Eric Trask and his k

their past. Only their beloved foster father's funeral could drag them back to the small town of Shaw's Crossing. Eric is haunted by the memory of GodsAcre, the doomsday cult in the mountains where they were raised and the deadly fire that destroyed it, but one memory still shines bright...Demi Vaughan. Her lush, sexy mouth, her stunning green eyes. Their hot fling seven years ago crashed and burned in the worst possible way, and she's still mortally pissed at him...and more gorgeous than ever.

Second chances...

Demi Vaughan did her best to forget Eric Trask. They told her from the start that he was a train wreck, and she hadn't listened. He'd broken her heart and derailed her life, and she'd be damned if she'd let him do it again, now that she'd followed her dream and opened her own restaurant. But the years that passed have only turned Eric into a more concentrated version of what he'd always been—a flint-eyed, brutally ambitious, hyper-focused alpha male hunk. Just taller. Harder. As intoxicating as hell.

Demi tries to withstand Eric's magnetic pull, but she can't resist the all-consuming heat between them. But an old evil still lies low in Shaw's Crossing, and Eric's arrival has shocked it back into life.

Now it's not just their hearts that are in danger. It's their lives...

Visit me at my website, http://shannonmckenna.com for news and updates, but the best way to stay in touch is to subscribe to my newsletter! Here's the link, http://shannonmckenna.com/connect.php, so you'll never miss a new book or a great promo! Plus, look out for a special gift from me to subscribers...a free Obsidian Files novel!

HEADLONG

THE HELLBOUND BROTHERHOOD
BOOK TWO

SHANNON McKENNA

PRAISE FOR SHANNON McKENNA

"Blends an intensely terrifying psychic thriller with a mind-blowing erotic romance."
—**Library Journal**, on *Fade To Midnight*

"Blasts readers with a highly charged, action-adventure romance . . . extra steamy."
—**Booklist**

"Pulse-pounding . . . with searing sex and raw emotions."
—**Romantic Times**, 4 ½ stars

"Shannon McKenna makes the pulse pound."
—**Bookpage**

"Shannon McKenna introduces us to fleshed-out characters in a tailspin plot that culminates in an explosive ending."
—**Fresh Fiction**

"An erotic romance in a suspense vehicle on overdrive . . . sizzles!"
—**RT Book Reviews**

"McKenna expertly stokes the fires of romantic tension."
—**Publishers Weekly**

"McKenna strikes gold again."
—**Publishers Weekly**

ALSO BY SHANNON McKENNA

The Hellbound Brotherhood
Hellion
Headlong

The Obsidian Files Series
Right Through Me
My Next Breath
In My Skin
Light Me Up

The McClouds & Friends Series
Behind Closed Doors
Standing In The Shadows
Out Of Control
Edge Of Midnight
Extreme Danger
Ultimate Weapon
Fade To Midnight
Blood And Fire
One Wrong Move
Fatal Strike
In For The Kill

Stand-alone Titles
Return To Me
Hot Night
Tasting Fear

Anthologies

All Through The Night
(with Suzanne Forster, Thea Devine and Lori Foster)
I Brake For Bad Boys
(with Lori Foster and Janelle Denison)
Bad Boys Next Exit
(with Donna Kauffman and E.C. Sheedy)
Baddest Bad Boys
(with E.C. Sheedy and Cate Noble)
All About Men
(a single author anthology)

1

E ric Trask stared over Otis's flower-heaped coffin. His jaw ached from clenching his teeth.

He couldn't skip his adoptive father's funeral, but couldn't help reflecting that this display was a huge waste of extreme discomfort. The old man was gone. He couldn't appreciate the gesture, and no one else around here gave a flying fuck if Eric was present or not, other than his brothers Mace and Anton, who stood on either side of him.

They hated funerals like he did. For all the same reasons.

Yet here they were. Shoulder to shoulder, grim and stoic as befitted the sons of the Prophet, as well as sons of Otis Trask. Both those men had been heavy into grim stoicism.

A big crowd of Shaw's Crossing inhabitants had trooped down to the cemetery in the frigid wind for Otis's interment, which wasn't that surprising. Otis had been the chief of police in Shaw's Crossing for many years and had been highly respected in that role.

Some of those people were giving the Trask boys the side-eye from across Otis's open grave. Not that they gave a shit.

No side-eye coming from Demi Vaughan, though. She didn't look at him at all.

Eric hadn't expected to see Demi here in Shaw's Crossing. He would have thought she'd be long gone, as far from her asshole of a father as it was possible to get.

But here she was, right in front of him. No time to prepare. To brace himself.

Looking at Demi gave him a hard, twisting ache in his chest. Different and distinct from the pain and shock of losing Otis. The feeling surprised him. He'd thought all that stuff from the past was buried deep and covered with concrete. He'd gone to great lengths to bury it. He'd even congratulated himself on how completely he'd gotten over it.

He hadn't. Like he needed anything else to humble him today.

On the plus side, being ignored by Demi left him free to discreetly ogle her, which was well worth doing. Seven years hadn't dimmed her glow. She hadn't gotten any taller, but her small frame had filled out, and every part of it looked great. Her full lips were painted a hot red and her long brown ringlets fluttered in the gusts of wind. He keenly remembered her hair's satiny softness and scent.

She looked sexy and tough in her snug black skirt. Black tights on her strong, shapely legs. High-heeled boots. A nipped-in black leather bomber jacket. Hot.

She still had that regal, indomitable look he remembered so well in those striking, pale green eyes. Clear, challenging. Demi Vaughan stared the world down fearlessly, calling out any bullshit she saw for what it was. Including

Eric's own.

It had made him hard, when it wasn't driving him fucking nuts. Sometimes both at the same time.

Demi stared at Otis's casket, not sparing him a glance, but Benedict Vaughan, her asshole father, made up for it with an unwavering glare.

Eric gazed right back. A look that silently said everything he needed it to say.

I know what you did. I know what you are, you lying piece of shit. And so do you.

Ben Vaughan's mouth twisted. His eyes slid away.

Vaughan himself, unlike Demi, didn't look so good. Seven years ago he could still have been called a good-looking guy, but not anymore. His face was puffy and bloated. His eyes bagged, his jowls sagged. Demi's granddad Henry Shaw, acknowledged king and boss of Shaw's Crossing, stood with them, but old man Shaw didn't glower at Eric. He just gazed at Otis's coffin with hollow, reddened eyes, hunched and sad in his black wool coat. Henry Shaw and Otis had served in Vietnam together. Marines. They went way back.

Eric forced himself to look away. Eye contact with the Vaughan/Shaw family was unwise. His long-ago fling with Demi had ended about as badly as a fling could.

Which was to say, with him in jail, looking at eight to ten. It had been a near thing.

Mace tapped his arm. "Pinstripes and hair grease at three o'clock," he said under his breath. "What's wrong with this picture?"

Eric spotted the guy instantly when he looked in that direction. He should have noticed the man already, but he'd been shamefully inattentive. Wandering down memory lane, gawking at Demi's hypnotic green eyes. He tried without success to place the stranger. A new arrival, a visiting relative, somebody's new out-of-town boyfriend?

No. 'Professional asshole' came off the man like a bad smell. He had shifty snake eyes. A hook nose. Balding, with a greasy black widow's peak. Bad skin, a pimp suit, and a restless, seedy urban vibe that was all wrong for Shaw's Crossing.

"His buddy's at nine o'clock," Anton whispered.

Eric assessed the other guy. Bigger than the first, beefy and bearded and thick in the neck. Cold, shuttered eyes. A brainless thug in a suit. The two were a matched pair.

"Assholes that Otis sent to jail?" he speculated under his breath.

"Maybe," Mace said. "Come to gloat over his corpse."

"If it was just one, maybe," Anton replied, his voice barely audible. "Not two. Bet they're packing."

"Yah think?" Mace said. "Good. Let's separate these shitheads off from the herd after and pick a fight with 'em. I need to vent."

The hungry flash of eagerness in his younger brother's eyes made Eric nervous. "No," he hissed. "We talked about this. In and out. No drama. Stick to the plan."

He forced his attention back to the service. The familiar verses made his stomach clench, just like the drone of the organ and the sickly smell of lilies at the funeral home. Otis's sister-in-law Maureen had organized all of that.

But when they lowered the coffin into the ground...God, he dreaded that part.

Eric and his brothers had declined to give a eulogy, their memories of Otis being their own damn business, so the eulogy had been given by the man who replaced Otis as chief of police after his retirement, Wade Bristol. Big, beefy guy in his late fifties. Eric remembered him all too well. Bristol had been the guy who arrested him and read him his rights while Eric was lying in bed in the Granger Valley Hospital Intensive Care Unit.

He didn't hold it against the guy. Bristol had just been doing his job to the best of his ability.

The eulogy Bristol gave wasn't bad. Comprehensive. No surprises. Bristol droned on about Otis's courage, his exemplary life, his heroic and highly decorated military service, his selfless dedication to the community of Shaw's Crossing, etc., etc. All of which was absolutely true and could not be overstated, even if you tried.

Only Eric, Anton and Mace heard the subtext. Thirteen years ago, everyone had told Otis he was a goddamn lunatic for taking on a three-headed monster like Eric, Anton and Mace, after all the bad shit that gone down at GodsAcre. Just because it was the right thing to do, and nobody else seemed to be willing to do it.

Taking not one, not two, but three big, strong, massively fucked-up teenage boys with extensive combat training and a bizarre upbringing into his home...it was a disaster waiting to happen. Otis would be murdered in his bed. Everyone was sure of it.

But they hadn't hurt Otis. The old man was tougher than boot leather. He'd kept them in line. They'd all survived. It hadn't been easy, but Eric and his brothers had kept it together. Graduated from high school. Eric and Mace had even gone on into the military.

It was afterwards that everything had gone to shit. When Eric ran afoul of Benedict Vaughan and Henry Shaw for daring to raise his eyes to their precious princess.

And not just his eyes. Another part had risen up, as

well.

Bad scene, all around. But in spite of everything, sex dreams about Demi Vaughan regularly jolted him out of sleep, panting and sweating and stone hard.

He'd gotten well away from that fucking place after the charges were dropped. Started his life fresh, far away from Shaw's Crossing. He'd worked like a bastard. So had his brothers, each in his own way. They'd promised not just Otis, but also each other. They would not be defeated.

They would make something out of themselves. Prove all the shitheads wrong.

They'd done it, for the most part. Built good careers. Lives for themselves, such as they were. Strange but true. They owed it all to Otis. Boot-leather tough, cantankerous, lecturing Otis.

It still seemed impossible that he could be gone. A stroke, they said, but Otis had gotten himself checked out, and recently. He'd bragged to them about being as healthy as a horse for his age. Just some arthritis. No reason that he wouldn't go on being his own ornery, opinionated, difficult self for decades to come.

And suddenly he was gone. With no warning except for that strange voicemail he'd sent to the three of them the night before his death. Not one of them had managed to get back to him in time.

He hadn't said that he was sick. Just that he had something urgent to tell them about GodsAcre, and that they needed to be in Shaw's Crossing to hear it. He'd sounded agitated. Afraid, even. Insofar as it was impossible to imagine Otis afraid.

But the mystery message had never been delivered. Otis had died on his own dining room floor. No warning.

Like all the people in the death cluster.

He tried not to dwell on that, but the thought hung heavy in the air and Eric was sure he wasn't the only person thinking it. Thirteen years ago, right before the GodsAcre fire, fourteen people in Shaw's Crossing had dropped dead in the course of only twelve days. All deaths had been unexpected, but there was no evidence of foul play. Like Otis.

Perfectly natural deaths...but for their suspicious timing.

The Prophet's Curse, the town called it. Sometimes to their faces.

It was the creaking of the ropes as they lowered Otis's casket down that set him off. Eric started struggling to breathe. His chest was being crushed in a vise. His head roared, his heart thudded, his belly heaved.

He heard coffin ropes in his nightmares. Thirteen years ago, they'd laid the victims of the GodsAcre fire to rest. So many coffins. All of them closed. By necessity, since the thirty-eight bodies inside them had been charred beyond recognition.

Nine of those coffins had been very small.

He felt like a container swiftly filling up with icy liquid. *Fuck.* After all these years, and it still got to him, as bad as it ever was. His throat was closing, chest squeezing, no air, vision dimming. Heart thudding, *boom boom boom.*

Guilt, clawing inside him. For surviving it. Not being able to save them.

"...Trask? Mr. Trask? Excuse me? Sir?"

The funeral director spoke with the tone of someone who'd asked the question more than once. When he saw he'd gotten Eric's attention, he gestured at the heap of earth that had been uncovered from the shroud of fake green grass.

Time to finish this.

Eric took a handful of earth and tossed it down. Dark, thick clods scattered over the gleaming cherry-wood coffin that Maureen, Otis's sister-in-law, had selected. His brothers followed suit.

From the corner of his eye, he saw the guy with the greasy black hair and his thuggish pal stroll toward the access road where the mourners' cars were all parked. Good. He wouldn't have to wrangle Mace out of provoking them. He didn't have the juice for that fight today.

"Let's get the fuck out of here," Eric whispered to his brothers.

"Oh yeah," Mace agreed fervently.

They wasted no time putting distance between themselves and the rhythmic shovelfuls of dirt hitting Otis's coffin. They'd opted to park on the rough dirt road on the far side of the cemetery, far from the paved road where the mourners usually parked, for the purposes of a quick getaway. Why not avoid the stiff, awkward, socially mandated conversations from the get-go? They were doing everyone a favor by sparing them that necessity.

They were so intent on their escape, the black granite obelisk that loomed suddenly before them took them by surprise. They all stopped in their tracks at the same moment.

Shit. Of all the fucking gravestones to stumble across today. It had been so long since he'd seen it, he'd somehow forgotten it was even here.

"Oh fuck." Mace cleared his throat. "That's just great. My cup runneth over."

They stood there like they'd all forgotten how to move, gazing at the list of names chiseled into the dark granite. Jeremiah Paley, 'The Prophet,' the charismatic leader of the survivalist compound where the three of them had grown up, topped the list. The rest of the adults that had died there followed him.

Nine children were listed at the end, in order of age. Youngest last. Little Timothy Paley. Aged three years. Eric still remembered Timmy's high, squeaky voice.

The kids born up at GodsAcre had never had birth certificates. There were no documents to consult, no registries, no living adults with reliable information about the actual biological parentage or possible relatives of the smallest burned bodies.

Only Eric, Mace and Anton could bear witness to the fact that those little ones had ever existed at all. No one else on earth remembered them.

Those exclusive memories were a strange and heavy responsibility.

So they had all been listed as Paleys. Eric, Anton and Mace had been Paleys, too, having become Jeremiah's adopted sons after he had married their mother. They'd borne his name until Otis Trask adopted them, a year after the fire. When Otis had offered them his name, they'd jumped at the chance. A fresh start, not tethered to the past.

A memory floated up from Eric's mind as his eyes moved over the engraved inscription. Some church in town had got up a collection to buy a proper headstone for the victims of the fire and the minister had asked the three of them if there was anything special they wanted engraved on it.

Without thinking, Eric had blurted out a fragment of Jeremiah's favorite psalm. The Prophet had chanted it every time he got up in front of his congregation at GodsAcre.

He trains my hands for war so that my arms can bend a bow

of bronze.

The Prophet never quite pulled that off, but it wasn't from lack of trying. Jeremiah had been crazy as all fuck, but no one could doubt the old man's commitment.

"Hey, you! Paley boys! Come to pay your respects to your psycho killer dad?"

They turned to see an older woman coming across the grass toward them. Her fuzzed gray hair was dragged back in an unkempt braid, and she wore a baggy sweat suit that had once been beige but was no longer. Her face looked caved in and her reddened eyes, sunk deep into bruised looking hollows, were wild and staring.

"No, ma'am," Eric said. "We're here for Otis's funeral. And our name is not Paley. We're Trasks now. Legally. For twelve years now."

"I don't give a shit what's on your driver's license." Her loud voice was slurred. "I know the truth. You can't bullshit me. I know what you are. You're garbage."

Eric waited for a careful, measured moment before replying. "Know whatever you want, ma'am," he said evenly. "And I'll do the same. Good afternoon."

But they weren't getting off that easy. The woman hustled toward them faster, a little unsteadily. Eric caught a scent of alcohol coming off her from yards away.

"You have nerve, coming here. See that grave?" She pointed behind herself, at a small headstone to the side of them. "That's my husband. My Malcolm. Do you know how he died? The Prophet's Curse, that's how. I put him in the ground and just a couple weeks later, the fucking bastard who murdered him gets buried right across from him. Now I have to look at your killer dad's headstone every time I come to see Malcolm."

"He wasn't our dad." Mace's voice was flat. "He was our jailor."

"Bullshit. Garbage. Otis couldn't see the truth, but the rest of us did."

"Don't worry," Anton said. "We'll be out of your face soon. We won't be back."

"Bullshit. Liars. Just like the goddamn Prophet." Foamy spit dotted her purplish lips as she staggered closer.

Eric exchanged alarmed glances with his brothers. Jeremiah Paley's combat training had wired them up for lethal self-defense, but they had no playbook for drunken, unhinged female senior citizens on the rampage. They were on uncharted ground.

"Linda, that's enough." Wade Bristol's gruff voice sounded from behind them.

They turned to see the older man huffing up the slope, red faced. "You're not making sense," he scolded the woman. "These boys weren't responsible for Malcolm's death. They were just orphaned kids. Malcolm died of a stroke. You know that."

"Stroke, my ass! It was the curse!" Linda yelled. "Fourteen people in twelve days, Wade! And now Otis? He had a stroke, too! Just like Malcolm! It's starting up again, see? Now their own goddamn foster father is dead. Just like all the others. There's some fucking gratitude for you, eh?"

"Linda, calm down. They didn't have anything to do with—"

"Garbage!" she yelled. "They're garbage, and their fancy fucking suits can't change that!"

"Thank you, ma'am." Mace flicked an imaginary speck of lint from his lapel and adjusted his jacket on his broad shoulders. "Glad you like the threads at least."

"Shut up, Mace. You're not helping." Wade laid a soothing hand on Linda's shoulder. "Linda, calm down. Try to—"

"Go to hell." She flung off his hand and lurched back, almost toppling over in the process. "All of you go to hell. Keep your murdering freak father company there."

They silently watched her totter down the grassy slope.

"You're not driving, are you, Linda?" Bristol called.

She flipped him off without turning. "Fuck you, Wade."

Wade cleared his throat self-consciously as Linda retreated. "Sorry about that."

"It's nothing we haven't heard before," Eric replied.

"Well, you shouldn't have to hear it the day you put Otis in the ground."

"Don't sweat it," Anton said. "At this point, we barely notice."

"Thanks for saving our asses, Chief Bristol," Mace said. "Nick of time, too. Don't know what we would have done. That dame woulda finished us."

The police chief gave him a quelling look. "Don't be a smart-ass. I buried a friend today, too, Mace, so shut your damn trap."

Mace's eyes went big and solemn. He made lip-zipping gesture.

Chief Bristol cleared his throat again and stuck his hand in his pockets. "So, ah...I just came over here to make sure you boys knew about the reception."

They looked at him blankly.

"Reception?" Eric repeated.

Chief Bristol grunted. "Figured as much. Since you don't answer calls and you came late to the funeral. And left

12

before anyone could shake your hand or offer condolences."

"We don't have a lot to say to people here," Anton said. "What with one thing and another."

Bristol harrumphed. "That's a real unfortunate attitude."

"I guess it is." Anton's voice was unapologetic.

"Hmmph. Well." Chief Bristol's eyes went to Eric. "So I know we've had some tense moments in years past," he said. "I sure hope you won't hold it against me."

"I don't, Chief," Eric said. "It's all good. Past and gone."

Bristol looked cautiously relieved. "Well, that's fine, then. I think it would be a real good thing, a real appropriate thing, to go to that reception. For Otis's sake."

"Maureen didn't say anything about a reception," Eric said.

"Maureen didn't organize it," Bristol said. "There's a buffet spread at the Corner Café. You should drop by. Show some respect for the people who respected Otis. I'm heading over there now. I expect to see you there."

Eric stared after the man retreating back. Bristol's lecturing tone stuck in his craw, but he figured it came with the job. Otis had been a lecturer, too.

But Otis had worn authority far better than most.

They watched Bristol's big, unwieldy body stomping across the grass toward his pickup. When the vehicle was lost to sight in the trees, they turned to each other.

"Well, damn. That came out of nowhere," Anton commented.

"Yeah," Mace agreed. "Reception? What the fuck? Who's paying for it? Not Maureen, that's sure, the cheapskate bitch. She's still pissed that Otis left his house and land and truck to us instead of her two boys. She'll never forgive him for doing that."

"This morning, I gave her back the money she fronted for the funeral expenses," Eric said. "But she didn't mention anything about a reception."

"Probably didn't want us to come," Anton said. "Did she spit in your eye?"

Eric snorted. "Not until the check was in her purse."

Mace shook his head. "I'm not going to any goddamn reception, no matter what Chief Bristol says. I feel like hammered shit as it is. Why dial it up?"

"Agreed," Anton said. "I can only take this place in micro-doses. I blew over my safety limit a long time back."

Eric gave them a withering look. "Can't handle a little fish-eye? Pussies."

"Say whatever you want," Mason said. "You can't shame us into this."

"Fine," Eric said. "I'll stop in alone. Just long enough to reimburse whoever paid for it. I don't want to be indebted to anyone in this fucking place."

Mace snorted under his breath. "Why? We didn't organize it. I wouldn't voluntarily give the time of day to most of these people, much less cheese cubes and fruit skewers. After what all those pricks did to you seven years ago? Fuck 'em all sideways."

"Not an issue," Eric said, through his teeth. "Gone and forgotten."

"I doubt that the majority of the people at that reception will have forgotten it," Anton said. "I heard you say 'in and out and no drama.' But if you keep engaging with these people, you're going to generate some drama. It's a mathematical certainty."

14

"That's where you're wrong," Eric said. "I'm just going in to write a check. That gesture works on drama like a fire extinguisher. Poof, and everybody's smiling."

"You cynical bastard," Anton said. "And if Demi Vaughan is there, or her acid-spitting dad? I saw him staring at you from the minute you walked into the funeral home. A check isn't going to work on that guy's drama. He hates you so damn hard."

The look on Eric's face made Anton raise a cautious, soothing hand. "Easy," he said gently. "I couldn't help but notice that she was there. Right front and center. You noticed her, too. In a big, obvious way."

"That is a big affirmative," Mace chimed in. "Obvious as all fuck."

"Not. Relevant." Eric bit the words out through his teeth. "Ancient history."

Anton let out a sigh, a worried frown between his eyes. "If you say so."

But they didn't move. Both his brothers just stood there, staring at him with those worried, searching eyes until he wanted to smack the living shit out of them both.

"So?" he urged. "Get lost, you two. If you don't have the balls to go with me, then stop lecturing and let me get this over with."

"Watch yourself." Mace's voice was grim. "Remember what happened when you last had dealings with these people. It didn't end well. It almost destroyed you."

"It came out okay. I'm fine. She's fine. We all survived. We're different people now. Besides, she probably won't even be there. I'll just go say hello and thank you, write somebody a check and walk out. Clean slate. And we are done with this place."

15

"Okay," Anton said. "Happy cleaning. See you back at the ranch."

His brothers strode off toward Anton's gleaming Mercedes GLS. They got in and drove away without looking back at him. His brothers. Dragon-scale armored bad-asses. They always acted like they didn't give a shit. Never let anyone see behind their masks.

But he saw beneath it. Because he was just like them.

Otis's death had cut them all off at the knees. The old man had been like one of those volcanic granite monoliths that jutted up out of the turf like a preacher's pulpit. Weathering the storms, never changing, never giving any ground. A touchstone, a landmark. The most solid, reliable one that he'd ever had, other than Anton and Mace.

Otis hadn't been afraid of them. That had been the biggest gift that anyone could have possibly given them. It might have saved their lives.

He still remembered the day Otis had told them that the paperwork was ready if they wanted to take the Trask family name. He wanted to show his boys how a man stepped up and did the right thing. How he followed through on his word.

That gesture had been a big deal for them. A new name. A fresh start as a Trask.

Aw, shit. Thinking about that had messed him up. Now a big fist was squeezing his throat hard enough to crush it. The world had never felt particularly friendly to him, even at the best of times, but without Otis in it, it felt like a ticking bomb.

Which was exactly how Shaw's Crossing had seen him and his brothers.

To be fair, the townspeople had good reason to think it.

With the intensive combat training they'd had since early childhood, he and Mace and Anton were fully as dangerous as the suspicious residents of Shaw's Crossing believed them to be. Probably more so.

But only Otis ever knew it for a fact, and Otis never told.

Old Jeremiah Paley had been a Vietnam vet. Delta Force. Trained to kill in every conceivable way. When he opened up GodsAcre to true believers, he trained the children who lived there for war. After the Scourge, they were to be the vanguard of virtue in the blasted aftermath. The army of the faithful. It was a great responsibility which required expertise in small arms, knives, hand to hand, marksmanship, strategy, explosives, military history, guerilla warfare tactics. Jeremiah had been a relentless teacher, and Eric, Anton and Mace had been his best students.

Before he went entirely nuts. In that final, awful year when everything had gone to shit.

Eric was surprised as he drove through the downtown area of Shaw's Crossing on his way to the Corner Café to see how the business district had grown. It was trendy and touristy now. He parked his car a couple of blocks away from the café and strolled past a number of high-end shops, noticing sports gear, jewelry, crystal art, fancy housewares, a bookstore, an art gallery, coffee shops, a taco place. Sushi, even, for fuck's sake. Marconi's Corner Café diner used to be the only place downtown for food. If you could even call it food.

The Corner Café looked different, too. Its decaying fifties era vertical neon CAFÉ sign was gone, replaced by a big carved, painted wooden sign. The big picture windows that fronted both sides of the street corner were lavishly decorated with grease-pencil color drawings. Autumn leaves, pumpkins, a witch on a broomstick.

It wasn't until he was right in front of the diner, in full sight of everyone crowded inside, that he focused on the words carved into the wooden sign.

Demi's Corner Café. The *fuck?*

Wade Bristol was inside, leaning over a buffet table. His face brightened when he saw Eric. He beckoned with a big hand piled with mini-burgers heaped on a napkin.

Benedict Vaughan saw him at the same moment, and choked on his wine. He grabbed a napkin from a napkin fan on the table, wiping his mouth, and flapped his hand at Eric in disgust. Shooing him off as if Eric were a raccoon knocking over garbage cans.

That fucking settled that. Eric pushed the door open and walked in.

Bristol lifted his glass to Eric. "Good to see you. Glad you decided to drop by. Anton and Mason chickened out, I take it?"

"You didn't tell me the Corner Café was Demi's." He could not control the accusatory tone that came out of his mouth.

"I'm surprised that Otis didn't tell you himself," Bristol said. "He loved eating here. The food is good. Much better than Ricky's ever was. Demi runs a tight ship. Great pie. And you need to talk to her anyhow."

"I do? Why?"

"She was the one who found Otis the other morning at his house. She was at the ICU with him when I showed up. And she was with him when he passed. She's also hosting this reception. All by herself. I just thought you should know."

Eric just stared at the police chief, his mind stalled out.

"I, uh…didn't know."

"'Course not. How could you know? You've been too busy making sure nobody ever got a chance to talk to you."

Then Demi turned her head and met his eyes.

The contact zapped his mind blank, his mouth dry. She looked right inside him with those wide, light green eyes, as if he were made of clear glass. Everything lit up. In one swift, blazing assessment, she saw everything he was. Everything he'd ever been.

Everything he'd tried so hard forget.

2

Just another guest. Keep busy. Keep smiling.
Slow down, heart. This speed is inappropriate.
Of course, her heart then galloped faster, out of pure spite.

"I can't believe he has the balls to just walk in here like nothing ever happened."

That was Dad, refilling his wine glass. From the looks of him he'd already had a few glasses, but she knew better than to comment.

"It's a reception for Otis, Dad." She kept her voice even and neutral, as was her habit when she had to speak to her father. "He's Otis's son. It would be strange if he didn't come."

"Otis was not his father." Wine glugged into Dad's glass. "Otis was his benefactor, not his father, which is more than that low-life ever deserved. Otis was crazy to take on those boys. They were ruined before he even tried to put his stamp on them. It was a blessing Moira was already gone when he took them in. Those wild animals in her house…it would have broken her."

Demi kept her mouth shut, ignoring him by force of habit. It was a struggle to find something to look at in her restaurant that was not Eric Trask.

Then her gaze landed on those funeral crashers she'd seen at the interment, who were currently stuffing their faces with bacon wrapped asparagus and salmon pastries. One of the men, the bigger one with heavy cheeks and the beard, caught her eye and gave her a big, unpleasant smile before his gaze dropped to her breasts and stuck there.

Those two needed to be told to leave, and her father needed to back off. She knew better than to defend Eric to him. But she just couldn't smile and nod anymore.

"What?" Her father's voice sharpened. "What's that look on your face?"

"It's just my face, Dad," she said evenly. "It's just me having my own opinion whether you're interested in it or not. You should recognize that look by now."

"Do not let him near you." Dad's voice was dangerously loud. "You know better."

"I'm fine. Don't worry. And now, if you'll excuse me..."

"Hey! Where do you think you're—hey! What the hell?" Her father caught up with her and grabbed her arm. "Do not go and talk to him! Are you crazy?"

"I'm giving him my condolences." His fingers bit deep into her forearm. "It's customary after a death in the family, remember? Mom taught me that."

She wrenched her arm free and made her way through the crowd toward Eric, uncomfortably aware that her father was following close behind. No way to get rid of him.

But the closer she got to Eric, the more her awareness of Dad's presence faded away. The hot vital energy emanating from him blotted out everything else.

Eric Trask made her restaurant look so much smaller. His size, his grace, that controlled, subtly predatory vibe. He seemed out of place. Too powerful and charged with energy for his environment. A sleek panther prowling through a henhouse.

He'd always been gorgeous. He'd been stunning in high school, and he'd been even more stunning seven years ago when he was twenty-four.

Now he was all that, but times ten. Leaner. Honed. The crinkles in the corners of his eyes were deeper, as were the sexy grooves carved around his mouth.

Eric seemed even taller than she remembered. His thick, dark blond hair was shorter, sleeker. No longer the shaggy, grown-out buzz cut she remembered.

Too bad she hadn't caught up a little in the height department. He was a head taller than…no, a head and probably some neck. Her eyes were on level with his collarbone.

Sometimes it sucked to be short.

His shoulders were massive. The shape of his powerful thighs made his suit pants look incredibly good. The elegant suit fit him perfectly. She could spot a costly, well-cut suit from a distance, but it was the lithe, hard body inside that made the magic happen.

His bright, silvery gray eyes burned into hers. She held herself as tall as she could, which wasn't very, and refused to allow herself to look away. Dad was hissing something unpleasant behind her, but she couldn't be bothered to understand him.

No one could expect her to. Not while walking straight into the force field of seething sexual readiness that had always surrounded Eric Trask.

She'd gotten off on that dangerous vibe back in her wild and foolish youth. Not anymore. Eric Trask had put a huge dent in her life. She'd learned her lesson well.

No one, but no one, would ever fuck her over like that again.

She had to make sure he understood that. She'd need a few well-chosen words for that purpose. She had no idea where the hell she was going to find them, or how she was going to string them together when she did.

Demi stopped far enough away to avoid any social confusion about a potential handshake, or God forbid, a hug or a kiss. She gave him a stiff nod.

"Hello, Eric." Her voice was little too high, but she got the words out.

"Demi." His voice was still so deep and rough, a little scratchy, like she remembered. It brushed over her. Sensual friction against the secret nerves inside her.

She shivered. *Oh stop it, Demi. Just stop. You can't.*

His throat worked. He was swallowing nervously. Good. She was glad he wasn't completely unaffected by this encounter. He should be ashamed of himself. Falling-through-the-floor ashamed.

"My condolences," she said. "Otis was a great man, and a good friend to me. He'll be missed around here."

He acknowledged that with a nod. "Yeah," he said. "Thanks."

The silence that followed was made even more uncomfortable by the fact that everyone else in the room had gone deathly quiet in an attempt to listen in.

"Have something to eat," she told him. "There's wine in the ice bucket over there, and beer and soft drinks in the cold case. Please, help yourself."

"Oh, yeah," Eric said. "About that. Wade told me you paid for the reception."

"It was my idea, and it was a pleasure," she said. "I was glad to do it. In Otis's honor."

"Let me cover the expense," Eric said. "Whatever you would have charged someone else to organize something like this. I'll write you a check right now."

"No, thank you," she said.

"I insist." Eric's voice was obdurate.

Her spine extended to its utmost, chin rising up. "You can insist all you want. It won't change a thing. Otis was my friend, and one of my best customers. This was my idea, and it'll be my expense."

Eric's brows furrowed. "Let us at least contribute. Me and my brothers."

"No, but thanks for asking. Do your brothers intend to stop by?"

Eric hesitated. "They're pretty broken up about Otis. They didn't feel up to company."

She nodded. "I understand. Please pass my condolences on to them, too."

"Will do," Eric said.

More silence. People edged closer, nibbling their tidbits, eyes averted.

Eric didn't seem aware of the intense interest surrounding them. He just studied her face with his narrowed silver eyes, and looked around, subjecting her restaurant to the calm analysis. Drawing his own inscrutable conclusions. Not that she cared. He could think what he liked. His opinion meant nothing to her.

His gaze stopped on the portrait of Otis she had set on

an easel next to a flower arrangement in the center of the room. It had been rendered in colored chalk on one of her menu boards, and it was an excellent likeness. Otis was unsmiling, gazing thoughtfully off into the distance. Elisa, the woman who had drawn it, had real talent. With minimal, economic strokes, she'd captured Otis's essence. His spare, craggy face and hook nose, his flat, uncompromising mouth. The toughness. The strength.

But his eyes were kind. The portrait caught it all.

Eric gazed at it for several minutes. "Who did the portrait?" he asked finally.

"One of my employees did that," she said. "Elisa Rinaldi. Isn't it awesome? I had no idea until this morning. Bruce Whitehorse found the photo for me in the archives of the Shaw's Crossing Chronicle and brought it over yesterday. I was just going to put that up on the easel. Then Elisa stayed up all night drawing that from the photo."

"It's excellent," he said.

Demi beckoned to Elisa, who was just emerging from the kitchen with a tray of savories. Elisa deposited her tray on one of the tables, brushed her hands on her apron and approached with a smile. She was a pretty girl, tall and slender with a thick braid of heavy dark hair hanging down her back and large golden brown eyes.

Elisa was a lucky find. She hadn't been at the restaurant long, barely three months. She'd stopped at the café one day and offered to draw decorations on Demi's chalkboard menus in exchange for some lunch. The drawings had proven to be gorgeous so Demi had offered her dinner and asked for more.

In the end, Elisa had stayed. She bunked in the little studio apartment Demi owned above the restaurant. Aside from the chalkboard art, she helped out with everything else that needed doing, from waiting tables to bookkeeping. The only thing Demi didn't like about having Elisa around was when she changed up the menus and had to erase the beautiful chalk drawings. That always hurt.

"Elisa, this is Eric Trask, Otis's son," she said. "Eric, this is Elisa Rinaldi, the artist who did Otis's portrait, as well as the other art work you see here. We keep her busy."

Eric shook Elisa's hand. "My compliments. It's excellent. Did you know Otis?"

"Only a little," Elisa said. "I haven't been working here long, but he came in here quite a bit. He was a wonderful man. I'm so sorry for your loss."

Eric turned back to the portrait. "You can't erase that picture."

Demi and Elisa looked at each other, taken aback. "Ah, okay," Demi said. "I hadn't really thought about it, but we certainly don't have to. I probably wouldn't be capable of erasing that picture if I tried."

"I want to buy it," Eric said. "Is it for sale? Can I put some kind of fixative on it?"

"Sure. I'll take care of that for you," Elisa said quickly. "And no, it's not for sale. It's yours, free of charge. Get Demi a new chalkboard for her soup menu and we're good."

"Please, don't worry about it," Demi said. "You're right, the picture is special and should be preserved."

"Thanks." Elisa's smile was brief and shy. "I'm pleased you like it, and that you want to keep it. Now excuse me. I have to put more ice in the wine buckets."

The two of them watched her weave through the crowded room, with an air of relief at escaping from their focused attention. Elisa was polite and friendly, but skittish and elusive. Demi was still waiting for the right moment to ask Elisa what her story was, but she was afraid that questioning her might startle the other woman away.

So she watched and waited. And wondered.

Eric watched Elisa emerge from the kitchen with bucket of ice. "Some cash would help out her emergency getaway fund," he commented. "Hiding out is expensive."

"Hiding?" Demi gave him a sharp look. "You don't know a thing about her. That's a big leap. She hasn't said word one to me about hiding."

"No one who's hiding would advertise it. She doesn't have to say it. It's written all over her. Whatever social security number she gave you, it's not hers."

She just blinked at him. "And is that any of your goddamn business?"

"Not at all. My apologies. Does five hundred bucks sound fair for the picture?"

"Eric, she just gave it to you. Didn't you hear her say it?"

"Right. Like you just gave the reception. At your own expense." He sounded irritated. "I want to pay for something, so I'll pay for this."

"Fine," she said. "Work it out with Elisa. It's none of my business."

"Wade told me it was you who found him," he said. "At his house."

Demi's throat tightened as she nodded.

"Otis's property is six miles out Vensel Road," Eric said. "What brought you out that far? There's nothing past his house. That road turns into a logging track less than a mile after you go past the house, until it hooks up with Long Prairie."

"I was bringing him pie," Demi admitted.

The grooves between his brows deepened. "Pie?"

"He had a sweet tooth. He liked my Dutch apple pie. It reminded him of something his wife used to make when she was alive. So I brought him a couple of pieces that morning. No one came to the door when I knocked, so I peeked through the window. Saw his legs stretched out on the floor. I broke the glass. Let myself in. Called the ambulance."

"Six miles on that old dirt road? Just to bring him some pie?"

Demi folded her arms over her chest. "Yes."

Let him wonder. She didn't justify herself to anybody anymore. Least of all him.

Truth was, she brought pastry to quite a few of her elderly ex-customers. She'd gotten into the habit a couple years ago, when old Georgia Visser, who lived down at the Kettle River Trailer Park, got macular degeneration and lost her driver's license. Georgia had used to come into the Corner Café twice a week to indulge in a slice of Demi's cream pies, so Demi made sure that some pieces of her cream pies came to Georgia, at regular intervals. It was a good excuse to check in, have a chat, connect. Georgia loved the visits, and the pie.

This experience at Otis's house reminded her too much of when she'd found Mom in her bedroom after her heart attack, three years before. She'd been sleeping badly ever since. "I wish I'd come earlier." Her voice had gotten thick.

Their eyes met. She felt a peculiar flash of emotion go through her, as if she'd tuned into some frequency that he was producing, and could feel what he was feeling. The pain he tried so hard to bury. He was an expert at hiding it, but she saw the dark and the cold, the howling emptiness in his eyes. She felt it intensely.

It took her breath away. Her ears rang. Heart thudding

hard and fast...

The moment passed. She started to breathe again. God, that had been awful.

Eric looked cautiously alarmed. He knew something had happened, but didn't understand exactly what.

Oh. Yes. Of course he looked alarmed now. He was looking over her shoulder at Dad, who loomed behind her, shooting daggers with his eyes.

Eric's gaze swept the room with a puzzled frown. "Hey, where's your mom?"

Her father inhaled sharply, but Demi cut in before he could speak. "She died about three years ago. Unexpected heart attack."

"I'm very sorry to hear that."

Another tense, awkward pause as Eric looked straight back into her father's face.

That was remarkable. Staring down the guy whose luxury car he had stolen and run off a cliff. With that hard, unflinching gaze. That must take steely nerve.

Eric looked back at her. "So you run a restaurant now," he said. "Last I heard, you were working for the family business out in Spokane. Cooking is what you always dreamed of, right? I'm glad for you. You finally broke the chains that bound you."

"Get out." Her father's voice was choked with rage. "Get the hell out of here."

"No, Dad." Demi made her voice stern. "This is my place, and you don't have the right to throw anyone out. And speaking of throwing people out, would you gentlemen excuse me? I have to go tell those funeral-crashing freeloaders over there to get lost." She seized her father's arm, tugging him. "Dad, come along and give me moral support."

"No! Stay away from them!"

She dropped his arm, startled by the panic in his voice. "Dad? What the hell?"

"Don't talk to them here." Dad's face was shiny with sweat. "It's inappropriate for the occasion. I'm not in the mood for ugly scenes."

The lines around Eric's eyes crinkled with silent amusement. "Could've fooled me," he said. "I'll remove them from the restaurant for you, if you want. My pleasure."

"This is no place for a brawl," her father snapped. "It's out of the question."

Eric shrugged. "A brawl is when both sides get in some licks and stuff gets smashed. It wouldn't be that way. They'd just find themselves lying in the gutter with a bump on their heads and no clear memory of what happened." He looked into her eyes. "I wouldn't mind blowing off some steam. Say the word, and enjoy the show."

She opened her mouth. Then words wouldn't come out of it, because he was smiling at her now, and oh, God. Those beautiful grooves around his mouth turned her totally nonverbal. Damn the man. She couldn't react to him that way. Could. Not.

"Demetra." Dad's scolding voice jolted her out of it. "You're not considering this, right? Tell me you're not."

"Butt out, Dad," she said. "No, Eric. Thank you, but I don't need any help managing my business. And I don't need to be rescued."

Eric's smile faded. "I didn't mean to make trouble for you," he said. "I just wanted to thank you for throwing the reception. You're sure you won't let me help? The reception, the freeloaders. Anything."

"I'm sure," she said. "But thank you."

SHANNON McKENNA

But Eric kept standing there, ignoring her father's muttering and gazing into her eyes. To her dismay, she started to feel it again. Tuning in to him. The grief, that sharp, aching clutch in her throat. Tears rushing into her eyes. Oh, for fuck's sake. Not now.

She reached out and placed her hand awkwardly on his shoulder. "I'm so sorry about Otis." Her voice vibrated so oddly, it hardly felt like her own. "I know how important he was to you."

Eric stared down at her hand like he couldn't believe it was there.

"For Christ's sake," her father muttered under his breath. "Just look at you. You never learn. I cannot watch this."

"So go home, Dad," she said. "It would be better."

Dad set down his wine glass on the buffet table and shoved his way through the crowd. People made way for him and then swiftly closed ranks, too intent upon the spectacle she and Eric were making to bother watching her father storm out the door.

Insane. She was actually touching him. Voluntarily. After everything that had happened. Everything he'd done to her. Breaking her heart. Trashing her life.

His body beneath the suit coat felt dense. Taut. Hot.

He covered her hand with his own. It was deliciously warm, the contact zinging through her body. He just kept it there. A deliberate, insistent pressure.

Sexual awareness rushed through her. Irrational, baseless pleasure, based on nothing but his eyes on her, the warmth and pressure of his hand. The back of her hand had never been an erogenous zone before, but now the contact pulsed and glowed and shimmered inside her, spreading out

31

from that point as if he were touching her between her legs, like only he could do. His immense skill at touching her. Natural as breathing.

She jerked back her hand and Eric rocked back slightly. His cheeks were flushed.

"Thank you," he said. "For helping Otis. And bringing him pie."

"Sure." She brushed away sudden tears. "Wish I could have helped more."

"I'll be back for the chalkboard picture after the reception," Eric said. "Before I leave town. Probably tomorrow. Day after, at the latest."

"Fine," she said. "I'll tell Elisa to expect you."

Demi stared after his broad back, his tapered waist, his incredibly fine, tight ass as he walked out the restaurant door. He walked the length of the picture windows, turned the corner and was lost to sight.

She shook with the urge to run to the door. Poke her head out and follow him, at least with her gaze. Her eyes felt hungry. She didn't want to waste a single instant.

Like she hadn't had enough of being poor dumped Demi, humiliated and abandoned. An object of pity and scorn. Fuck that.

She'd be dignified if it killed her.

3

Eric slowed down on the sidewalk on his way to the car when he spotted Benedict Vaughan on the sidewalk, about a block ahead of him. Vaughan stopped, appalled, to stare at Eric's gleaming black Porsche 991 GT3.

Vaughan's bellowed profanity could be heard all the way down the block. He punctuated his outburst by kicking one of the tires.

In the meantime, Eric ducked into the recesses of the brick entryway to the old brewery, which had been transformed into a trendy, steam-punk themed pub. He waited there, well out of sight. Not hiding, just avoiding drama. Like a fucking grown-up.

Vaughan was drunk, hostile and riled up. Talking to him would inevitably end in conflict. What could it help, or change? Both of them knew the truth. There were no revelations to be had. Ben Vaughan would never admit to wrongdoing. Why should he? He'd won that round and Eric had lost. End of story. He had to let it go, and lurking in an entryway to avoid conflict was what letting go looked like today.

In and out, no drama. And maybe, just maybe, he and his brothers could get the hell of this town before the Prophet's Curse had time to wind itself up and start fucking with them again.

He hoped Vaughan wouldn't key the Porsche. Though it would serve Eric right if he did. Driving that particular car into this town was a direct eye-jab to the guy. Blatant provocation. The car said everything Eric felt about what had happened seven years ago. How badly he still wanted to punish that lying, scheming asshole.

Breathe. Wait. Don't be a dick. Walk away. Live your goddamn life. Don't fuck it up again.

Up ahead, he heard the hollow thud of a car door closing. A motor started up. He heard the grind and squeal of tires against asphalt. Vaughan was driving away. Angrily.

Free and clear. He let himself exhale, and was about to step out onto the sidewalk to head toward his own car when he heard the hushed voices approaching.

"...having a shit fit, right out on the street. Fuckin' alkie asshole. He could get wasted and start blabbing and blow everything." A man's voice, deep and rough.

"Can't really blame him for freaking out." This voice was soft and oily. "Gotta hand it to that fuckface. He's got some balls, driving into town in that fuckin' Porsche. Like he's spitting right into Benny's fat face."

"Yeah. Dumb fuck had it coming." The two chuckled together.

"Did you see that look he gave the girl back in the restaurant? I'm-gonna-fuck-you-and-you're-gonna-like-it. It was beautiful. Made the dumb bitch all quivery and wet right

34

in front of her dickhead dad. And then the Porsche. Poor Benny's probably bustin' a blood vessel right about now."

Eric eased out of the shadows of the entryway, peering past the wall. Just an instant was enough to confirm his suspicion. The men speaking were the funeral freeloaders. Widow's Peak and his buddy, the slab-faced bearded guy with no neck.

No-Neck went on talking. "Can't blame the guy. I was lookin' at her, too. I wouldn't mind givin' some to that girl myself."

"Take a number and get in line." Widow's Peak's voice was sharp. "Anybody hits that, it's gonna be me. I got seniority. But the boss won't sign off on that yet, so put it out of your head. We're lying low for now."

"For now," No-Neck said. "When the time comes, I don't care if you go first. I don't mind sharing…long as I get to watch."

The two men snorted in ugly laughter.

"The boss'll be pissed that those assholes are back in town," No-Neck said.

"I know," Widow's Peak said. "Lucky for us, he'll come down on Benny first. Here, you drive. I gotta text the boss."

Keys jingled as they were tossed from hand to hand. "Where to?" No-Neck asked.

"Where do you think? We rattle old Benny's chain. He needs a pep talk."

The car doors shut and the engine roared. From his spot behind the brick pillar, he saw a big black SUV pulling away.

Eric's body buzzed with alarm. No time to think this through or figure out what it meant. They'd been talking about Demi and he had to know more. Right fucking *now*.

He stepped out onto the sidewalk, catching the taillights of the SUV before they turned, on their way to shake down Benedict Vaughan.

Back away slowly, meathead. Do not fucking touch it. Don't you dare.

There it was, the voice of reason in his head. But those guys had slimed Demi. Fantasized out loud about gang-raping her as soon as their boss gave them free rein. What in the *fuck* had he just heard?

One thing was sure. Demi was in danger, because her prick loser of a dad had put her there. Wow, what a shocker.

And now—*move.* He sprinted to his car, regretting the self-destructive impulse that had made him drive here in the Porsche. He liked to think he had nothing to prove to anyone in this town, but the Porsche gave him the lie. It was too damn noticeable. Even to the people who didn't know the whole fucking tragic saga of his life.

Too late for regrets. He knew how to get to the Vaughan mansion, but even if he hadn't, he could see that black SUV heading up Osborn Grade toward the heights.

He followed it, driving right past the turn-off for Cedar Crest Drive, then parking off the street on a little utility road that led off to nowhere in the woods. The car was visible from the street if you were looking on purpose, but he hoped that no one would have reason to look. It was right where he'd parked his old car, the Monster, on that fateful night seven years ago. Not a thought to be dwelling on right now.

But he couldn't avoid thinking it as he cut through the woods. He'd memorized all the vantage points of the Vaughan house's security cameras on the screens he'd seen, that night he'd spent in that house while her folks were gone.

The night he'd been trapped, framed. Almost killed.

Don't think about it, he reminded himself grimly. This wasn't about that. This was about Demi's safety and the assholes who meant her harm. That was all he was considering here.

His own history, his issues with Vaughan, all of that was completely off the table.

He skirted the back yards of three other luxury homes before coming up behind the Vaughan lot. The largest house, the biggest lawn, the stateliest shade trees.

Demi had showed him the best route to stay out of the camera's view. It came back to him, as clear as crystal. After all these years of trying so hard to forget.

The goons' black SUV was parked right in front of the house. The two men had been banging on the front door, and were now coming around to the side porch.

"Hey! Benny!" Widow's Peak was calling. "We know you're in there. We saw you heading home, and we see your car in the garage. Come out and talk to us. Or else we'll just come on in. You decide."

Widow's Peak wasn't even trying to be discreet. The neighbors could probably hear every word he said at that volume.

The door to the side porch opened. Eric crouched down, the young fir boughs screening his face, edging forward until he saw Benedict Vaughan framed in the doorway. His mouth was drawn downward, like a man in chronic pain.

"Keep your goddamn voices down," he hissed. "I told you to park around the block and cut through the back if you have to talk to me!"

"Benny, my man. Nice to see you, too," Widow's Peak said. "Nice buffet at that reception, huh? I was sure hungry after all that burying. That sexy girl of yours can lay a spread like a fucking boss. Besides being hotter than hell. Can I marry her?"

Benedict just scowled. "What do you want from me?"

"Aw, Benny. Be nice. I'm asking to join your family!"

"You shouldn't be here," Benedict insisted. "Anyone driving by could see you!"

"What, are you ashamed of us, Benny?" It was No-Neck speaking. "Felix, I think that Benny's ashamed of us."

"I think you're right, Rocco," Felix said, his voice mock-sad. "Aw, Benny. You cut us to the quick. After all these years. All we've been through together."

"Stop fucking around with me and tell me what he wants," Benedict growled.

There was an ominous silence as Felix and Rocco looked at each other.

"What he's always wanted. From the beginning." The mock friendliness was gone from Felix's voice. "What he bought and paid for when he bailed you out of that mess in Tacoma. You know your job description. You ensure us the privacy we need, by any means necessary. You're not delivering on your promises. The boss isn't pleased."

"There's no way I can control the situation completely." Benedict sounded hunted. "I tried for years to buy that place. The property is worthless, even for grazing. That stubborn bastard said no just to spite me."

"Yes, we know. You tried to get sneaky, but he was on to you."

"I don't know why he was so fucking pig-headed about it—"

"Because he smelled a rat, Benny. Because that's what you are. A rat. You fucked it up. All this loss and suffering, it's

38

all on you. Loser."

"It's not my fault that I—"

"No one is interested in your fucking excuses. The boss least of all. You're a fuck-up. If you can't do your job, you're a liability."

Benedict shuffled back a step, shrinking back toward the shelter of his house. "Are you threatening me?"

Felix and Rocco exchanged evil smiles.

"I don't know, Benny," Felix said softly. "Do we need to?"

Benedict's hands went up in a swift, placating gesture. "No. No, you don't need to do anything. I'll fix it. I'll take care of it."

"You do that. Or else we will. In ways you will not enjoy."

The two men took their time strolling away. Benedict waited, supporting himself by the door frame, until he heard their engine start up. He emerged onto the porch, peering out to make sure the car was really pulling away.

Then he lurched forward and vomited over the porch railing into the rosebushes.

He draped over the railing like a limp rag, spitting and coughing. Finally he pushed himself up, wiping his mouth and cursing as he went inside.

Eric was unable to move. His body hummed with combat readiness, but he had no one to fight. No place to put the adrenaline. It made him feel like his brain was on fire.

Benedict Vaughan was in over his head and getting squeezed. Well and good. Couldn't have happened to a nicer guy. Eric wouldn't give a shit, if not for Demi.

Any threat to her, anything at all, was unacceptable.

He wondered what Vaughan was supposed to do for

these assholes, but dismissed the thought. Who cared. The details were none of Eric's business. Properties, privacy, whatever. Let the guy drown in his own shit. He'd done it to himself.

But Eric couldn't let him pull Demi down with him.

Problem was, Eric was the last person she would ever believe, convinced as she was that he was a thief, a liar, and a user. Plus, he had every reason in the world to nurse a grudge against her father. His credibility was for shit. On every possible level.

Also, having been here at all, at Vaughan's house, spying on him from the bushes—that looked bad in and of itself. Like, restraining-order bad.

But even if she didn't believe him, he had to say something. At least the information would be registered in her mind, even if she dismissed it. She'd be on her guard.

He had to tell her what he'd seen. Then run like hell before she ripped his head right off his neck. Or had him arrested. Again.

On the bright side, she couldn't possibly think any worse of him than she already did.

4

"Sorry, sir, but we're closed today for a private event." It was Tasha speaking, after the bell over the restaurant door tinkled. Demi pricked up her ears from the kitchen.

"I know. I'm here to talk to Demi."

Eric's voice. Deep, scratchy and resonant. Beautiful. Inappropriate excitement exploded through her body. She took a second to chill it down before she emerged from the kitchen, where she'd been packing up takeaway trays of buffet leftovers.

Eric stood by the door, waiting. Tasha gave her a questioning look.

"Hi, Eric. It's okay, Tasha. You can go ahead and take off. Do you have the delivery list straight? And the addresses?" She piled the last of the cardboard trays into the box and carried it out into the restaurant floor.

"Right here on my phone," Tasha assured her. "Dorothy Pilcher, Rodrigo Santiago, Georgia Visser, Rodney

Bellows, Anne Fogarty and Betty Trumball. Right?"

"Exactly." She passed the box to Tasha. "And the last two trays in the box are for you and your folks. Make sure to give the one with the big blue sticker to Betty. She and her daughter are both diabetic, so there are no sweets in that one."

"Got it. Blue sticker for Betty. Thanks for the goodies for Mom and Susan."

"Can I carry that out to your car for you?" Eric asked Tasha.

"No, that's cool. I got it. Thanks, though. I'm off." Tasha gave Demi a speculative look, then gave Eric a longer, more appreciative one as she bumped the door open with her hip and maneuvered the box through it.

The two of them watched Tasha stow the box in the back of the Mazda that was parked right outside. Tasha got in, beeped a farewell and drove off.

Eric was the first to break the silence. "I recognize those names," he said. "All the people on that list are senior citizens. With limited means. Is this like Otis's pie?"

Demi felt oddly defensive. "They're all people who I'm sure would have liked to come to the funeral or reception or both, but couldn't for whatever reason. I wanted to include them. So what brings you back so soon? I expected you tomorrow or the day after for the chalk portrait."

"Decided to take care of it now," Eric said. "If I can."

"I see. Wait a sec. Elisa!" she called out.

Elisa came out of the kitchen, wiping her hands on an apron. "Yes?" She saw Eric and gave him a smile.

"Could you spray that fixative onto the portrait now?" Demi asked. "Is it a quick thing, or is it a process that takes time?"

"Oh, it's quick," Elisa assured her. "Let me run it

upstairs and I'll do it for you right now. Hang on. I'll be right back."

She disappeared out the side door that led to a breezeway through the building, leaving the two of them alone in the front of the restaurant. Locked in a breathless silence.

Eric dug into his pocket and put a wad of cash down onto the counter. "I stopped at the bank machine," he said. "Got some cash for her."

"She'll refuse it," Demi said.

"She can give it away. Or donate it to anyone she wants. Not my problem."

"You are one stubborn guy," Demi observed.

"Yes, I am."

More silence. It took fortitude to short-circuit her natural instinct to fill the silence with pleasant, face-saving chit-chat, like her mother had taught her to do. Let him fidget and squirm. Let him be exactly as uncomfortable as he deserved to be.

"It's nice of you to send those trays of food to the shut-ins," he said finally.

"Just good business," she said crisply.

"If you say so."

"Speaking of trays of leftovers, I can make one up for you and Anton and Mace, too. Seems appropriate, don't you think?"

"No, please don't worry about it," he said quickly.

"Hah. Too bad. Joke's on you. Protest all you want." Demi pulled out one of the big, wide paper cartons and set to work with the slices of pepper roasted beef. "Give it away or donate it to anyone you want, but you have to take it. That's my passive aggressive way of guilting Anton and Mace for not dropping by the reception."

"You can't guilt those two," Eric said. "They're impervious."

"I see. How about you?" The words flew out of her mouth before she realized how unprepared she was to hear his answer.

Eric was quiet for a long time before replying. "I'm more subject to guilt than either one of them," he said.

Demi snorted under her breath. "Well, that's unfortunate. For you."

"I suppose," he said.

She shoveled stuff haphazardly into the tray, feeling her face go hot. "Well," she said finally. "I have a bunch of things to deal with in the kitchen, so I'm going to leave you here to wait for Elisa on your own." She placed the tray next to him. "Take this when you go. Give your brothers my best, and have a good evening." *And a nice life. And fuck you very much.* She spun around and marched away.

"Demi, I have to talk to you."

She stopped short with her back to him. The cheerful banter of the kitchen staff came suddenly into the foreground, along with the clatter of pots and pans and cutlery.

"No, Eric," she said. "We don't have anything to talk about."

"It's important. And urgent. Please."

"What about?" She still couldn't move. It was like every muscle in her body had contracted to stone-hard tension, waiting for his answer.

"I don't want to be overheard." Eric moved toward her. His voice was quiet, but its depth and resonance hummed through her, as if she was a bell that had been rung.

Or was still ringing, more like.

He stopped, almost close enough to touch her. She could feel that quality he projected. The heat. That overwhelming energy that hung around him like a force field.

"Can we go into the meeting room?" He gestured toward the room off to the side where she put the birthday parties. "It's private."

She stepped back. "No, Eric." Her voice vibrated with anger. "We cannot go into the meeting room. There is nothing private between us. Say what you need to say to me, and make it quick. I'm busy."

"It's about those funeral crashers that were in here earlier," he said. "The ones I wanted to throw out."

"What about them? They turned out not to be a problem. Much less of a problem than you. They left right after you did."

"I know they left," Eric said. "I saw them in the street. I also overheard what they were saying to each other."

Demi gestured impatiently. "Yeah? So?"

"They were talking about your dad. They were going to put the squeeze on him. The way they said it, they had to go rattle his chain. Give him a pep talk."

Demi's blood chilled, in every part of her body. A horrible, sinking feeling. Her ears started to ring. "About what?"

"That part wasn't clear," he admitted. "Some job your dad was supposed to do for their boss. Something involving buying some property, ensuring privacy. For some reason, he hadn't done the job like they wanted him to."

"Okay." She nodded, biting her lip. "And this is your business exactly why?"

"I only made it my business when I heard them mention you."

She inhaled sharply. "Me? What did they say? I don't even know those guys!"

"They didn't say it directly, but from what I heard when they were talking to him, it sounded like they were implying some threat to you if he didn't deliver."

"Talked...to him? To my dad, you mean?"

Eric nodded.

She narrowed her eyes. "Let me get this straight. You're telling me that a couple of mobsters shook down my dad. Out on the street. In front of you, of all people."

Eric's face tightened, as if bracing himself. "No," he said reluctantly. "It didn't happen out on the street. And they didn't see me. I heard your name mentioned as they got into their car and I got curious. So I, uh...followed them."

"I see," she said. "To where?"

An agonizing pause, and he finally came out with it. "Your dad's house."

Demi realized, after a few beats, that her mouth was open. She forced herself to close it. "You went to my dad's house," she repeated. "And spied on a conversation that he had with these men."

Eric nodded again.

"Where exactly did you overhear them? Did you put your ear to the door?"

"I was out back, behind the pool house in the trees," he admitted. "They were in the back yard. Your dad was on the side porch. I heard every word."

"I see." Her voice felt deadened and flat. "You mean, you were hiding in the security camera's blind spots. The ones that I showed you years ago."

"Yes," he said.

Demi couldn't control her face. She could barely feel it.

46

She turned away, and spoke without looking at him. "I hope you understand how sick and twisted this is. Sneaking around my dad's house. Spying on him. I should call the cops on you."

"Please don't," he said. "I heard them say your name. I had to do it."

"It is still not your business." Anger shook her voice. "Even if they were plotting to fucking murder me, it would still not be your business. You abdicated the right to be interested in my welfare many years ago. Your interest now is unwelcome."

"I knew you'd feel that way," he said.

"Then why the hell did you throw this in my face?"

"You needed to know." His face was stubborn. "You need to be on your guard."

"I am," she told him fervently. "After a lifetime of being my father's daughter, plus a very memorable three-day affair with you? You better believe I'm on my guard. I'll be on my guard until the day I die."

"You need to be specifically on the alert for those guys. It's not safe for—"

"Don't pretend you care about my safety. And don't you dare use that to justify getting anywhere near me or my dad, you sick, manipulative bastard."

He nodded. "Understood." His voice sounded strangled.

"I just don't get this," she said. "Are you actively, deliberately trying to get into trouble again? Do you have some twisted psychological complex?"

"I had to," he said simply. "I believe in doing the right thing. Even when it hurts."

That hurt, like a blow to the chest. "Get the hell out of

here."

"Demi, I just want—"

"Go!"

He backed toward the door. "I'm sorry I upset you. Just please, watch your back."

"I do. It's a trick I learned from tangling with you. Your great and lasting gift to me. I always watch my back. I can't ever stop. So don't worry, I'm covered. Get out."

He was almost out the door when Elisa opened the door, the chalkboard in her hands. She glanced from Demi to Eric, bewildered. "Sorry about the wait," she said. "I had to wait for the spray to dry. It's probably okay, but you should try not to touch the surface for a few more minutes, just to be sure." Her voice petered out as she sensed the weirdness in the air. She turned to Eric. "Do you…still want it?"

Demi sighed, gesturing at Eric. "Take it," she snapped. "Be quick about it."

Eric took the picture from Elisa's hands. "Thank you," he said gravely. "I left the money on the bar."

Elisa looked distressed. "I told you, it's not for sale. Please don't—"

"Just take the thing and go, goddamn it!"

Utter silence followed Demi's savage outburst. Silence from the kitchen. No more water spraying, clanking pots, jabbering or giggling. Everyone was holding their breath.

Elisa's eyes were wide with alarm.

"Sorry," Eric said quietly. "About all of it."

He went out the door, holding the chalkboard gingerly by the edges, and disappeared into the gloom.

Demi covered her face with her hands and fought for control. She felt Elisa's slender hand on her shoulder.

"Demi," she said. "I'm so sorry."

"I'm the one who's sorry. I didn't mean to yell. Just…give me a minute."

Elisa waited without a word, patiently leaving the weight and warmth of her hand on Demi's shoulder until she pulled one hitching breath, then another, into her chest.

"Have you ever thought you knew someone, and then found out that they were someone completely different?" Demi's voice was tight and shaking. "And I mean, night and day different."

Elisa squeezed her shoulder. "Yes," she whispered.

Something in her tone made Demi turn to look at her. Elisa's eyes were wet. They wrapped their arms around each other and hung on.

When Demi finally released Elisa from the shaking hug, her own face was wet, and she needed tissues, urgently. She took care of her own goopy nose, then passed the tissue packet to Elisa, along with the pile of fifties that Eric had left on the bar. "Take this."

"Demi, I—"

"I would count it as a huge favor if you would not argue about it. Please." She looked over at Gomez and Alba, her latest hires for the kitchen staff, who were peeping through the kitchen entrance with wide, worried eyes. She whipped off her apron. "Would the three of you close up for me? I just need to go hide out for a while at home."

"Of course," Elisa said.

"No problem," Alba chimed in. "Go on home. We got this. See you tomorrow."

Demi grabbed her jacket and her purse and hurried out into the chilly, windy gloom outside. Dead leaves swept and whirled in the gusts of wind. She looked in every direction to make sure that Eric wasn't still lurking out there.

Headlights approached. Her guts went heavy and cold with dread...until she saw who was driving. An older lady with a big cloud of frizzy hair. Not the funeral crashers.

Then she could breathe again, and steady her wobbling knees.

Well, wasn't that lovely. Something new and fresh to feel uptight and paranoid about.

Eric Trask was just the gift that kept on giving.

5

Anton was putting his box of Otis's framed photographs into the back of his Mercedes GLS when Eric pulled up outside Otis's house. They'd agreed that Otis's wildlife photos and camera equipment were the only personal items that they'd keep, and the rest of Otis's stuff would be donated to the thrift store charity in town. Last night they had drawn lots for first and second dibs and had then taken turns choosing their favorite photos until all photos, cameras and lenses were sorted into three piles to be carried away.

Heavy clouds were massed in the darkening sky. Trees on the mountainside tossed in the wind. Eric sat in his car and watched as Anton slammed the back of his SUV closed and leaned against it, crossing his arms over his chest. The wind ruffled his thatch of brown hair. Longer on top, buzzed short at the sides. Otis had hated that look. Punk-trash, he called it, but Anton had serenely ignored Otis's fashion dictates.

Rain beaded Anton's long, black leather coat. His face

was grim, and his dark eyes were shadowed with exhaustion. None of them were sleeping for shit.

Eric got out of the Porsche and watched Mace finished duct-taping a square of cardboard over the broken pane of glass in the door that Demi had broken to get to Otis.

Mace came down the porch stairs after he finished and strolled toward them, spinning the roll of tape on his forefinger with a big, manic grin that fooled no one. The back of his hand was gnarled and shiny from the burn scars that covered it.

"So?" he asked. "How did it go? Did Shaw's Crossing clasp you tenderly to its bosom? Were there shrimp puffs and pigs in a blanket? Did you write your check? Was there drama?"

"The Corner Café belongs to Demi Vaughan now," Eric told them.

His brothers exchanged alarmed glances.

Anton whistled softly. "I'll be goddamned. So there was drama after all. I'm sorry now that I didn't go. We missed the floor show. Bet it was something."

"So?" Mace asked. "What went down? Did Benedict Vaughan and Big Granddaddy Shaw try to lock you up again?"

"Vaughan made threatening noises," Eric said. "But he has bigger problems than me."

"Bet you didn't even notice the dad and granddad," Mace said. "Not with Demi Vaughan offering you trays of luscious finger food held up to the level of her cleavage."

"She wasn't showing off her tits, Mace," Eric said through his teeth.

"No problem," Mace said cheerfully. "I can fill in the blanks with my overheated imagination."

"How about you don't."

Mace looked taken aback by his brother's tone. "I had no idea you felt so strongly about it," he said. "Since you're so completely over the whole thing, like you say."

"Demi was the one who found Otis," Eric said.

That wiped the smile off Mace's face.

"What the hell was she doing way out here?" Anton asked.

"Being neighborly," Eric said. "She came out to bring him some pie that morning. Saw him through the window, laid out on the floor. She broke the window. Called the ambulance. Stayed with him at the ICU until he died. Wade told me about it."

"So," Mace said, swallowing hard. "Good, then. He didn't die alone."

In the silence, the pine boughs swished in the gusts of wind. A drift of dead leaves scudded across the muddy dirt road around their feet.

"And this information is relevant to us exactly why?" Anton asked finally.

"Don't be an asshole," Eric replied. "It's not relevant to anything. I just didn't want to be the only one who knew it."

"Thanks for sharing," Mace said sourly.

"You're fucking welcome. But that wasn't the end of my adventures in Shaw's Crossing today. Remember the funeral-crashing goons?"

"Oh, shit." Anton looked like he was bracing himself. "What did you do?"

"They were at the reception. Benedict Vaughan's got himself mixed up with some thugs, and apparently, he owes them. Now they're squeezing him. I overheard them saying ugly things about Demi."

Anton and Mace's faces went blank with shock.

Anton was the first to recover. "Excuse me? And how do you know all this?"

"I overheard them talking to Vaughan at his house. I heard Demi's name mentioned when they were walking past me on the street, so I followed them to find out what they were up to. That's where they ended up."

"Benedict Vaughan's house," Mace repeated, incredulous. "You followed a couple of thugs to Benedict Vaughan's house and spied on his shit? We only left you alone for a couple hours! Have you lost your fucking mind?"

"I wanted info," Eric said, defensive. "I don't care if Vaughan goes down in flames, but I don't want him dragging Demi down with him."

"Dude," Anton said heavily. "You keep messing with these people, and the only one going down in flames will be you."

"I don't intend to engage with them," he told them. "I'm backing off from the whole thing, I promise. I just stopped by the restaurant to warn Demi, in case they —"

"You *told* her that you stalked her butthead dad?" Mace put his hands in his hair. "Do you have a fucking death wish? They'll put your punk ass in jail for real this time, and I wouldn't blame them!"

"It was the right thing to do," Eric said stubbornly. "I had to tell her."

"Did it occur to you that Demi might not want to know just how much of a fuck-up loser her dad is?" Mace said. "She might have been better off in happy ignorance, but you just had to burden her with this knowledge. What a prince. Real altruistic of you."

"She is in danger," Eric said, with cold emphasis. "I

had to warn her. In any case, it's a done deal, so forget about it. I don't think she's going to call the dogs on me now."

Mace let out a harsh laugh. "When it comes to Shaw's Crossing, expect the worst. This place is poisonous. Let's leave right now. Before shit gets ugly."

"We need to be here tomorrow," Eric said. "We have to call the thrift store truck to come pick up Otis's stuff, remember? Plus, we have those appointments with Otis's estate lawyer and the real estate agent. I saw Terry Cattrall at the funeral home yesterday and he said he could go up to GodsAcre tomorrow and out to Otis's property the morning after, so we can go ahead and put them both on the market. Let's finish this."

Anton squinted at him. "You should be more anxious than any of us to get out of here, but you're dragging your feet. Makes me wonder what the fuck is going on inside your head. What are you holding out for?"

"Nothing," Eric said impatiently. "Don't make a big deal of it. I just want to see this all through so we can put this place behind us for good."

"We can leave a key for the thrift store people," Mace said. "They can do their thing without us. We got what we wanted from the house. Put your box of Otis's pictures into your car and boom, you're done."

"If there's more business with the real estate agent or the lawyers or whoever, I'll pay for them to fly up to Seattle," Anton said. "I'll buy everybody's meals, put everyone up in a nice hotel. My expense. Fair enough?"

Eric just shook his head. "I have this feeling," he admitted. "Like an axe is about to drop. Like I'm holding my breath. Waiting for something."

"It's the Curse," Mace said grimly.

"It's also Otis's message," Anton said. "We're never going to know what he wanted to tell us. We have to let it go."

"Yeah, and let go of Demi Vaughan, too, while you're at it," Mace murmured.

"I'm not hanging on to her!" Eric snarled.

The hand Anton ran through his dark hair made it stick up wildly. "You're scaring me, dude," he said. "But I can't stay, even to babysit you. I can't fucking breathe in this town. Otis was the only good reason to be here, and he's gone. So for fuck's sake, come on. Let's shake the dust of this place off our feet."

"Yeah," Mace said. "The Curse is biting your ass already. It'll chew you up and spit you out if you stay here longer."

"Agreed," Anton said. "We should all run. But you should run the fastest."

"Like fucking rabbits?" Eric said bitterly. "I can't. Goes against my training."

The rain was now pattering down, but they all just stood there, unmoving, as Eric's reproach rang in the air.

"We were trained for a different reality than the one we actually have to live in, brother," Mace said finally. "Call me a rabbit if you want. I'm not ashamed to run."

"I'm not leaving," Eric told his brothers. "Not until business is taken care of."

Anton shook his head. "You're the one who is doing the crazy shit when our backs are turned. You're the last one who should hang around."

"So how about the two of you could dig out your balls from wherever you buried them and stay with me," Eric said. "Just for a couple of days. Short-term pain, long-term reward. The more we delegate, the longer all of this will take. Don't

56

flinch from pain and you'll be invincible, remember? Jeremiah's favorite saying. Man up, guys."

But Mace was already shaking his head. "I'm tired of pain." He sounded exhausted. "I need a break. I'm out of here."

"Same," Anton said. "Sorry, man. Gotta go."

"Fuck you both," Eric said, through his teeth.

Mace threw his shoulders back, staring up at the sky. "It's late, and this rain is getting worse," he said. "Gotta get on the road. I'll go get my stuff."

"Chickenshits," Eric said.

"Bwawk, bwawk, bwawk," Mace clucked as he went back inside the house.

Anton rattled his key fob in his hand. "Text me," he said. "Let me know what happens with Terry Cattrall. And the lawyer."

"Sure," Eric said. "I'll keep you informed."

Anton had the grace to look uncomfortable. "Don't be such a hard-ass," he said. "You shouldn't stay here either, and you fucking know it. You of all people."

"Yeah, right. Drive safely."

"Do not, I repeat, do not get anywhere near Demi Vaughan," Anton said.

"Get gone," Eric said. "The look on your face is pissing me off."

Anton lost no time. The big black Mercedes GLS bumped and bounced painfully hard over the washboard ruts as his brother accelerated around the curve.

His youngest brother knew better than to make eye contact when he came out of the house with his box of photos in his arms and his duffel bag slung over his shoulder.

Mace put his stuff into the back of his rented car. "I got

a flight out of Portland tomorrow morning," he said brusquely. "Back to Africa. Gonna be a long night. See you."

Eric knew better than to ask what Mace was doing in Africa. His brother ran a small, specialized mercenary army and his services were in high demand, but the actual work he did was best not scrutinized too closely.

"Watch yourself out there," he said gruffly.

"I always do, brother. You do the same. Stay safe. And hey. Fuck the Curse."

"Yeah," he replied. "Fuck the Curse."

Mace got into his car. A rev of the motor, a grinding spray of gravel and mud, and Mace's taillights retreated swiftly down the winding road and were lost to sight.

The wind was picking up, whipping the trees angrily.

Inside, wind howled mournfully in the eaves. The old house creaked and groaned. Wind rattled the square of cardboard Mace had duct-taped into the window frame in the door. Eric opened up the cases of electronic gear he'd brought with him, fired up his laptop and router, and sought the refuge of deep concentration. When it worked, it let him float in a tranquil place inside his own head. Dreaming up app design, coding, sifting data. Solving problems and anticipating new ones.

He liked his work as a tech entrepreneur. Otis hadn't approved of their career choices, but Otis was a one-note guy when it came to vocation. If a job wasn't in agriculture, construction, engineering, law enforcement or the military, for Otis it was parasitic white-collar bullshit. Doctors were exempt. Lawyers got an extra dose of scorn.

Mace's work as a soldier-of-fortune was at least comprehensible, if a little too morally flexible for Otis's comfort zone. But Anton's DJ fame and his chain of decadent nightclubs had baffled Otis altogether. As had Erebus Inc., Eric's app design company.

They all made spectacular money, which had helped to reconcile their adopted father. Even so, Otis had seen Eric's business as frivolous and suspect. Selling smoke and mirrors, stuff with no substance. Who knew, maybe Otis was right, but Eric still liked what he'd created. More importantly, it kept him too busy to get in trouble.

Idle hands do the Devil's work. Old Jeremiah used to say that whenever he found them loafing. Mostly during that last bad year, after the old man started tripping out on hellfire and pestilence. The hellfire theme had picked up a lot of steam after Mom died.

It got even worse after Redd Kimball showed up and started egging Jeremiah on.

That was when all the vaccinations started. Every day, they'd been forced to line up for a fresh injection from Kimball. A daily needle full of what-the-fuck. They'd felt like human pincushions.

He tried not to think about what might have been in those shots. The past was done and gone. They'd all survived this far.

GodsAcre had always been weird, but it had morphed into something dark and different after Redd Kimball showed up. It had been lonesome and boring up there for sure, even before, but running wild in the mountains with Mace and Anton had been good. He'd loved the hunting and fishing and swimming. He'd been four years old when Mom brought him there. Anton, five. Mace only two. He had no clear memories from before. GodsAcre had been his whole world.

After Mom died and Kimball showed up, the place had turned into a dystopian prison camp. Jeremiah's rambling sermons had completely lost their thru-line. They'd turned into endless, incoherent rants against an amorphous, evil 'them.'

And GodsAcre had started losing people fast right around then. They'd gone from well over a hundred people down to the final forty-one diehards, at the end.

The ones who got away before the fire were the lucky ones.

Then they'd saved Fiona in the nick of time after Jeremiah had agreed to let that prick Kimball marry her when she was only fifteen. He and Mace and Anton put a stop to that. Then the Curse came down, full force, and things got apocalyptic real fast.

Unwelcome memories flooded in on him. Fire and pain. Smoke and death. He knew why Mace and Anton wanted to run. They didn't want to remember it either.

Jeremiah said that only the pure of heart would be spared the cleansing fire. Ironic that the three of them were the only survivors of the GodsAcre fire. There was nothing pure about them. Selfish, sinful, pleasure-loving sons-of-bitches, all three of them. Anton had named his chain of nightclubs 'Hellbound,' and Eric and Mace understood why.

Anything to prove that old madman wrong.

He paced around the place, twitchy and restless. Looked through his box of photos. Some were of birds and animals, some were of the three brothers. Otis's favorite breed of wildlife, he used to joke. He stopped to stare at photo of Mace, naked to the waist, chopping wood. A red-tailed hawk. A spotted owl. Anton, diving into the swimming hole. A cougar prowling the length of a fallen log.

The loud, labored tick-tock of Otis's grandfather clock was driving him nuts.

He didn't want to think about the past. Ashes in the wind. It should stop haunting him. *Fuck* this.

He took his jacket off the hook. A hike over the ridge would get him to the highway that wound down that valley and into Shaw's Crossing. There was a roadhouse bar there. The Hi-Way House. He'd go on foot. He knew the way, even in the dark. Jeremiah had insisted on teaching them to keep their bearings in the woods at night. Darkness, rain, snow, no adverse conditions were an excuse for getting lost. Not for the vanguard of the army of the righteous.

Besides, he planned to drink a fair amount of alcohol tonight. He never drove when he drank. And the Hi-Way House was no place to park his Porsche.

The walk would blow off excess energy. Sex would be better, but there was only one woman in the world that interested him right now, and she hated him with all the force of her being.

The Hi-Way House was a dump, but there would be tequila shots. Loud music. Maybe even some devolved, hairy biker types spoiling for a fight. There was an art to pissing people off and he wasn't half bad at it when he applied himself.

Maybe he could provoke a big bunch of them all at once. Get a little workout. Drain some poison.

A guy could hope.

6

*B*e on your guard.
I believe in doing the right thing. Even when it hurts.
You broke the chains that bound you.

Eric's words had been echoing through Demi's mind all day. Now that she was home in her quiet townhouse with no interference, they bounced around in her mind like a freaking pinball machine. She didn't know which of his outrageous statements to be pissed off about most. There were so many. Too much to process.

Do the right thing, hah. The balls on that guy. That he actually dared to say word one about the chains that bound her when he was the one who had forged them.

The truth about Eric had been hard to accept. She'd had to break the whole thing down into bite-sized pieces and force herself to swallow it one little bit at a time, and it had taken years to work through it all. Years.

To think that all that painstaking hard work and determination could be undone in an instant by a single smoldering glance. Damn that seductive, arrogant bastard.

His actions had made no sense to her at all seven years ago. She'd been so confused by what he'd done. She knew how smart, hardworking and ambitious he was.

But stealing your girlfriend's father's trophy car, chugging booze in it, speeding on a narrow mountain highway with it, and running it off a cliff? That was stupid. Crazy.

There was no arguing with facts. It was a matter of public record. They'd fished Eric out of Kettle River more dead than alive. He'd been a few hundred feet down the steep slope of the canyon directly below Dad's stolen, totaled Porsche, which had snagged on some trees on the hillside. He had alcohol in his system. He and the wrecked Porsche both stank of tequila.

Actions spoke louder than words. Eric's actions had been one long, rage-filled yell.

The only way he could have gotten the keys to Dad's Porsche was when she'd sneaked him into the Vaughan house seven years ago while her folks were gone on their weekend getaway. She'd invited him over for a hot secret tryst. She remembered the entire episode in exquisite sensual detail. Second by second. Kiss by kiss.

Then they had a big, ugly fight. She'd lost her temper and thrown him out.

He must have grabbed Dad's Porsche keys off the pegboard in the kitchen as he went out the door, but she hadn't seen him do it. She'd been too busy blubbering on the landing of the staircase, her feelings all hurt from their fight. Boo-hoo. Poor her.

Her mother had insisted that Eric had a brain development issue. A lack of impulse control, probably the result of the severe trauma in his past. It was tragic, and Mom was so sorry for him, but that didn't excuse him from having to face the consequences of his actions. And ultimately, it was a blessing that Demi had seen who and what Eric Trask truly was before she got in too deep, right?

Right?

In the end, it was Demi who had paid for Eric's fuck-up. Dad, ever the schemer, had swiftly figured out a way to use the situation to his advantage. He'd agreed to drop the charges against Eric—in exchange for full compliance in Demi's career goals.

The conditions: She gave up the prized restaurant internship she'd won at *Peccati Di Gola*, the hottest new restaurant in Seattle. She gave up her plan to study at the Culinary Institute. She agreed to work hard and train for a leadership position in the family business, Shaw Paper Products. And she would never communicate with Eric Trask again for any reason. If she met those conditions, Eric walked free.

That part about not communicating with Eric wasn't hard to comply with. She'd rather die than see that lying loser again. But the rest of it…well.

It had been hard to swallow.

In retrospect, she should have said no. From the very start. She should have said fuck you to all of them. Followed her dreams and never looked back. She should have left that idiot in jail to rot like he deserved. She would have been doing the world a favor.

But she couldn't leave him in a cage. Not when she had the option of freeing him.

She'd caved, and she'd been angry at herself ever since.

Aw, crap. Enough already. Ancient history. No point

thrashing it out again. She put on another dash of mascara, leaning toward the window to wipe a smear from under her eye. The Trask Effect was working its wicked sorcery on her even while Eric wasn't physically in front of her. Just knowing he was out there somewhere made her body feel more female. It made her dress more seductively, walk with a sexier sway to her hips.

Look at this outfit she'd dug out of her wardrobe, for God's sake. Tight, clingy shirt, a push-up bra, ass-flaunting jeans? What the fuck was that about? Her hair was even hanging loose. She never wore it like that these days. And she'd put on the highest-heeled boots she owned, just because her neck ached from looking up, up, up at Eric Trask.

She never dressed sexily in Shaw's Crossing. Running a restaurant kept her too busy for a social life in any case, and for sleeping, too, for the most part. Besides, the dating pool around here was a shallow one, and she herself was a cynical, defensive, suspicious, uptight bitch when it came to men. Or so she'd been told, post-Eric. More than once.

A side-effect of always being on her guard. Bummer for her, but there it was.

Still, she was going out tonight. For air, alcohol and noise. Angry heavy metal live music would have suited her mood perfectly, but she wasn't going to find any in Shaw's Crossing. She'd have to make do with twangy country rock at the roadhouse.

The parking lot was unusually full at the Hi-Way House. Some popular local band was playing tonight. Demi shoved her way through the crowd to the bar, perched on a stool and yelled for a beer. The place smelled of booze and old frying grease. The live music that blared from the room with the stage sounded muddy and garbled. Someone had spilled tequila.

The smell unleashed vivid sense memories. Eric had brought tequila to their tryst that night. They'd done the whole ritual; salt, shot, lime. She'd never loved the heavy, bitter taste of that liquor, but once Eric Trask's hot, demanding kiss tasted of it, well. It was all the tastes of life rolled into one. Bitter, salty, sour. The sweetness of his kiss. The burn of fire, the sting of danger, while his gorgeous body moved insistently inside her, driving her to explosive pleasure.

Oh yeah. After that night, she definitely 'got' tequila.

She hadn't touched it since, and avoided any cocktail that contained it.

Demi sipped her beer and watched the dancers gyrating in flickering bluish light on the dance floor, wondering what the hell she'd hoped to accomplish by coming here.

Then the door opened and Eric Trask walked into the place, like an answer to her question.

Their gazes locked instantly. *Click,* like magnets coupling. Not even a split-instant's chance to slip away unnoticed.

Just like that, it happened again. Energy raged through her body. Fireworks went off in her head. She couldn't think, move, breathe or see anything but him.

Oh crap. She didn't want this feeling. Make it *stop.*

He walked toward her. As luck would have it, the woman sitting on the bar stool next to her slid off and headed out onto the dance floor, giggling with her friends.

Eric approached, standing by the empty stool. His leather jacket was damp and cold and his hair was wet. He smelled like wind, rain, and himself.

"Looks like Fate," he said. "You can't seem to get away from me today."

"You're wrong," Demi said. "I do whatever the fuck I want. Nobody forces me anymore. Not even Fate."

"Good for you," he said. "I'm going to sit down on this bar stool. Do whatever you want, but I'm really hoping that you won't get up and walk away."

She stared into his eyes. "One single word about that crazy shit you did today at my dad's house, even one, and I'm gone. Like a shot."

"Agreed," he said. "Not a word. Like it never happened."

He slid into place on the stool, angling his body toward hers.

"I didn't expect to see you here tonight," she said.

He had to lean close to hear her in the noise. Close enough so she could smell his shower soap and aftershave and the cold air clinging to his leather coat. "I'd say the same thing about you," he said. "Doesn't seem like your kind of place."

"I don't have a lot of choice in this town," she said. "It was a long day. I wanted a drink and enough noise so I couldn't hear myself think. I don't like my thoughts right now."

"Same for me. Until now." Eric gave her a slow once-over that made her body tighten with hot sensual awareness, a sensation as intense as it was unwelcome. He beckoned to the bartender. "Tequila," he called out. "Gran Patron Piedra. Two shots."

The guy slapped two glasses down on the bar and filled them. He shoved over lime slices and a salt shaker.

Eric downed his first tequila shot swiftly, and pushed

the other in her direction.

Demi looked down at it. Her heart sped up, loud in her ears despite the pounding music. After all these years, every detail of that episode in her bedroom was so intensely vivid in her mind. She wondered if he remembered it as clearly as she did.

"You have got to be fucking kidding me," she said.

Eric studied her averted face. After a moment, he took the second shot and tossed it back himself. "Guess I deserved that."

"Don't," she said sharply. "Don't even lift the lid."

She clutched the neck of her beer, white-knuckled, and took a sip, refusing to meet his eyes. Playing it oh, so very cool. She could care less. He was welcome to get up and walk away if he wanted. Screw it. She'd barely notice.

But then the silence got so long, it started to annoy her. "Oh, for God's sake, Eric," she finally snapped. "What is your damn problem?"

"I'm just trying to think of something to say to you that won't lead into a danger zone," he said. "And I'm coming up blank."

"Well, think harder. And don't make such a big goddamn thing out of it. I'm just any old high school classmate that you haven't seen in years. You know. Where have you been? What have you done? Small talk. Chit chat. You can do it. I know you can."

"Small talk? For real? Us?"

"Especially us," she said.

He sighed. "Damn. I guess I can give it a shot." He studied her face for another long moment. "So. Been a while."

"Sure has," she agreed.

"I never thought I'd see you settled here. I thought

68

you'd get the hell out of this town. Like me."

Demi sipped her beer as she considered her answer. "I did leave."

"But not to cooking school. Isn't that where you were headed?"

She shook her head. "I gave that up," she said. "I ended up working for Shaw Paper Products for a few years. The center up in Spokane, like you heard."

"So they finally got you. They wrestled you down." He hesitated. "For a while, at least."

"Yeah. I gave it my best shot, but I finally bailed. It's not like it was a death sentence or anything. It just wasn't my thing. After Mom died, I finally managed to make Granddad understand that my heart would never be in it."

"And then you opened the restaurant? You went back to your original idea?"

"Not exactly," she hedged. "Demi's Corner Café isn't haute cuisine, like I was dreaming of, but I like it. I sling great hash, and I'm my own boss. And business is good."

"I still remember those kick-ass sandwiches you made at the Bakery Café," he said. "I wish I could try your food now."

"You had your chance, buddy," she told him. "We prepared tons of tasty food for the reception today. It was wasted on you."

He smiled briefly. "With that death-glare your dad was giving me? How was I supposed to swallow food?"

"Lightweight," she scoffed. "I learned to perform all essential activities of daily living while under the influence of that death-glare. I'm living proof it can be done."

"Good for you," he said. "For real, I mean. Congratulations on doing your own thing. No matter the odds."

There were a thousand different things she could say in response to that, but she squelched them with savage effort. *Keep it light. Don't get into it. Just don't.*

"Thanks. Same to you." Her voice felt strangled.

He nodded, and gestured to the bartender, lifting the two shot glasses and sliding a couple of bills across the bar.

"How about you?" she asked. "Where did you go after…everything? Did you go back to the Marines?"

"No, I was all done with that. I went to Las Vegas for a while. Did some security work in the casinos for a couple of years while I finished designing my app. Then I launched it, and started a company."

Demi waited to reply while the bartender refilled the shot glass and tossed another couple of chunks of lime onto the plate. "Started a company," she repeated slowly. "That means nothing by itself. What does your company do?"

"It solves problems."

She laughed. "Oh. So, you're what? A fixer?"

His eyes narrowed. "Is that what you think of me?"

She gave him a mysterious smile. Messing with his head was kind of fun. "I don't know what to think of you unless you're more specific," she said. "Solving problems? Come on, Eric. It sounds kind of ominous. It could mean anything."

"It doesn't mean anything like that. It's very straightforward."

"Oh really? Tell me."

"Remember that work-flow app I was designing seven years ago? That's my flagship product. I named it Aion. I've launched a lot of new apps since then. I'm an entrepreneur, Demi. Boring, legitimate business. Products, launches, spreadsheets, databases, taxes. I'm not a bagman for some mafia overlord, for fuck's sake."

Ooh, she'd gotten under his skin. "Okay," she murmured. "Sounds...respectable."

"It is," he said forcefully. "One hundred percent."

Then his words sank in and she turned back to him, genuinely startled. "Wait a sec. Aion, you said? Your company designed the Aion app?"

"No," he said. "I designed the Aion app, alone and unassisted. Then I started a company to help me market it. Now I have a team that works with me, and we've done Helios, Eos and Pallas since then. Nyx is our latest. I just launched it a couple months ago. It's doing well. You've heard of them?"

"Of course I've heard of them. Especially Aion. Shaw Paper Products started using Aion right before I stopped working there. I remember all the buzz. Everyone called it a big game-changer. Everybody uses those apps, Eric. They're huge."

"Not everyone," he said. "Not yet. We think there's plenty of room for growth."

"Well...wow. In any case, that's impressive. So who is 'we?'"

"My team. My company." He reached into his pocket and handed her a business card.

It was very simple. Heavy, cream-colored stock. An embossed logo. Erebus, Inc. Eric Trask, Owner and CEO. A phone number, an email, and a QR code.

"Owner and CEO," she murmured. "Of Erebus. Look at you. You hit the bigtime."

"Go ahead, look it up online," he said. "My picture's right there on the masthead. Suit and tie, the whole deal. I clean up nice when I make an effort. You'd be amazed."

"No, actually, I'm not amazed at all," she told him. "I knew nothing would keep you down for long."

He gave her a long, searching look. "Thanks," he said finally.

"For what?"

"For thinking that. Not many around here would. And thanks for talking to me right now. Like a normal person. After…everything that happened. It's generous of you."

She struggled with that for a minute, but kept her reply rigorously bland and pleasant. "Otis expected the best from you, too. He was very proud of all three of you."

Eric looked away. A muscle in his jaw pulsed. He took the second shot glass that sat in front of them on the bar, and lifted it. "To Otis," he said.

"To Otis." She took a sip of her beer while he downed his shot.

"Well, well. Look what crawled out from under a rock and decided to go out drinking," said a sneering voice behind them. "Eric-fucking-Paley. The Prophet's spawn."

Eric spun around on the bar stool. Boyd Nevins stood behind them.

"The name's Trask," Eric told him.

Boyd had been two years ahead of her in school, in Eric's class. He'd worked for Shaw Paper Products in Spokane at the same time she did and was now the director of Shaw's distribution center in Granger Valley. He'd come on to her every chance he got back in her Spokane days, and since he'd moved back he'd made it plain that he was still interested, but she hadn't returned his interest. Boyd was good looking, smart, ambitious, all that good stuff, but she just wasn't feeling it. Not even a flickering spark of curiosity.

Then again, that could just be because Boyd was the walking, breathing embodiment of everything Dad, Mom and Granddad had always wanted for her. That could be what turned her off. Which was unfair, but hey. What could you do.

"Hey, Boyd," she said. "What's your problem?"

"Is he bothering you, sweetheart?" Boyd didn't take his eyes off Eric.

That made the hairs on her arms prickle. "I'm not your sweetheart," she replied. "And no, he isn't, so walk on by."

Boyd ignored her, still addressing Eric. "I saw your brothers gassing up at the station earlier," he said. "I figured you'd be hauling ass out of town right along with them with your tail between your legs. But no. Here you still are. Guzzling booze like the drunk thief loser that you are. Tequila, no less. I guess that's appropriate."

Eric just looked at him without saying a word.

Boyd made an abrupt lunging gesture toward him. Eric didn't flinch.

"What?" Boyd barked. "Get that dick look off your face. Fuckhead."

"I'm just wondering how you live with yourself," Eric said. "You must have tied yourself into knots to justify what you did. Maybe you're weak and someone forced you. Or you're greedy and someone paid you. Or you're an asshole sociopath and you don't care. Who knows. In the end, you just don't deserve that much thought."

Boyd's eyes glittered. "Time to go, Prophet's spawn. Up you get. Right foot, left foot."

"Really? You sure about that?" Eric slid off the stool and stood up, looming a full four inches taller than Boyd. "I got plenty, if you want some. But I don't think you're up to it. I don't want to waste my time on a dickless coward like you."

Demi looked from one to the other, horrified. "Holy shit! Guys! What the hell is this about? Cool it, both of you!"

"Maybe you don't understand," Boyd said to Eric. "I represent a lot of people in this town, many of whom are in this bar right now. We want you to get gone. Right now would be a good time. So fuck off."

"Boyd, what the hell are you saying? He just buried his father! Stop being a dick!"

Eric was so completely still, it unnerved her. "Since you know who these people are, do me a favor," he said softly. "Call them all together right now. I'd be happy to discuss any issues they may have with me all at once. We'll save time that way."

Boyd's mouth twisted. "I can take you alone."

"If you want." Eric's eyes roved around the crowded space. "Outside." He glanced at Demi. "This will only take a minute. Save my seat." He gestured to Boyd. "After you."

And off they went, just like that. Both men headed toward the door to…to do what? To go pound on each other in the parking lot?

Oh, please. This could not be happening. "Eric! Are you fucking kidding me?" she yelled after them.

She was talking to empty air.

Bad idea. Back away. Don't indulge yourself. Don't be a dumb asshole.

There it was, the voice of reason in Eric's head. It sounded a lot like Otis, but it didn't stand a chance tonight. The beast inside needed to move and flex, or he'd snap.

Boyd's had this coming. For years. Shit-eating liar. He

needed a pounding and tonight was his big night. Hell, the guy had literally invited him to do it.

And what was left of his self-control had already been fatally compromised by staring at Demi Vaughan. Those bright, direct eyes. Those curves of her full, sexy lips. The way that shirt hugged her tits. Her husky voice. It made his cock pulse with lust.

And then that prick Boyd just walks up and volunteers himself? How the fuck was he supposed to turn down a gift-wrapped opportunity for payback like that?

He and Boyd danced around each other. A ring of hollering onlookers began to form in the pool of harsh orange light cast by the streetlight in the parking lot.

Boyd came on with a roar. Obvious as all fuck. And slow. Eric whipped to the side, tripped him, flipped him.

Boyd landed hard on his back in a mud puddle, splashing the onlookers. They bellowed and roared, urging him to get up and try again.

Boyd did so, staggering slightly and wiping mud out of his face.

"Fucking lowlife. Shoulda stayed gone," he snarled as he came on again.

Eric blocked the wild and obvious blows easily. He jabbed a hard punch directly to Boyd's nose, then drove a knee up into his crotch.

Boyd reeled back with a grunt of pain and bounced off someone's car.

Shit. There would be no satisfaction in this. No blowing off of steam. This was just taking out the trash. Which just infuriated him more.

Cheated again.

Boyd glared, panting heavily. Eric beckoned with his

fingers. Best to finish this up clean and fast. Before he lost his temper and ended up actually hurting the guy.

Boyd charged, screaming, eyes bugged out. Eric pivoted, seized and twisted Boyd's wrist and arm and used Boyd's own momentum to send the guy soaring.

Crunch, Boyd hit the hood of someone's car. He slid down, leaving a dent and a lurid smear of dark blood from his broken nose. He landed heavily, face down in a puddle.

People rushed to the guy, pulling his face out of the water and trying to revive him. Eric was glad they were on it. He didn't want Boyd to drown in a puddle, dickhead liar or not. That would complicate his life in stupid ways.

And there he was. Standing there, buzzing with unspent rage, at the mercy of his own bad choices. He looked at the people still ringed around him. "Anyone else want to kick my ass?" he demanded, beckoning to them. "Bring it."

Gazes slid swiftly away and the muttering group dispersed. Fucking useless. All of them.

Demi emerged from behind the crowd as it melted away. She looked appalled.

His fighting buzz drained away. There was only grief and self-loathing beneath it.

He shouldn't have scolded his brothers for running. They were lucky they both had a functioning instinct for self-preservation. This place made him as dumb as a fucking rock.

Eric turned around and headed toward the dark highway.

7

Eric left the pool of light cast by the parking lot streetlamp.

Demi ran to her car. She pulled out onto the highway, and caught sight of Eric on the road ahead in her headlights, just as he left the roadway to plunge into the dense forest that covered the mountainside.

She pulled over and rolled down the window. "Hey! Trask!" she yelled.

He was already lost to sight in the shadow of the trees. "Let me be, Demi," he called back.

Uh-uh. He didn't get to sulk after throwing his tantrum in the parking lot. She got out of the car and yelled in his direction. "Get back down here right this minute, Eric!"

"Stay away from me. Everyone told you to, and everyone was right."

"Oh, shut up. For real? You're running away like a little bitch. All sorry for yourself. Who would have thought that Otis Trask's son would be such a pansy-ass wuss."

"I'm warning you, Demi. I'll be shitty company tonight."

"I'll do it, okay?" she said. "Since you're so goddamn desperate."

A puzzled silence. "You'll do…what?"

"You begged for someone to kick your ass back there in the parking lot, remember? You desperately need it, and it looks like I'm the only one who's willing to oblige you. So get your ass down here so I can start kicking."

There was a rustling sound, and Eric appeared at the edge of the forest.

"You?" he said. "You're going to kick my ass?"

"With pleasure," she said. "You want punishment, you're in the right place. I'll kick your ass right into next week."

A wary, reluctant smile flashed across his face. He hesitated for just a moment, then started down the slope toward the highway. "Okay, then," he said. "If you're offering."

They got into the car. Demi rolled up the windows against the cold wind and splattering raindrops and got back on the road.

He kept giving her surreptitious glances as they drove, until she couldn't stand it anymore. "What?" she demanded. "What's with the sideways looks? They bug me."

"Just wondering how my ass will be kicked," he said. "You know. In what way, on what level, how hard. I'm intrigued. Maybe even a little afraid."

"Be afraid," she said crisply. "I'll come up with something very severe. You just sit there and sweat while I devise a fitting punishment for all your sins."

He grunted under his breath. "Good luck with that."

She wasn't sure what he meant by that, so she let it pass. Rain pattered down even harder. The wipers squeaked in the charged silence.

"You good to drive?" he asked. "How long were you at the bar before I showed up?"

She shot him a narrow look. "You're suggesting that I'm driving drunk? *You?*"

"Just wondering," he murmured.

"I got to the bar a few minutes before you did. There's two thirds of a beer still sitting there on the bar. My first. And that's offensive as hell, coming from you."

"Didn't mean any offense. Slow down anyway. The road's not in great shape."

"Do not lecture me, Trask."

He made an impatient sound. "For fuck's sake, Demi. Please. Out with it. Whatever's on your mind."

"You don't know?"

"Of course I know," he said. "Just get it out where we can see it. Please."

She considered her reply as she negotiated the sharp turns, and then slowed down at the bridge at the turn-off for Kettle Canyon Road. "I told you not to lift that lid."

"Not an option, if you want to kick my ass," he told her. "We never got a chance to hash this out seven years ago. Let's do it now."

She bumped over the wooden bridge and made a hard right on to Vensel Road. The car started to climb up the steep grade. "I don't know if I should even start."

"You already did, right or wrong. So talk to me."

She drove along the bumpy road for several minutes in stony silence before she finally nodded. "Just remember," she said, her voice tight. "You asked for this."

"Yes," he said.

"Okay, here goes nothing. You *prick.* You betrayed my trust. You used me, lied to me and made a fool of me. I let you inside my family home, and you took the keys to the Porsche when you left, stole my dad's car and crashed it, practically killing yourself in the process, which makes you both suicidal and insanely stupid. It was a dick move in every way. And yes, I'm still extremely pissed."

"That's not how it went down," Eric said.

"Oh, please," she scoffed. "Don't even try. They found you at the scene. At the bottom of the canyon. Two hundred feet directly below the wrecked car. They measured your blood alcohol level. You and the Porsche both stank of tequila. You had the fucking car keys. Your blood was all over the seat and the steering wheel. What gives?"

"So you never got my letters."

"You mean, physical letters, from the post office? No, I did not get letters from you. I left Shaw's Crossing while you were still in jail, and I didn't come back for years."

"I wrote to you while I was in jail," he said. "I wrote afterwards, too. The emails bounced, and the phone number was out of service, and you blocked me on the socials, so I wrote letters to the only address I had. I guess your parents intercepted them."

"I wouldn't have read them even if they hadn't," she said.

He nodded. "So you never heard my side of the story."

"What side? You have no side. The facts speak for themselves. What could you possibly say?" Her throat felt tight to the point of pain.

"The facts aren't the whole picture. The facts they gave you are incomplete."

She slowed to bump over the noisy cattle guard. "Fine," she said. "Complete them, then. Entertain me. Tell me your side. Start with that night at my house. After our fight, when you took Dad's car keys off the pegboard by the kitchen door."

"I never took those keys," Eric said. "I'm not a thief. Or an idiot."

Demi let out a slow sigh, gritting her teeth. "And so it begins."

"Hear me out, Demi. Please."

"I will," she said, through her teeth. "Go ahead. Let me have it."

"I was set up," Eric said. "The whole damn thing was staged."

She glanced at him, bewildered. "Excuse me? Staged? By who?"

"Just let me tell you how it went for me. Then draw your own conclusions."

"Fine. Tell me."

"After our night together, I walked out to the car," he said. "I found all four tires on the Monster slashed. I should have just called my brothers, but it was four in the morning and I couldn't bear the shit I knew they would give me. So I hesitated."

She nodded. "And then?"

"Then I saw a black Porsche coming up behind me. Just like your dad's. It pulled over, and it was Boyd Nevins driving. He offered me a ride to the crossroads."

"Boyd Nevins?" She gave him a startled glance. "The hell?"

"Seemed strange to me, too. He gave us no end of hell back in high school, so it was weird that he would offer me a ride. But I was tired and miserable and I didn't want to hear what Anton and Mace were going to say. I wasn't thinking straight. Plus, I wanted to get the Monster away from your house before your folks came back from their trip. I didn't want to make more trouble for you."

"And you drank, in the car? They told me it was drenched with tequila."

"I did not drink," he said. "The tequila in my system was only what I drank when I was with you. But things got strange really fast. Boyd asked if he could use my phone. He made a call, and started going through the streets downtown at insane speeds. He ran a light at the crossroads and went up onto the Narrows Bridge at ninety-eight. Then he threw my phone out the window on the bridge. Over the railing and into the river."

Demi's mind went blank. Of all things she might have expected to hear, this was not one of them. It was full of implications she couldn't begin to process yet.

"Okay," she said slowly. "And then?"

"I told him to stop and let me out and he sped up even more. I'd given him the tequila bottle when I got in, and he was chugging it and laughing like a lunatic. I thought maybe he was on coke or meth. He had the look."

"Eric, that's insane," she said.

"I know it is. At that speed, if I'd tried to take control of the car I would have killed us both. He got up over a hundred and ten. Then I saw the gloves."

"He wore gloves? In July?"

"Latex gloves," Eric said grimly.

She shook her head, and couldn't stop shaking it. The things he said wouldn't go in. Wouldn't process. They were breaking up into a confused jumble. Bottlenecked.

Everything he said was just...senseless.

"We got all the way up to the trailhead at Peyton State Park. He pulled into the parking lot and got out. Smashed the tequila bottle down on the door of the Porsche. He got into a pickup that was parked there and drove away, leaving me soaked with tequila. With no phone. With your dad's Porsche."

Demi regretted opening this can of worms with everything in her. But what the fuck had she expected from Eric, with his track record? Sincerity? An apology? Hah.

True to form, he'd given her a load of bullshit. He blamed everyone but himself. There would be no closure or forgiveness. Just more stupid, senseless lies.

"I knew that I was going to be accused of stealing that car," Eric went on. "I couldn't call anyone. I was afraid to leave the keys and walk away. It would have taken me hours on foot to get back to town. I was even more afraid of getting caught driving it." He stopped, eyeing her. "Demi?" he prompted. "You still with me?"

"Finish your story, Eric."

"I decided to risk getting closer to town, at least to the nearest phone, so I could call the cops. My plan was to call the cops from the Gas&Go. Call Bristol and throw myself on his mercy. So I took the Porsche out onto the highway."

He stopped speaking for so long, she gave him an impatient glance. "And?"

"A big Humvee came up behind me and started ramming the car."

"Excuse me?" she said blankly. "What the *hell* did you just say?"

"You heard me," he said. "I went as fast as I could. The bastard finally knocked me off the road. The car caught on the trees on the side of the canyon. That saved my life. I was hanging there, upside down, when I heard those guys from the Humvee climbing down toward me. They were talking about finishing the job. So I opened the car door and fell. I woke up at the Granger Valley Hospital, all fucked up. And under arrest."

It was clearly her turn to say something, but she had nothing.

She blurted out the first words that came to her. "Eric, do you think I'm stupid?"

His head shook slowly. "I think you are anything but."

"But you still expect me to believe this? That someone tried to...to *kill* you?"

"I don't expect a damn thing." He sounded weary. "I know how crazy it sounds. I just wanted you to hear the truth from me at least once. Nobody else believed me either. Not Chief Bristol, not the judge, not my public defender. Not even Otis. He wouldn't speak to me for three years afterwards. Only Mace and Anton believed me. Boyd had a rock-solid alibi and they had all the time in the world to clean up the crime scene—"

"Who is 'they?'"

He shrugged. "Whoever put Boyd up to this."

She took a deep breath and just said it. "Sounds like you're implying that it was my dad."

He was quiet for a moment. "Means, motive and opportunity," he said finally. "The set-up was perfect. I'd been in the house where the keys were kept. You and I had argued right before I left. I had good reason to be angry at your dad. I looked bad."

"Eric," she said. "I know you two hate each other, but this is way over the top."

"Seemed severe to me, too," he said. "As much as he hated me being intimate with you. But that's what happened."

"You're saying that my father organized a hit," she said. "That he arranged for his own car to be destroyed. That he paid somebody to run you off the road. You could have been killed. You almost were. Which would have made my father a murderer."

"I know it sounds improbable," he said.

"Oh, no. You left 'improbable' way back there in the dust, Eric. You're now squarely in the realm of ridiculous, offensive, insane, and shut-the-fuck-up."

"I understand that you might not want to—"

"I have no illusions about my dad, believe me," she said. "I wasn't even all that surprised at what you told me at the café earlier. I know he's been mixed up in some shady things in the past. But my dad's brand of misbehavior falls short of murder. He's a guy who likes money, power, status. Not killing. Never speak about this to me again."

"Okay." He looked away. "Sorry. I shouldn't have said anything. There was no point in upsetting you after all these years."

Bitter laughter shook her. "Oh, please. Are you for real?"

"Yes, absolutely. To a fault. I don't tell lies even when I should. I couldn't plead guilty to a thing I didn't do, not even for a shorter sentence. I thought about it, but it would have broken me."

"Your life didn't get broken," she said.

"I know," he said. "I couldn't believe it when your dad dropped the charges. He's the last person in the world that I would expect to have a change of heart."

"He didn't," Demi said coolly. "He would have left you

to rot in prison with the greatest of pleasure. That was me."

His head whipped around, gaze fixed on her. "What do you mean, you?"

"Dad and I struck a deal. He agreed to drop the charges. If I gave up the internship, and cooking school, and accepted a job at Shaw Paper Products, you walked free."

Eric looked dumbfounded. "Holy fuck. Demi...*fuck*. I never knew—"

"Of course you didn't know. It was none of your damn business. But we've gone far enough down memory lane tonight. Let's drop it, okay? I learned some important things back then. Maybe you did, too. Let's put a rock on it."

"Why?" he demanded. "Why do that for me? You had no reason to think I deserved it."

She shook her head. "Damned if I know. I've been asking myself that question ever since. But it's fine now. I like my restaurant, my house, this town. I like my life. It's all good. I have no regrets."

"If you say so. Still, thanks. You saved my life by doing that. I just never knew you paid such a high price for it."

"Oh, don't overdo it," she snapped. "It's not like he banished me to the salt mines."

Eric shut up after that. After too much quiet, she looked over and found him was studying her intently, as if he were trying to memorize her.

"What?" she snapped. "What is it now?"

"Your hair," he said. "I'm glad it's still so long. That's how I remember you. All that beautiful wavy brown hair flowing down your back. Curly ringlets bouncing at the bottom."

Demi cleared her throat. "Eric," she murmured. "Don't."

86

"Sorry," he said. "I'll stop."

"Actually, I was thinking of cutting it really short. A pixie cut. Easier for work."

A smile flashed across his face. "What, to punish me?"

"I see you still have that bad habit of making it all about you," she said. "I don't take your likes and dislikes into account when I groom myself."

"Of course not." He sounded almost amused at her snark.

They had turned the corner onto the last stretch of road, and the silence took on a hot, buzzy, brain-melting charge that made her search vainly in her mind for a change of subject. Something neutral, that wouldn't explode in her face.

She saw the fenced field that marked the beginning of Otis's property, and it came to her at last. "Oh. There's something I wanted to tell you, before I forget again."

"Yes?"

"When I found Otis that morning, there was a brief period that he seemed lucid, before the ambulance got there," she said. "He grabbed my hand and kept on saying the same word, over and over. He said 'lock, lock, lock.' He seemed anxious for me to understand. Does that mean anything to you?"

Eric thought about it for a moment, and shook his head. "Can't think of anything," he said. "Just that I wish I'd been there for him."

"I'm glad that I was," she said.

"Do you play the martyr often?"

She bristled. "Excuse me? What do you mean by that?"

"It seems to be a theme. Sacrificing your dreams to get me out of jail. Driving miles of bad road to deliver pastry to lonesome seniors. Staying in the ICU with someone who isn't even your own relative. Throwing a reception in Otis's honor at your own expense and refusing to be reimbursed. Did you do that for him just because my brothers and I didn't?"

Her spine stiffened in outrage. "Are you feeling reproached, Eric?"

He shrugged. "Maybe."

"Tough shit for you," she said. "I will continue to do my own thing with no regard for how you feel about it. Don't bother feeling obligated or guilty. I'm a busy woman. I won't even notice."

"Ouch," he murmured. "Burn."

"You'll forget all about it in no time back in the big city. Where did you finally end up, anyhow?"

"I have apartments in a few different cities," he said. "I move around a lot for work. San Francisco, Seattle, New York and Los Angeles. I guess you could call San Francisco my home base."

She whistled. "Seriously?"

"I travel a lot." He sounded defensive. "And I don't like hotels. Not enough privacy."

"You don't have to justify yourself to me. So you're leaving soon, right?"

"Yeah, probably tomorrow afternoon. Day after tomorrow at the latest. I have appointments with the estate lawyer and the real estate agent, and then I'm gone. This place..." He shook his head. "It makes me do dumb things."

"Like bar fights?"

His gaze slid over her body. "Among other things."

They had reached Otis's driveway, and Demi's headlights reflected off the back of a parked car. She braked, and stared at the gleaming black Porsche in stunned disbelief.

"Holy shit," she said. "*This* is your car?"

"It's just a car, Demi." But he didn't look at her as he said it.

"Seriously? With all the thousands of makes and models of cars to choose from, you chose an exact replica of my dad's Porsche? The one you almost killed yourself crashing? It's even the same fucking color!"

"Yeah. But my leather interior is black, not cream."

"Oh, stop. Why would you get the very make and model of the car that screwed up your life so badly? That's twisted."

"I don't know," he said. "It's like armor, I guess. Like riding into this town in a tank. I need to make it clear to everyone that I don't need to steal other people's shit. I can buy my own."

"I should think so. That car must have cost, what, three hundred thousand bucks?"

"With all the extras, more like three-fifty," he admitted.

She was taken aback. "So you're rich. Of course. You designed Aion, Eos, Nyx. You own homes in four different cities. You can afford that car, and ten more like it."

"I do okay."

She rolled her eyes. "That Porsche is a big, expensive chip on your shoulder."

"I suppose. Not a damn thing I can do about it."

She parked right in front of that obscenity of a car and killed the engine, careful not to look in the rearview mirror. She was going to have to put the Porsche completely out of her mind to make this work. As well as this entire train-wreck of a conversation.

Because in spite of all the crazy bullshit she'd just heard, she was still going to do this. Deliberately, and in the face of her own good sense. She knew who this lying, delusional bastard was. What he was capable of. And she still wanted him in her bed.

One last time. On her terms. She would use him, exactly the way he had used her. Then she would move on, and let him go for good.

Then she would finally be done.

They sat in the darkness. The air hummed with the things she'd forbidden him to say. But he wasn't making a move on her.

Damn. She could feel the sexual tension. It was thick enough to cut. She'd counted on him being a selfish, oversexed opportunist. That he would come on to her as a matter of course. That, at least, should have been a sure thing.

Then again. She'd just scolded him brutally. Told him in ten different ways that he was a delusional asshole and a lying prick. He could be forgiven for deciding she was more trouble than she was worth.

God knows, he wouldn't be the first to come to that conclusion.

Or maybe it was even simpler than that. Maybe the truth was, after seven years, he could take it or leave it. And he'd decided to leave it. His prerogative.

Keep it dignified, girl. You don't need the worthless bastard. You're fine.

"Get out of the car," she said abruptly.

Eric didn't move. "What did I do?"

"Nothing," she said. "Which tells me everything I need to know. If you don't have the balls to make a move on me now, there's no point in me being here. Get the fuck out, Eric. Go back to your fancy luxurious life and don't try to—"

Her words cut off into a gasp as he kissed her.

8

Demi's lithe body vibrated with emotion. He slid his fingers into the thick, glossy hair at the back of her head, and her silky locks slid luxuriously between his fingers. Amazing softness. Sweet, mysterious scents. The deep shiver of response in her body.

She wanted this. In spite of hating him. In spite of everything.

He tasted the sweet, tender heat of her mouth, his lips moving slowly over hers as he waited for another cue. In the darkness, he couldn't read her expression. His hand closed around her hair, but he didn't pull her toward him. Not yet.

He had to be so fucking careful. Every word, every move was fraught with danger. Charged with need. The stakes impossibly high.

As bad ideas went, this one took the prize. She hated him. She believed the absolute worst of him. He was doing his best to armor himself against that.

But he couldn't keep his guard up if he was fucking

her.

He didn't speak. The way things were going for him tonight, it was better to shut up and just let the pull of unsatisfied lust that still throbbed between them speak for him.

They stared at each other. He didn't dare to breathe.

Demi barely moved, but on some level, he felt the energy shift as a deep, wordless impulse nudged her forward again. Oh so slowly...leaning toward him. *More.*

Fuck yeah. Anything. As much as he could get.

He slid his hand into the warmth of her open jacket to snag her waist and tug her closer. She responded by climbing over the center console to straddle him, face to face. Pressing her soft sexy heat against his stiff, aching cock. Pure, agonizing bliss.

She smelled so good. A vital, flowery hot sweetness that made him drunk and desperate. Her full, luscious lips opened against his, her tongue flicking, dancing with his. Her hair fell around them like a fragrant cape. He wanted to rip her clothes off. Touch and grip and tongue every part of her. All the details that had haunted his dreams for seven goddamn years.

She was trying to get a grip his leather jacket, but her hands kept slipping on the thick, damp surface. He wanted to feel the clutch of her hands. He took a second to shrug it off and she seized him immediately, fingers sliding into his short hair, clutching the back of his neck as he kissed her ravenously.

He felt like he'd die if he took his mouth away.

She was so smooth. Lithe and hot. Her soft, lush tits right under his face. She moved on him, rubbing her ass seductively against the stiff bulge of his cock. Staring into his eyes. That look of fearless challenge in her eyes made him burn.

"You're all hot and sweaty," she said. "From that stupid caveman fight."

"Yeah, I guess."

"That was a dumb thing to do."

"Yeah. Right. Absolutely." He would have agreed to anything with Demi undulating over him like that. Kissing him like she wanted to eat him up.

He ran his hand down over the curve of her hip, settling it on top of her thigh, hyper-alert for signs that he was pushing too hard. Overcompensating for all the missed chances, the hopeless wanting.

She wasn't pulling back. She rose up on her knees, arms around his neck, clutching his back, nails digging in as their desperate, furious kiss raged on. She ground her hips over him, and the breathless, gasping sounds she made were so sexy, he was about to come then and there.

He leaned away, gasping for air. "Wait a second. Let's pace ourselves. You're going to make me explode."

"Nope." Demi just shrugged off her jacket, tossing it behind her, and pushed up her shirt, revealing the smooth curves of her belly and a fresh cloud of her hot perfume. "I don't feel like waiting."

"You're killing me," he ground out, sucking in air as her hips pulsed sensually.

"Suffer," she whispered, lifting the shirt higher, above her low-cut, lace-trimmed bra. Her gorgeous tits spilled out. Tight nipples pressed the sheer fabric. "Fight for it."

God, yeah. He was all over her, hands, lips. Cupping the plump, heavy curves of her breasts. Her velvety heat overwhelmed him. The taste of her skin against his lips.

Her breath stuttered off as he dragged the stretchy cups down to free her nipples, licking and nuzzling hungrily. She moved sinuously in his grasp, gasping for air.

So sweet. So hot. Her hair, coiled against his chest, his face.

He went at her belt with shaking fingers, jerking it open. Then the buttons of her jeans. He couldn't pull them down far the way she was straddling him, but he got them down far enough to admire her sheer black lacy panties and slide his hand down inside to stroke her mound right above her clit, circling and teasing.

She danced against his hand, pushing herself against him, and pushed her own jeans down farther. He pressed his face against her breasts, licking and suckling as he teased his finger beneath the elastic and delicately probed inside against her hot, silky pussy lips, sliding along the length of her tender folds. She grabbed his wrist and pushed against him with a wordless moan, demanding more.

So he gave it to her, sliding slowly into a tight, clinging paradise. Slowly finger-fucking her while he suckled her breasts, her collarbone her shoulders. He liked how her nails dug into him. The sweet sting of her hunger.

She could have anything she wanted. He was helpless to deny her. She was so responsive. Those moans and sighs and arching shivers of pleasure with each bold caress and the hot liquid kiss of her pussy around his fingers was driving him crazy. He diddled her clit with his thumb. Slowly, slowly…around and around…right there, that was the place. He insisted and insisted…doubling down on the perfect sweet spot, listening to her body with every cell in him, waiting for the moment…and oh holy *fuck*, yesyesyes…

She went rigid with a sharp gasp. Made a tight, keening

sound. Her pussy clutched his fingers hard with every wrenching jolt of pleasure.

So sweet. Oh please, yes. He could do this for-fucking-ever.

When it finally subsided, she was draped over him, limp and trembling. Damp with sweat. He waited patiently until she looked up into his eyes.

Then, deliberately, he slid his hand out from between her legs, and sucked his fingers, licking off every lingering bit of her hot sex juice.

She tasted so right. Rich and sweet and sexy. Perfect. Ready for him.

"Please," he said thickly. "Let me lick you. Let me fuck you. Make you come ten more times. Or a hundred. Please."

She drew in an unsteady breath, reached down, and jerked up her jeans, buttoning them. Buckling her belt. Tugging down her shirt. Shaking back her hair.

"Not yet," she said. "Too easy."

Stopping right there, when she wanted so desperately to continue, took more willpower than anything Demi had ever done. It would have been so easy and perfect to tear off all her clothes and just mount up, letting the cool night air caress her bare ass. Shirt hiked up, her breasts bouncing in his face as she rode his thick, hard cock all the way to sweaty, screaming completion. Right there in her own car. Oh God, yes.

But she was so close to losing control. The windows were all fogged up, her hands shook, her body shook. She felt mortifyingly close to tears. Which was unthinkable.

And she had to be careful with him. Everything had to be just so. Studied and staged and planned. Choreographed down to the last move. It would be very tricky, to get what she craved while keeping her inner self locked up safe and tight.

She could not let herself be vulnerable to him. Not for one second. No tender feelings allowed.

She couldn't let him draw her into his trap. And it was so hard to resist the pull.

Eric groaned, deep in his throat. "Easy? You're playing games with me."

"Oh, Eric. You have no idea." She reached down and ran her fingertip slowly down the length of his stone-hard dick still trapped in his jeans. "I have not even begun to play games with you."

"Remember the time we made love in my car, after we hiked out of Lindsay Springs?"

"I don't want to talk about the past."

Eric nodded. "Right. Forgot. Sorry."

But it was too late. That particular Pandora's box of memories was open now, and they were so vivid. That time in the car when he first told her that he loved her.

She clambered back over the console and into the driver's seat, careful not to look at him as she gathered her thoughts, organized her words.

"I know you're leaving soon," she said slowly. "And you're not coming back."

"That's why I hesitated to make a move. You're not the sort of woman who only wants a—"

"Wrong," she said.

He frowned. "Huh?"

"You have no idea what kind of woman I am," she told him. "You never did. You were just a clueless boy."

"Ahhh…okay. If you say so."

"You don't know what I want until I tell you," she said, her voice cool.

"I'm listening," he said.

Her entire body hummed with emotion. She felt it vibrating in every part of her. Fingers and toes, lips, eyes, breasts. Everywhere.

"We have some unfinished business," she said.

He let out a low laugh. "Yah think?"

"So let's finish it."

"In a weekend? Just like that?"

"Not a weekend," she said swiftly. "One night. I'll never see your face again, am I right? Because that's the only reason I can even consider doing something so crazy."

He just sat there in the dark, silent.

"Say it," she said, more harshly. "Is that right?"

A long pause, and he nodded reluctantly. "Yes, I am leaving. I'm not coming back. You'll never see my face again. Are you satisfied?"

"Let me just state the rules. It's just sex. No talk of the past. We don't mention what happened between us before. What you did, what you didn't do. We don't talk about Boyd, or my dad, or his Porsche, or your Porsche, or the accident. None of it."

"I don't see how we can just cut off—"

"One night to settle our accounts, and neither expects or hopes or even thinks about more than that. Swear it."

"Demi, this is not what I—"

"Swear it or get the fuck out of my car."

He let out a sharp sigh. "Fine. I won't ask for more. Will you come inside?"

She hesitated, eying Otis's dark farmhouse. "Not here,"

she said. "Not tonight. It's too soon. And too easy."

"I've got no problem with easy," he said.

"Meaning what?" she asked. "Me? I'm easy? For climbing on top of you and coming all over your hand?"

"That moment will go down as one of the highlights of my life," he told her, with absolute sincerity.

"Nice try, but still, no. Not here. It's just too easy."

Eric laughed shortly. "Tell me one thing about this fucking day that was easy."

"Pounding Boyd into the mud didn't look like a towering challenge for you."

Eric let out a snort of disgust. "Don't remind me. I've hated that lying prick for all these years for fucking me up. In my revenge fantasies, he gave me a better fight. In real life, he came apart on me like a wet paper bag. What a goddamn anticlimax."

"We took a turn into the no-go zone," she said. "My bad. I said his name first."

"Right. No talk about Boyd." Eric gestured toward Otis's house. "What's wrong with here? Comfortable bed, clean sheets, total privacy. We're already here. We've already started the foreplay. It's great. What more do you want that we can't have here?"

She shook her head. "I just gave you a ride home," she said. "I'm not bringing sex conveniently to your door all served up on a silver platter."

He considered that for a moment. "I'll make it worth your while."

"You already have," she told him. "And even so. Not happening."

"Your place?"

"Hell, no. I don't want anyone to see that godawful car

parked outside my house. And I'd be justly embarrassed if anybody witnessed me doing anything this stupid and self-destructive."

"Ouch," he murmured.

"Get your feelings hurt if you want to. I don't care. This is between you and me and it needs to stay secret."

"Your guilty pleasure," he said. "Just like old times."

"I suppose," she said. "If it bothers you, take a pass."

"Hell, no. There's a motel on the strip mall down in Granger Valley, if you want anonymous. The Savoy Suites, one block past the dollar store. It'll smell like a thousand old cigarettes, but I for one will not notice."

"Hmm," she murmured. "Sounds kind of dirty and illicit."

"You say that like it's a bad thing," he murmured.

She almost smiled, in spite of herself.

"I don't care where we go," he said. "Dictate any terms you want. Jerk me around. Make ridiculous demands, play mind games with me, make me pay for all my sins. Do any damn thing you want. Just let me fuck you until you scream."

She lifted her chin, going for the mysterious and merciless femme fatale vibe, but she still had to swallow to keep her voice from wobbling. "You think you can take it?"

"Yes," he said. "If you're dishing it out, I want some."

She looked at the tracks of the raindrops trickling down the windshield for a minute. "Tomorrow night. Spruce Tip Island. Meet me there."

Eric looked dismayed. "Not tonight?"

"I need time to plan," she said.

"For what?" He sounded baffled.

She shrugged. She was under no obligation to explain to him how risky this was for her peace of mind. "I'm working early tomorrow. Tomorrow night is better for me."

"Spruce Tip," he repeated. "The island down at the far end of the lake, where your folks had the cabin, right? I can't drive to an island."

"So find a boat," she said.

"Otis had a boat." He sounded dubious. "If the motor still works. It's ancient."

"If it's too difficult, then don't come." She kept her voice light. "But I'll get there around seven tomorrow evening. Don't come before that."

"Okay. Seven o'clock, Spruce Island. Give me your phone number, in case I—"

"No. I don't want your number on my phone. My phone is a tool for the real world. This is just a secret fantasy. No connection with reality."

"It's gonna feel real tomorrow in Otis's leaky old fishing boat," he said ruefully.

"Your problem, not mine. Sweet dreams."

Demi didn't permit herself to look back as she drove away.

9

"I'm sorry I can't assess both properties today, Mr. Trask," Terry Cattrall said, his voice apologetic. "GodsAcre is pretty far up Kettle River Canyon, and you know how the roads are. Plus I have a conflict later in the evening, so…"

"It's okay. And call me Eric," he said, for the third time. Terry was a stocky, round-faced man with the pale, nervous looking eyebrows and small rimless glasses. Eric vaguely remembered the guy from high school. He'd been couple years younger, in Demi's class. "I can arrange to be at Otis's property tomorrow morning to let you in."

Terry looked relieved. "Great. I got the impression at the funeral that you were real anxious to get on your way today, but I couldn't fit it into my schedule yesterday, so…"

"I'll stay until tomorrow. But don't come too early. Say, ten-thirty?"

"Ten-thirty's great for me. So, shall we ride up together

now? We can take my Jeep up to the property. It'll probably handle better on that road than...that." Terry waved a reverent hand in the direction of the Porsche, parked right outside the storefront window of McCabe Realtors.

"I'm not going up to GodsAcre with you," Eric said.

Terry looked startled. "But don't you want to walk me around the place?"

"You have the site map," Eric said. "It's not like I need to let you inside locked buildings. There are no buildings. There's nothing to show you but the land. You can look that over without me. Everything's gone."

"Oh." Terry blinked, his brows furrowed. "Well, ah...I suppose that's fine, then."

"You can't get lost," Eric told him. "Kettle Canyon Road doesn't have any turn-offs. It hugs a cliff-face pretty much the whole way up. Set your odometer at the Narrows Bridge, and when you hit 12.5 miles look for a road on the left that leads into a narrow canyon. I'm sorry to make you go there alone, but I don't go up there. Not for any reason."

Terry's face reddened. "Of course you wouldn't," he murmured. "I'm so sorry."

"It's okay. Give me a call once you're there, if you have questions. I'll be happy to answer them, or walk you through the place at a distance."

"Yes, of course. I hope you understand, though, that GodsAcre probably won't demand the price you might have hoped for, given the size of the property. With the remote location, the fire damage, the poor condition of the roads and of course the tragic history, it'll be—"

"Of course," Eric said. "We know all that, and we don't expect it to be an easy sell. We just want it to be someone else's problem."

"We'll do our best, you can be sure of that. It's too bad Otis didn't go ahead and sell the place when he had the chance."

"Chance?" Eric stared at the other man. "What chance?"

Terry looked bewildered. "You mean…you didn't know about those offers?"

"What offers? When were they made?"

"Well, ah…" Terry's voice trailed off. "I was under the impression that Otis would have told you. I don't want to be opening any can of worms here, you understand, putting my foot in my — "

"Just tell me about the offers, Terry."

Terry looked hunted. "Ah, the only one I witnessed first-hand was about three years ago, about a year after I started working here. It was Bob Nagy's project, and I remember overhearing him telling Otis that he was crazy not to take the offer. That the land wasn't good for anything but hunting, maybe some timber, and he'd never get an offer anything close to that price again. Bob knew that you three wanted nothing to do with the place so he urged Otis to just sell it and be done with it. But for some reason, Otis wouldn't bite."

"Who made the offer?" Eric asked.

"To be honest, I couldn't tell you. Yesterday after I talked to you at the funeral, I came back here and looked all over for the records, but I cannot seem to locate them, not in our file cabinets or our computers. All those documents are just gone. It's the darnedest thing. But I'll certainly keep looking. I seem to recall Bob complaining about other offers coming in, too, before I started here. Offers that Otis had also refused."

"He never said a word to us about it," Eric said.

"I'm, ah...sure he had his reasons," Terry offered timidly.

"I'm sure he did. Is there any way I can talk to Bob?"

"Well, um, no, unfortunately. Bob died of a heart attack about three years ago. Not long after this last offer was made, actually. He was just about to retire. It was real sudden, and he didn't have any history of heart disease, but I guess that's how these thing go sometimes. His widow Agnes moved down to Santa Fe last year to be near her daughter."

A chill of dread shivered up Eric's spine. He pushed it away. All this bullshit about the Curse was superstitious crap anyway. Self-indulgent, magical thinking that could drive him crazy if he let it. He wasn't giving into it. He'd left all that garbage behind him.

"Well, then." Terry's voice took on a hearty tone. "Guess I'd better be heading out. I need to be back by four at the latest. My wife Deborah and I are having a special dinner date up at Cooper's Corner tonight. It's our fifth wedding anniversary."

"Congratulations," Eric said. "You can't be late for that. Call me if you have questions."

"Will do," Terry assured him.

Eric followed the guy out and watched him climb into a late model blue Jeep and tap the horn lightly in farewell as he drove away. The icy sting of autumn burned his ears, and the smell of frost was in the air.

He glanced up the street, where he could just see Demi's café a couple blocks up the way. He was tempted to go get coffee. Maybe a piece of that pie Otis had liked so much. But he had the feeling that any approach on his part would be perceived as violating the boundaries that she had set.

He did not want to fuck this up.

Even shifting his thoughts to Demi didn't chase away the chilly weight inside him. A strange sense of dread. A looming shadow but he couldn't see what cast it.

And he was sending Terry Cattrall up into that dark shadow all alone.

Oh, for fuck's sake. It was just an abandoned property. Nothing up there would hurt the guy. Terry would do his job and come back down. End of story.

But who the hell could have made those offers? And why? GodsAcre had so many strikes against it. It was uniquely undesirable.

Yet for some reason, Otis had refused all of the offers.

He wished he could talk to Otis. Not even so much for solving the mystery. Just for the comfort of seeing the old man's face. Hearing his gruff, no-nonsense voice.

He got into his Porsche, wishing he'd driven Otis's four-by-four pickup into town, but he'd already loaded Otis's old fiberglass fishing boat into the back of it, to haul to the last boat ramp on the shore of Shaw Lake.

Which was still very far from Spruce Tip, which was way the hell out there at the tip of the lake. In that crappy little boat with its ancient, bad-tempered two-stroke outboard, it could end up being a real adventure tonight, but fuck it. If worst came to worst, he could row. Or swim.

He could have rented something big and sleek and fast at the marina, but people would notice and start to speculate. He couldn't risk that.

If Demi wanted him to be her dirty secret, a dirty secret he would be. Lady's choice.

He spent the rest of the day tinkering with the ancient outboard. When he was marginally satisfied with how it functioned, he went on up to the bathroom to make himself presentable. Shower, shave, scent, fresh clothes.

He was heading out, Otis's keys in hand, when the landline rang in the kitchen.

Everyone in town knew Otis was dead, so that call couldn't be from anyone local who had known him. Anton and Mace texted him if they wanted to communicate. Terry and the estate lawyer had his cell. He had no reason to talk to anyone else around here other than Demi, and Demi had declared a no-phone zone.

Curiosity dragged him back to the kitchen, just as Otis's deathless eighties relic of an answering machine picked up the call.

It clicked and whirred. A high, nervous female voice spoke. "Hello? Have I reached Eric Trask? I hope you're there, Mr. Trask. It's Deborah Cattrall? Terry's wife?"

He hit the button that opened the speakerphone line. "Hi, Deborah. This is Eric. What can I do for you?"

"I'm so glad I reached you." Deborah's voice was tight and thin. "I would have called your cell, but only Terry had that number, so I looked up Otis in the phone book."

"I'm glad you caught me," Eric said. "How can I help you?"

"Well, um, I was just wondering if Terry had contacted you." The words came out in an anxious rush. "When I called the office, they told me he'd gone up to GodsAcre to do an appraisal after he met with you. And he was supposed to be home by now. Over two hours ago. But he's not back, and he's not answering his cell, and that's not like him."

"Hold on." Eric pulled out his smartphone and checked it. "I don't have any calls or texts from him."

"We had a date, for our anniversary dinner. It's just so

strange for him to not be home by now, and to not call me. We're too late to make it to the restaurant now. It's just so weird that he won't answer, you know?" Deborah hesitated for a moment. "There's a tracker on his phone," she said miserably. "It's up there. Near GodsAcre. It's on the road. And it's not moving."

"How far away?" His creeping dread swelled into alarm.

"Um, I'm not sure. Below the Upper Falls. So, I'll just, um, drive on up there, I guess. See if he maybe…had trouble with the car? And the phone?" She paused for a moment. "At the same time," she finished, voice quavering.

"It'll be dark soon, and the road is bad. I don't think that's a great idea. I'll go up and have a look around myself," Eric heard his own voice say it while the rest of him, the selfish, sex-crazed part that was wild to go to Spruce Island, howled silently in protest.

Deborah sounded scared. He couldn't let her drive up that bad road in the dark, not with the sick cold knot forming inside him.

He'd be damned if he'd throw Deborah into that black hole, too.

"I'd appreciate it," Deborah's voice trembled. "I hate to bother you, but I just don't know if my little car would be up to that road."

"Don't worry about it," he said. "I'm familiar with it, and I have Otis's four-by-four. Give me your cell number. I'll go on up there and take a look around for you."

Deborah did so. He finally managed to hang up over her thank-yous, and stared grimly out the kitchen window.

He'd fucked himself left right and sideways. Even if he didn't have a smoking hot date for wild, mindless sex with the woman of his dreams on Spruce Tip Island, he would do any crazy, desperate thing to stay away from GodsAcre.

He hadn't seen the place since the fire. It was haunted by the screams of the doomed. The thought of going up there made him physically sick.

But Terry did not seem like the type of guy who would blow off an anniversary dinner with his wife. His phone was motionless on Kettle Canyon Road. And Eric was the lazy, selfish dickhead who'd sent the poor guy up to that ill-omened place. Alone.

They had all thought it was hugely ironic that he, Anton and Mace, being the only survivors and bearing Jeremiah Paley's name at the time of his death, had fallen heir to the GodsAcre property. Like it or not, that blackened ruin and the land it was built on actually belonged to them. God help them.

Luckily for them, Otis had managed the property. They all stayed well away from that hellhole.

Now he was about to see the GodsAcre ruins, lonesome and ghostly in the autumn twilight. He'd be lucky if he managed to keep down his fucking lunch.

Don't flinch from pain. Hah. Old Jeremiah's command rang in his head as he got into Otis's four-by-four and headed down Vensel Road. Otis's gas gauge showed a third of a tank. That should get him up there and back.

He hesitated for one final moment at the turn-off to Kettle Canyon Road. The last time he'd taken this road was when he'd taken Demi up to Lindsay Springs for their scorching tryst at the waterfall. More emotionally charged memories.

Gravel slewed under the tires as he turned onto the road and punched the gas.

Kettle Canyon Road was rougher than he remembered. His belly felt colder and heavier with every lurching mile. Otis's boat slid around in the back of the pickup, thumping and rattling as he climbed.

Higher and higher. Endless, grinding switchbacks. The trees got shorter, the road narrower. Signs of coming winter were all around. During the winters of his childhood, they had sometimes been snowed in up there for months at a time. They often got eight to ten feet of snow at that elevation, and when they did, they lived like the end of the world had already happened. For all they knew, it had. The Prophet had stockpiled food, fuel, medicine, solar panels, machinery, medical equipment. After Kimball arrived, Jeremiah had invested in a fully equipped med lab in the caverns. Eric didn't know where Jeremiah's money had come from, but he must have had a lot of it to build and acquire all that stuff.

As he came closer to the level of the Upper Falls he slowed down. Something caught his eye as he rounded a hairpin turn and he ground to a halt in the thick mud.

A fringe of young pines separated the rough dirt road from the drop-off to the steep, rocky slope of the draw below. What he'd seen was a ragged gap in the fringe of trees, like a missing tooth. Three of the trees in the middle were broken in half.

He got out, trying to breathe down the sickening upwelling of ugly memories. That Humvee knocking Vaughan's Porsche off the cliff with him inside it, seven years ago.

Crashing through the trees. Snagging on a few more halfway down the steep slope.

Those trees had just barely stopped the car's fall. He'd hung by a thread.

He saw fresh tire marks in the mud. Deep, wet and obvious. They led up to the edge of the road right in front of the broken trees. The tracks did not display any attempt to brake or turn. Clean and straight. Right angles to the edge…and right off.

Pale splinters of fresh wood stuck up from the three broken trees. Eric could smell the tang of fresh pine-sap in the cold as he peered over the edge, his heart thudding.

He saw the glitter of broken glass on the steep, rocky slope, and far below, Terry's blue jeep in the canyon below. On the edge of Kettle River. Upside down. Crumpled.

There had been no trees on this slope big enough to break Terry's fall.

Eric pulled out his phone and called 911.

"What is the nature of your emergency?" the operator asked him.

"This is Eric Trask," he said. "I'm up on Kettle Canyon Road, about two miles below Upper Kettle Falls. I'm looking down at the scene of a car accident. Someone went off the road here and fell pretty far. It looks bad."

"Is anyone there in need of medical attention?"

"I'm hiking down now to see. If the driver is alive, he's definitely going to need medical attention, so tell them to hurry. There's a red Ford four-by-four parked on the road. That's your landmark."

"Please stay on the line, sir, so we can—"

"I can't. I need both my hands to climb." He cut off the call, looked at the glow of sunset and went back to the four-by-four to fish out the flashlight Otis kept in the glove box. He clambered over the edge, welcoming the mental concentration needed keep from falling as he half scrambled, half tumbled down the rocky mountainside.

The busier his mind, the better. He didn't want to think about Terry and Deborah's anniversary dinner, or the Humvee knocking the Porsche off the road. Green trees crunching, branches rushing past him, upside down. Or Otis, cold and stiff in a box in the Shaw's Crossing Cemetery. Or the roar of flames licking the trees in the darkness.

And the screaming. It never really stopped. It was always there, waiting for him whenever his mind was idle. The Curse, following him like a faithful hound.

I'm so sorry, Deborah. I should never have sent him up to this godforsaken place.

"Terry!" he yelled "Terry? Can you hear me?"

No response, not that he could have heard one over the roar of the water rushing down the draw to join with Kettle River.

The closer he got to the Jeep, the less hope he had. Terry's car had tumbled end over end multiple times. It was flattened and twisted, every window shattered.

Eric had to crawl over piles of logs, tangled branches and the enormous tumbled boulders of the river to get to the Jeep. He steeled himself as he crouched to peer inside.

Oh God. He turned away, and his ass landed heavily on a rock as the strength all rushed out of his legs.

Terry was definitely dead. He hung upside down in his seat belt, neck broken, head half crushed, his face streaked with blood. His eyes were wide and blank. Surprised.

There was no point, but still he reached inside, feeling at the base of Terry's throat for his pulse. There was none. His blood felt tacky, almost dry. It was all over for him.

Then there was nothing left to do but sit with Terry's body as the dusk deepened, the river rushing and roaring in his ears.

Another man dead. His young wife a widow. And Eric was the gutless asshole who'd sent the poor guy up here to die. The same, exact death that had almost claimed him seven years ago. He'd cheated the Curse of its prize. It had taken Terry in his place.

No. He had to stop thinking this way or he'd go nuts. Jeremiah-style nuts.

The roar of the stream couldn't drown out the screaming, the crackle of flames in his mind. There was no fire anywhere near, but still he smelled smoke. He was choking on it. He wanted to bellow and roar, smash and break things, but there was no point.

Everything was already broken.

It was full dark before he saw the blue and red police flashers crawling slowly up the hill. He waited until the flashers stopped moving near where he had parked the truck, and turned on the flashlight, signaling the cops until they trained a powerful searchlight down the hill, pointing it at Terry's crushed Jeep.

He waved to them, stepped out of their blinding pool of light and started to climb.

He didn't remember the slog back up. It was like he watched from someplace very distant while some other guy made that effort, clawing his way back up that steep, muddy slope. Once he reached the top, he had a conversation with some cops, a man and a woman. He'd known their names in another life, but not tonight.

He didn't know if he'd been coherent, or if he'd babbled nonsense. An ambulance followed. Too late for Terry. The ambulance attendants tried to make a fuss over Eric, but he waved them away. When everyone was looking elsewhere, he got into Otis's pickup and took off. In the rearview, he saw someone running after him, shouting for him to stop.

He just kept on driving.

10

Benedict Vaughan stepped out in front of her from behind a van, blocking the gate to the marina. Demi was so startled, she almost dropped the shopping bags full of food trays that she carried. She stepped back awkwardly. "Dad! What are you doing here?"

Her father gestured toward her car, which she'd left parked across the street. "I came to your house, but you were driving off just as I pulled up. I wanted to talk to you."

That made the alarm bells jangle. Coming to see her? Dad never came to see her.

He had that same sweaty, clammy look she'd noticed at the funeral yesterday, and his eyes were puffy and reddened. "Dad, are you okay?"

"I'm fine," he said impatiently. "It's you I'm worrying about."

She raised her eyebrows. "Don't worry. I'm fine."

"Are you? I heard you were out drinking last night with that…that person."

"That's nobody's business," she said, with studied calm. "Don't listen to gossip."

"I heard he was in a bar-room brawl. That Boyd Nevins ended up in the Urgent Care because of him. This is the kind of person you want to party with?"

"Boyd had it coming," she said. "I was there. Boyd was the instigator."

"Of course you would come to his defense," he snarled. "Of course."

Demi took a deep breath, and let it out slowly, counting down. "Dad," she said evenly. "Please. Let's not do this."

"Believe me, I would rather not. But you force my hand, Demetra. Every time."

She shook her head. There was no point in starting an old argument, but there was a question burning in her mind that only Dad could answer, and it just came out of her.

"Speaking of Boyd," she said. "There's something I have to ask you. Eric told me he never took the keys to the Porsche. He said that Boyd was driving it that morning. That Boyd picked him up, took him to Peyton State Park, and drove off and left him there. He also says he was forced off the road by a Humvee while he was bringing the car back. Why did I never hear that side of the story?"

Her father's eyes went wide with outrage. "Because it's ridiculous!" he sputtered. "He'd say anything to gain your sympathies. That's the most farfetched thing I ever heard. Boyd was somewhere else at that time, and fully accounted for. This man is supposed to be relatively bright, isn't he? You'd think he'd come up with something a little more believable than that! I'm embarrassed that you'd even take it into consideration!"

"You never told me Eric claimed that Boyd was driving

the Porsche."

"Of course not. Why should I? It was a bullshit claim. Quickly shown to be completely false. It didn't deserve to be repeated."

Dad's face was turning that eggplant color that indicated the danger zone. She edged away from him, gripping her bags. "Well, okay. I just had to ask. Oh, by the way. I'm taking the boat out to Spruce Tip tonight."

"Tonight? By yourself? I don't think that's safe."

"It's been an intense couple of days, and the island relaxes me," she said. "It's a beautiful sunset. Look at the colors on the water. I've done it many times. I'm an old pro."

"In the middle of the summer, maybe!"

"It's fine now," she soothed. "The lake is very calm. There's good cell reception out there these days. Absolutely nothing to worry about."

Already she was kicking herself for telling him. He would never have known if she'd just taken the boat and gone. Now he might forbid her, which would be complicated and stupid.

"Okay, honey," he said. "Of course. Go ahead to the island. Just be careful, all right?"

Demi stared at him, disoriented by his sudden change in tone.

"Uh...uh, great," she faltered. "Thanks. Talk to you tomorrow, Dad."

"'Night, honey."

Honey? Since when had Dad called her 'honey?' Twice in the last minute.

She forced a smile and a nod, hoisted up her bags, and headed down the wooden walkway. When she got to the boat slip and turned around, he still hadn't moved.

He had made a lot of huffy noises about Boyd, and the Porsche. But he'd never come out and said, in so many words, that what Eric said wasn't true.

Just that it wasn't probable.

He giving her that raw, hollow-eyed stare again. She'd noticed it periodically for the last few years. Even from here, it creeped her out. It was the look of a guy whose dire predictions had all come horribly true.

Despair, but no surprise.

Benedict watched until he lost sight of the boat. He got into his car and sat there, frozen, until he started feeling self-conscious. People were starting to notice him.

He put his phone to his ear. That looked better.

Demetra had just thrown him the life-saving rope he needed. But it came at a price.

He had tried once before to get out of this trap back when Elaine was alive. But Elaine couldn't accept the danger they were in. He still remembered her eyes, full of shocked horror, after he confided his escape plan for the two of them.

It was extreme, yes. Risky. But Elaine wouldn't even consider it. She'd wanted to run to the police, call the newspaper. Blow the whole thing wide open. She had no fucking idea what they were dealing with.

Well, she'd certainly found out.

Elaine had insisted on kidnapping insurance for Demetra when she was a child and Shaw Paper was booming. At the time, he'd thought it was paranoid, but if his father-in-law wanted to fork out the premiums, why not? It was Henry's money. The old man could afford it. Henry adored

Demetra and indulged all of her whims.

Henry would pay any sum to get his granddaughter back. Six million was the cap on the policy. The insurance company would pay up eventually, so it wouldn't be stealing. At least, not from his father-in-law, who would be fully reimbursed. In good time, once Demetra was home again safe and sound. No lasting harm would be done.

Six million was a fresh start for him. Far away from this shit-pile of a town. It was also his only hope of survival, at this point.

It should never have come to this. Eric Trask would have left on his own if Demetra hadn't lured him to stay seven years ago. Benedict had been instructed to make Shaw's Crossing a living hell for the Trask boys, and he'd done his job. The other two young men had hightailed it out of there right on schedule, as soon as they graduated. But not Eric. He'd come back, after his stint in the Marines, and attached himself to Demetra.

It was a catastrophe but Benedict handled it. At least, he thought he had.

He was still reeling from Felix's last call. *Eric Trask is accident prone. Everyone knows that, thanks to you. Be real sad if a beautiful young woman got caught in the accident along with him.*

He was doing this for Demetra, too. To keep her safe. Desperate times, desperate measures.

He dialed the number, wondering if it was still valid. The line clicked open. Benedict heard just the faint, wet rasp of breathing.

"Ah, hello?" he said. "I need to speak to Sayer —"

"Who the fuck are you?" A nasal, reedy voice. Not Sayer's.

"I'm Ben. I contacted you about three years ago, and

I—"

"I remember you. The asshole who chickened out at the last minute, right?"

"I didn't chicken out. I had a problem with my wife, and she—"

"Stay on the line. I'll see if he wants to talk to you."

Click, and he was listening to country music on hold.

Six minutes ground by. He was about to start up the car the when the voice came back on the line. "Call this." He rattled off a number.

"One second. Let me just grab a pen and you can repeat—"

"Don't write it down, asshole!"

"Okay, okay," Benedict soothed. He entered the number wrong four times before it finally rang through.

The line clicked open. "So it's you again." The rough, scraping voice he remembered. "Changed your mind? Again?"

"Ah, yes. I was hoping to put our old deal back on its feet."

"You fucked me over. And now you want the same deal? Hah. That's funny."

"I'm sorry. It was unavoidable. This time it'll go through. I'm completely committed, and there's no one trying to stop me. But it has to happen tonight. Out on the lake, at Spruce Tip Island. Tonight's your perfect opportunity."

"Tonight? Hah. You pricks think I just pull this stuff out of my ass?"

"Ah, no. I never thought—"

"Four times the old fee. For the rush, and my inconvenience. In advance."

Benedict did some calculating. "Twice the fee," he

countered. "Third up front, the last two thirds when I pick her up."

"You have the cash?"

"Same cash, shrink-wrapped in plastic. I never even touched it. But I'll need time to find the rest of the money."

"Not if it's tonight." Sayer clicked his tongue. "Three times the fee. Last offer."

"Done," Benedict said. "She'll be at the cabin on Spruce Tip Island, at the end of the lake. No surveillance cameras, no cars. There's nothing out there."

Sayer grunted. "Right. Now I gotta find a fucking boat?"

"One more thing. There may or may not be a man with her tonight. Eric Trask."

Sayer whistled. "That same punk you had me run off the road? You must hate that motherfucker so bad."

Benedict gritted his teeth. "I'm not sure if he'll be there. But if he is, I want you to, ah…take care of him."

Sayer paused for a moment. "Ben," he said. "A hit job is not a little extra. You know that. It's a whole different thing. A whole different fee schedule."

"So don't kill him, then," Benedict said desperately. "Just, ah…rough him up. Incapacitate him. Leave him tied up. Wear masks. Just be sure to, ah, tie him up really well. Duct tape, rope. Something like that."

Sayer grunted thoughtfully "He gonna give us trouble?"

"I doubt he'll be armed. He has no reason to be. None he's aware of."

"Military training?"

"He was in the Marines for a while, I believe."

"Fuck. Six times the original fee. Half up front tonight."

"I don't have the—"

"I need more men and I have to pay 'em. We on?"

"We're on," Benedict said numbly. "And, ah, be careful not to hurt her, right? I mean, try not to terrify her too much. It's not necessary to be violent, or—"

"Losing your nerve? You want me to tuck her into bed and sing her a lullaby?"

Sayer's lascivious tone made Benedict's skin creep. "I just want to be sure you understand that she's not—"

"Shut up. I'm a fucking professional. Bring the money to the drop point, and stop jerking yourself off. Look for my text." The line went dead.

Benedict sank back against the car seat, shaking. If Eric Trask did go to Spruce Tip tonight…if the kidnappers succeeded in beating and binding him…then maybe, just maybe, he could finish this himself.

He would personally make sure that Eric Trask never found out any more about what was going on in Shaw's Crossing. Once and for all.

Felix and his employer would have no more reason to punish him. No reason to pursue him when he disappeared. He just had to man up. Take matters into his own hands.

Along with a knife, or a rock, or…something.

He was furious at Demetra for putting him in this awful position. Forcing him into doing this in the hardest, ugliest way possible. Maximum pain, fear and violence.

But she'd brought it on herself. Just like she always did.

11

It was her own damn fault, getting all wound up thinking that Eric would show up and make all her fantasies come true. At least the strictly sexual ones.

But evidently, it wasn't happening.

Demi had run the gamut of the feels. Giggly teenage flutters while she showered and depilated and lotioned and plucked and perfumed herself, made up her face and blew out her hair and picked out the sexy little nothings to wear under her clothes.

Then the trip out over the lake in the glow of sunset. She felt so connected, so alive. Her whole body buzzed with endless possibility. She fussed over the food she brought. Lit a fire to take the damp and chill out of the cabin. Put fresh, crisp lavender scented sheets on the bed.

After making such a big fucking deal about making him work for his treats.

Aw, whatever. She was human, and this was Eric Trask. She forgave herself.

At least until the next phase began. The one that involved watching the clock.

That phase morphed, with agonizing slowness, into staring out at the moon on the undisturbed water as her heart and stomach sank lower and lower. Watching the minute hand crawl around the clock face. Then the hour hand. Again and again and again.

No boat appeared.

Then the gamut of other feels began. Anger at him for making a fool of her again. Fury at herself for falling for it. For wanting him at all. Compromising herself. She knew what he was, but she just hadn't cared. Not if he fulfilled her stupid fantasies.

She deserved to get dinged for being such an idiot. God, she'd almost started believing him about Boyd driving Dad's Porsche, after Dad sounded so weird about it.

She wanted so badly for Eric to be telling the truth. Even though that opened a lot of other very dark possibilities that she wasn't quite ready to consider yet.

But the truth was the truth. It didn't give a shit what she wanted.

And the real truth she had to face was just this. That clock, tick- ticking loudly in the enormous silence.

Then came the final phase. Swallowing that bitter pill...again. Every rejection and failure and shortfall, every time she'd felt stupid and not good enough, all rolled up into a big, fat wad and shoved down her throat.

She, of all people, should have known better than to do this to herself.

To hell with him. Life went on. She'd meditate on the moon tonight. When the moon set, she'd move on to the stars. She'd contemplate the dawn when that came around.

The lake was beautiful. Alone or accompanied, beauty was always a comfort.

And tomorrow, she'd go right back to work. Unchosen. Untransformed. Unfucked.

She'd told him right up front to take it or leave it. He'd left it, just like he had before. Now she was all surprised and hurt about that?

Grow up. Get some dignity. Boo-hoo, poor her. There were worse things, but she didn't want to dwell on them. She wished she'd gotten that man's fucking phone number after all, just so she could have the satisfaction of blocking it. *Boom.* Take that, dickhead.

Demi went out to sit on the sheltered back patio rather than the deck that fronted the lake. The wooden deck furniture was cold and damp, and the moonlight seemed chilly and ghostly once all the brilliant sexual excitement was drained out of it.

The moon set. The stars came out. Cold sank into her bones until her teeth rattled in her head. Screw this shit. Time to go inside. Have her sulk-fest by a crackling fire with hot chocolate. She'd take comfort where she found it. Brownies always helped.

She was in the kitchen, about to sip her cocoa when the knock sounded on the door. Excitement zapped her so hard she jumped, sloshing hot liquid onto her hand.

The knocking continued. "Demi? Hey! You in there?"

She looked up at the clock, which she'd stopped allowing herself to do somewhere around a twelve-twenty AM. It was now one-fifteen. She wiped her stinging hand on her jeans and stood there, frozen in doubt.

Holy shit. He was actually here.

But please. *Hours* late? It was humiliating. Really, it had taken him that long to decide if a night of wild, unbridled sex with her was worth the effort?

Fuck's sake. Enough already.

"Go home, Eric," she called. "It's late for me. I need to work tomorrow. Bye."

"Demi, open the door. I'm sorry I'm late. But I—"

"Sorry? Six hours? Really, you were that ambivalent about my invitation? It occurs to me that I never actually asked you if you were involved, or engaged, or even married, for that matter. Sloppy of me."

"I'm not married or involved with anyone. Open the door so I can explain."

"No. Follow your original impulse, which was not to come at all. Get lost."

Dead silence followed that. She couldn't even breathe.

Crash. The door burst open and Eric Trask stepped into the entryway. He saw her in the kitchen. He stood there, swaying on his feet, covered in mud.

The look in his eyes scared her.

"Eric?" she said. "What the hell? Did something happen? Are you hurt?"

"Not me." His voice was a rasp of exhaustion. "I went up the mountain toward GodsAcre tonight, looking for Terry Cattrall. He went up to appraise the property. Didn't show up for a date with his wife. She asked me to go check on him. His Jeep went off the cliff. So I hiked down into the canyon to see if he was alive."

"And…?"

He tried to speak, but his voice caught in his throat. He shook his head.

"Oh, Eric." She set her cup down on the table.

"Deborah was about to drive up there herself to look

for him, but I thought that was a shitty idea," he said hoarsely. "So I told her I'd go."

Demi knew what that must have cost him. Just the thought of that place made him grit his teeth. She nodded, waiting for more.

"I knew he was gone as soon as I looked down. The Jeep was crushed. But I went down to check anyhow." He shook his head. "Then I went see Deborah. To tell her."

Her eyes fogged up at the desolation on his face. "Oh, Eric. Oh, no."

"Chief Bristol would have done it eventually, but she would've been waiting up all night, fearing the worst. Not knowing. And I couldn't tell her on the phone. That seemed wrong, too."

She pressed her hand to her mouth, which had begun to shake.

"I didn't know what to say. In the end, I didn't have to say anything. She saw it on my face. But I couldn't just leave her there all alone. I waited until her mom and sister drove over from Granger Valley. Oh, for fuck's sake. Demi. Don't cry. Please don't."

"I can't help it," she said, sniffing back tears. "It's not up to me. Or you."

"Bitch me out, like before," Eric pleaded. "Scold me. Be a scary man-eating femme fatale. That I can deal with. But not tears. Not tonight."

The grief in his eyes cut her to the bone. Eric flinched away from her gaze as if he couldn't bear to be seen.

The silence was awful. This whole thing had gone completely sideways. Her plan only worked if everything stayed super-light. It had just gotten terribly, shockingly real.

A night of fun, hot, playful sex was one thing. Actual

intimacy…God, no.

"I would've called if I could," he said. "I'm sorry I'm so late."

"Never mind that. Sit down, before you fall down." She jerked a chair out from the table. "Here. Sit. Right now. You look kind of gray."

He lowered himself into the chair. Demi pushed the cup of steaming hot chocolate across the table in his direction. "Drink that," she directed, seizing a bottle from the counter.

"I really don't need to—" He stopped, as she sloshed a generous shot of bourbon into the cup. "Oh. Well, then. If you put it that way." He took a deep swallow. "Thanks."

He looked so miserable. Oh, to hell with it. She gave into the impulse and sat down on his lap, wrapping her arms around his neck.

He jerked back in the chair. Cocoa slopped all over the table. "Don't."

She got back to her feet and stepped back, hurt and confused. "What? Don't touch you? Then what the hell are you doing out here?"

"I don't fucking know," he said. "I shouldn't have come at all. I'm afraid it's starting again. I don't want you caught up in it."

"What's starting? What the hell are you talking about?"

"The Curse." His voice sounded hollow. "I can feel it closing in on me. It'll hurt anything I touch. I don't want it to hurt you."

His words provoked a deep chill of fear inside her, which pissed her off. "You mean the Prophet's Curse?" she demanded. "You can't be serious."

Eric rubbed his face, not meeting her eyes. "I tell Terry to go up to GodsAcre, and immediately, he dies. Otis sends us a voicemail late at night telling us he has to talk to us about GodsAcre and the next day, he dies. Bob Nagy fields an offer for GodsAcre three years ago, which Otis refused. He immediately has an unexpected heart attack. I don't know, Demi. The way things are going, you might be smarter to stay away from me."

"Well, that goes without saying," she said wryly. "But not because of some stupid fucking curse. Give me a break, Eric. You should be ashamed of yourself."

"I never said it was rational," he said wearily. "It wasn't rational thirteen years ago either, but people still died. A lot of people, Demi. I just don't want to hurt you."

Demi let out a short laugh. "Too late, Eric. That ship has sailed."

They stared at each other in the heavy stillness.

"At least you're still alive," he said. "I have that to be grateful for."

"Don't be an asshole," she said. "This isn't about you. The bad, random shit that happens to people? It doesn't all originate with you, Eric. The universe doesn't revolve around you. You...aren't...that...powerful. Get it through your thick head."

An almost-smile twitched his mouth. "Do you get tired of being such a hard-ass?"

"No, actually. It never gets old." She wiped her eyes with the backs of her hands, wishing she'd skipped the damn mascara, and glared at him, tight-lipped. "Truth time. You didn't come to the far end of Shaw Lake in a crappy little fishing boat in the middle of the night just to tell me to stay the hell away from you. You could've told me tomorrow. Or just left town without a word. You didn't do that."

He swallowed hard and shook his head.

"You're just feeling guilty about still wanting this. Even after what happened tonight. It makes you feel selfish and frivolous. That's why you're hesitating."

He started to speak, but Demi held up her hand. "I am so sorry about what happened to Terry," she said. "But it doesn't change anything about this."

"You don't think?"

"No," she said. "You came out here for one thing only." Demi plucked the cup from his hand and placing it on the table. She swung her leg over his legs and sat down, straddling him and cupping his face in her hands. "So take it."

Game on.

Eric seized her, pressing her lithe body closer to his aching cock, and kissed her with savage urgency. Her mouth opened and their tongues flicked, twining. He groaned under his breath as she rocked against his erection, pressing against his throbbing bulge with a sigh of longing.

Closer. He cupped her ass with one hand, sliding his other hand down to circle her clit with his thumb. Feeling for it…until he got it just exactly right. Her breath got ragged and sharp. Little helpless gasping noises. *Yes.*

Just like the last time he touched her. Only more.

He got it right, again…and again…and again. Righter, every time. The pulsing got deeper, the pace got faster. She clutched his shoulders, head thrown back, her luscious lower lip caught between her teeth. Lost in her own pleasure.

That's how it'll be when I'm inside you. I'll fuck you so good. Slow, fast, below, behind, on top, whatever you want as long as it lasts for-fucking-ever. As long as you come and come. All night long.

He couldn't say it. No sexy, seductive patter tonight. He was at her feet. Wordless, panting, desperate. He wanted to lose himself in her. Forget what had just happened.

Just let the pain go. Fall into her arms and never come out.

Her thighs tightened, squeezing around his. He gripped her ass and pulled, feeling his way toward her first climax. That was how it had to be with Demi. She had to come before he even got her clothes off. This had to be best-ever sex. Unmatchable.

If this was all they were going to get for the rest of their lives, he'd make it count.

He kissed her like his life depended on it. She was life itself, the hot, the wet. Astonishing salt-sweetness. Warm lush softness. The strength in her slender frame. The impossible, velvety softness of her warm skin, the plump heft of her tits. His hips surged and bucked under her squirming body, pushing her up to the edge…

And over it. She arched back with a cry as the orgasm wrenched her.

Its echoes pulsed against his own long-suffering dick. A distant, teasing throb that aroused him so sharply, he teetered on the edge of losing it.

Breathe it down. Don't open your eyes. Do…not…fucking…move. Not one muscle.

Okay. He was cool. He dared, very slowly, to open his eyes.

Lust surged at the sight of her. Head flung back, a sheen of moisture on her flushed face, her eyes closed. She licked her lips. They gleamed, lush and soft.

His dick twitched with eagerness to get on with it.

Demi's head lifted slowly, and she sagged forward, leaning her forehead delicately against his. It was a tiny point of contact, but suddenly his forehead was an erogenous zone, and the point was a tingling glow, spreading outward. Filling him with heat and light.

"Hey," he said. "You good?"

"Yes." Her lips curved in a sensual smile. "Incredible."

Eric stared at the sexy swell of her bottom lip. The sensual gleam as she licked them again. That hot red color. Flushed and full. He wanted to touch every inch of her. Every detail of her bone structure. He wanted to explore every warm, silky dip and swell and hollow and curve of her skin with his lips, his tongue. In his mind he could still feel her snug, silken wet pussy clinging to his caressing fingers, like his finger was a cock, and she was taking him in. Slick and deep and willing.

So responsive. Burning for him. It blew his mind. Humbled him.

"So," she murmured. "Now what?"

"This is a good starting place," he said. "We can move any direction you want from here. Erotically speaking."

"Yeah?" Her eyes were dilated, heavy-lidded. Smiling. "Such as?"

"You tell me," he said. "Ladies' choice."

Her laughter sounded breathless. "You want me to spell it out for you? Or do you have a pre-set menu for me to choose from?"

"If you need one, sure. Go a la carte, if you feel like it. Be as specific as you want. I stand ready to fulfill any desire, any fantasy." He slid his hand down into the waistband of her jeans, stroking the exquisitely smooth, fine texture of her ass cheek, then pulled her back into a swift, hard kiss. "Or if you don't want the responsibility of choosing, you could just go with the special of the day."

He felt her lips curve against his cheek. "Tell me about the special."

"With the special, you just let go and trust me to get you there," he explained. "Point me to any horizontal surface, let me get your clothes off, and I'll just make you come all night long. Hands, tongue, cock. All over you, kissing and licking and sucking and fucking you. As long as you want. It stops when you say. Starts again when you say."

He felt her tremble in response. "That's quite a sales pitch for the special."

"I'm good for it," he said. "Making you come makes me feel like a god. I'm so motivated to make it good for you. You would not believe my steely resolve."

Demi reached down between her legs, wiggling back until she could grip his aching penis. "Very steely," she murmured. "Inspiring as hell." She gave his stiff erection an appreciative pat, and slid off his lap. She took his hand and pulled. "Come on."

He followed her through a door leading to a steep white-painted staircase. At the top were two doors facing each other.

She pushed open one of them. The attic bedroom was dim and shadowy. A small, glowing rock lamp let off a reddish glow like firelight. There was a double bed with an old-fashioned quilt, lace-trimmed white sheets. A turned-down bed. Pale and pristine.

Eric looked down at himself. For the first time in several overheated minutes, reality intruded as he registered the mud-caked boots, his sodden, filthy jeans.

Demi was waiting for him to enter. But he couldn't get

anywhere near snowy linens or heirloom quilts in this condition. "I'm filthy," he said. "I'll ruin this place."

"There's a bathroom where you can wash up," she said. "I'll show you."

She led him into a connecting bathroom with a sloping attic ceiling. Reached up onto the shelf for a white towel, thought better of it and tossed him a navy blue one.

"Leave your stuff in here," she said.

She left him in there, peeling off his muddy clothes and contemplating his own face in the big mirror. It reminded him of the look they all had after the GodsAcre fire. That bottomless-pit look of someone who's seen things he can't un-see, no matter how fast he ran. No matter how compelling the distraction.

He turned the shower as hot as it would go and scrubbed himself until the muddy water ran clear and clean. Tonight would be different. If anything on earth could heal him, Demi could. He would fill his eyes with her. Fill his mind. Tough and prickly and guarded as she was, she was still pure magic for him. She had the power. He craved it. Craved her.

He was hers. Always had been. Nothing held back, no matter the cost.

He was all in.

12

Demi paced the room, listening to the shower in the other room. Pictured him gloriously naked in there, hot water running down his perfect body. She couldn't breathe.

Two options. She could strip down right now and flaunt her bare naked body to him when he walked out. Or else she waited to get her clothes peeled off.

Both options had their unique appeal.

In the end, she got busy pulling her clothes off, not being the type to wait around for others to decide how things were going to go. She'd invited him here for sex, plain and simple. It made no sense to be all fluttery and demure about it now. And it was late, after all. They had no time for coy, time-wasting crap.

The lingerie was another mini-dilemma. In the end, she stripped it off, too. It no longer felt like the right vibe for this encounter. Tonight wasn't going to be a light-hearted, teasing seduction involving peach-colored lace or French cut lace-trimmed panties. Her naked boobs alone would have to do the heavy lifting. Fortunately, they had some raw stopping power all on their own. She'd make full use of that fact.

In fact, she could hardly wait.

The shower stopped. Her heart was in her throat already, but swelled up in there, in that final flash of girlish panic.

Oh please. Just stop. She was no longer the clueless girl she'd been when they were together before, all dazzled by his smooth, sensual bedroom moves. She was a grown-ass woman who knew exactly what she liked.

She could run this show herself. She sat down, her fingers biting nervously into the foam mattress, sliding over the white sheets.

The bathroom door opened. Eric snapped off the bathroom light and emerged, wreathed with drifting, scented steam, the blue towel wrapped around his hips.

No surprise, but still. Holy crap. His body, whoa. Not that she'd forgotten how stunning he was.

Eric took her breath away even when fully clothed. Naked, the effect was even more intense. Big and broad. Taut sinewy muscle. Thick-shouldered, heavy-chested. That tangle of dark hair on his chest, threading down in a damp line over his lean belly.

He looked at her naked body, and a flush rose on his face. He tried to speak, and just swallowed. She'd intended to say something teasing to break the tension. Nothing would come out. The silence was deafening.

Eric was the first to find his voice. "You're so beautiful," he said hoarsely.

The towel was tented out over his erection. He let it drop.

Oh. Good Lord. That was one beautiful penis. Broad, thick, blunt, jutting from his thatch of hair, high and proud. She'd admired it before, at great length...but still. Wow.

"Do you have condoms?" he asked. "I was going to pick some up, but..."

"I brought a few with me." She reached for her purse on the bedside table and pulled out the three-pack she still had stashed in the bathroom cabinet back at her house, back from her more hopeful dating days. She'd been in a cynical sex drought for a while now. She wasn't even sure how long it had been, and was too distracted by his stunning presence to do the math now.

Eric took the three-pack and shook one out. She plucked it from his hand and laid it down on the bedside table. "Don't tell me you're going to shrink-wrap that excellent thing before I even get a chance to play with it," she said. "That would not be fair."

His words broke off into a gasp as she grasped his cock and squeezed. Broad and hot and smooth. Stiff and pulsing in her hand. She loved the shudder that racked him. The tendons standing out in his throat, the tension in his jaw. His throat moving as he tried to speak, failed, swallowed. "Oh God," he rasped. "Demi."

Yeah. That was the reaction she was going for. Her hottest fantasy. Eric Trask helpless, gasping, fighting for control. It made her feel so powerful.

And she desperately needed to feel powerful with his man.

Demi reached around to grip his hard, muscular ass, and pulled him closer, twisting her hands sensually up and down the length of his shaft. Close enough to drop a kiss on the tip of his penis. He smelled sweet, like shower soap. Hot, spicy and fragrant. She licked him, tasting the salt-slick of his pre-come. Liked it intensely. Went for more, lapping him, slowly, luxuriously. Sliding her tongue all the way around his cockhead.

He groaned, holding her head. "Wait." His voice sounded strangled.

She looked up, still caressing him from root to tip with slow, sensuous strokes of her squeezing hands. "Why wait? Don't you like it?"

"I fucking love it. But this wasn't what I had in mind. My plan revolves around making you come. If there's oral sex happening, I want to be the one giving it. At least the first few times."

Demi looked up through her lashes. She flicked the tip of her tongue over the slit at the end of his penis. Tried a long lapping stroke up the length of his shaft.

His hands tightened in her hair. Her hands tightened around that thick shaft.

"So this isn't on the a la carte menu?" She circled the tip of her tongue around and around the pool of slick fluid, spreading it with her fingertips to make his reddened cockhead gleam like polished stone. Licking the sensitive opening—flicking up, down, and slowly around. "Sucking on that big, stiff beautiful cock…that's off limits?"

She pulled him deep into her mouth. No easy feat, as blunt and broad as he was. But she got into a rhythm, and took him deep, suckling hard on the out-stroke, until his fingers in her hair began to shake and his ass muscles clenched to steel under her hand.

It drove her crazy. His eyes, watching her pleasure him.

"Don't make me come yet," he begged. "I want to come with you."

She looked up at him. "You can time when you come so precisely? Impressive."

"I can try." He sank down to his knees in front of her, pushing her knees apart, and leaned forward, grasping her hips and dragging her closer. One hand stroking her ass cheek, sliding up to the small of her back, the other hand sliding up her thigh.

He stroked the folds of her pussy. She was so turned on from the kissing and petting and sucking, the flaunting of his outrageous male gorgeousness, that he didn't need to do a thing more. She was ready for sex right now. She'd never been so primed in her life.

But he put his mouth to her anyway. Had to live up to all that big talk, she supposed. Not that she was complaining. His tender, skillful tongue lapping over all her tender inside bits was delicious. Intensely erotic, licking and thrusting and caressing her everywhere. Taking his time, exploring every fold. Loving on her clit. He'd always known exactly what kind of touch melted her, made her shiver and gasp...and then soar.

The long, intense orgasm wracked her endlessly, wrenching and sweet. She collapsed over his back afterward, damp and panting. His hot, muscular shoulder tasted salty. Her hair clung to him.

She'd never responded to anyone like that. It wasn't just his technique. It was Eric Trask himself. He just rang her bells. It was like she was programmed to crave him. Like no one else would do.

But she didn't want to think about what that might mean. Not now, anyway.

One mind-blowing revelation at a time.

They stayed locked together, hearts throbbing in tandem. His face pressed against the silky smoothness of her thigh as he fought for control.

Get a fucking grip. Condom now. Get the condom. Can't wait any longer.

He felt around for it and almost knocked it off the bed. Good thing he'd already opened the envelope before, clumsy as he was now. His body shook as he rolled the latex on. Emotions he couldn't name. He didn't want to know what they were. He just wanted inside her, where he could forget everything inside that tight, hot well of perfection inside her. Kissing her, rocking her. Cock and tongue, thrusting madly together.

Lost in her.

Demi scooted back and tossed the covers open. Reclining against the white pillows. She reached for him and pulled him down onto herself, her lithe body so smooth, her strong, shapely legs opening wide. The tender pink and crimson folds poking out of her sexy pussy lips were so beautiful. Soft and glowing with arousal. Shining with sex juice. The mouthwatering scent of her made his heart race and his head spin.

He was wordless and shaking as he stroked her pussy reverently, teasing between the delicate folds to plunge deeper, finding her slick, clinging depths. He caressed her clit, sliding the tip of his dick to spread her juice all around. He wanted her so wet. Slippery soft. He circled her clit with the blunt head of his penis, teasing her.

She made an impatient sound and reached for his ass, yanking him in. "Now," she said, breathlessly.

"Now," he agreed, nudging himself inside her slick folds.

Then came the long, slow, delicious shove into that snug hole. It made them both groan. Demi rocked her hips against him, her lip caught between her teeth. Raising her hips to take more of him. Offering herself and demanding everything he had in return.

He had no choice but to give it to her. It was hers already. Always had been.

Her eyes challenged him. She saw so much of him, and she wanted him anyway.

He had to shut his eyes to keep from going to pieces. Shaken to the core. She was tight and small. He had to be gentle. He'd never had to fight so hard for self-control as he fought with her.

He caressed the taut little bud of her clit with his thumb as they settled into a deep pumping rhythm. A tight, rocking slide. So damn good, having his dick squeezed and kissed and caressed by her clinging body.

He meant for this to be slow, controlled. All about pleasuring her, but a storm was blowing up inside him. It raged out of control. He had to get closer. Deeper inside. He was driven brutally onward by that blind, desperate urge.

All he could do was hold on to her for dear life and fuck like a maniac.

She held him, fingernails raking his back and biting into his ass, her legs wrapped tight. She cried out something, but he was beyond understanding words. He just needed more, more, more. Her. She was the whole universe.

Something cracked. Broke wide open inside him. He went off like a volcano.

When he came to his senses, he was collapsed over her.

Drenched, heart thudding.

As soon as his brain switched back online, so did the fear. Her face was turned away from his. Eyes closed. Just the beautiful, sharp jut of her perfect cheekbone. The sensual curve of her smooth cheek, her jaw. The glow of pink, the damp sheen.

She still held him, hugging him close. She hadn't let go, or shoved him away. He could still feel the muscles of her pussy quivering around him. Her thighs shook, still twined around his. Her heart thudded against his. Her chest, bucking for air.

Duh. Of course it was. He was huge, and he was crushing her. For fuck's sake.

He rolled to the side, pressing the small of her back. Holding her against him to keep his penis inside. He wanted to stay inside her forever.

Demi rolled away onto her back, detaching from him. Stretching with a luxurious sigh. Back arched, tits out. Damn, she was so beautiful, it hurt his eyes.

But she wasn't looking at him.

Eric sat up, holding the extremely full condom on with his fingertips. Looking around the room for a solution to his dilemma.

"Bathroom," Demi said lazily. "Waste basket under the sink."

He went to take care of it and caught a glimpse of himself in the mirror, wincing away from his own reflection. That look in his eyes. He didn't want Demi to see it. The pain, the fear. Unquenchable hunger. She unleashed something dangerous in him.

He still remembered how it felt to be with her years ago. Crazy magic. Anything had been possible. He could even beat Shaw's Crossing if he had Demi. He was kissed by fate. She was the smartest, sexiest, most special woman alive and he could do anything, be anyone, with her at his side. He wasn't nailed down by the bad shit in his past or marked by the Prophet's Curse. Demi could lift the spell. He'd been convinced.

He'd been so fucking wrong. And in the end, it was Demi who had paid the price.

He walked into the room and waited. Demi was stretching in the rumpled bed. She looked over and gazed up at him, perplexed. "Everything okay, Eric?"

"Yeah. Uh…how about you?" Damn. If he had to ask.

"I'm fine." Her voice was husky, relaxed and low. "Never better."

She lifted up the quilt, beckoning him in. God, yeah. He slid in between the sheets and groaned with pleasure as the heavenly warmth of her closed around him. Every part of him that touched her reacting wildly to the silken texture of her hair, her soft skin.

His dick sprang to attention. Demi glanced down with a swift smile. He shifted it so that it lay flat, not prodding her belly as he pulled her closer.

She murmured in appreciation, squeezing him. "That was prompt."

"You inspire me. Hotter than hell."

"Glad to hear it," she said.

He searched for words. "I'm sorry that I, ah…lost it, back then. I don't usually —"

"Stop it right there," she said. "I don't want to know your sexual habits."

"Okay." Eric hooked his leg around hers and slid his hand up over her hip. His hands shook with his intense awareness of her. The shockingly smooth texture of her skin.

"We could take another run at it," he said. "Unless you'd rather sleep. Or talk."

Her green eyes were full of laughter. And he was trying so hard to play it cool.

"Eric," she said. "Please. I didn't drag your poor tired ass all the way over this lake in Otis's old fishing boat in the pitch darkness to sleep. Or talk."

Eric dug his fingers into her hair and lifted a lock to his face, inhaling its warm, sweet smell. "Does that mean we don't get to talk?"

She looked wary. "Talk isn't in the scope of this encounter, Eric."

"Not on the menu, huh?"

"Nope," she said crisply. "Sure isn't."

Eric stroked her back, memorizing the curve of her waist. He was trying to fix every detail into his sense memory. "Being a hard-ass again?"

"Just looking out for myself. Orgasms are fine. Bring 'em on. Talking, not so much. You're leaving this place and never coming back, and I don't blame you. What is there to talk about?"

He grunted under his breath. "Whoa. That's harsh."

"I suppose so. But it's the only way this can work for me."

And in a flash, he felt it. Like a movement caught out of the corner of his eye. Feelings she wouldn't dare let him see.

The stakes were high for her, too. She didn't dare let down her guard.

He slid his arm around her waist, clamping her body against his and rolled over onto his back so she was sprawled over him, laughing. "Huh? What the hell?"

"How about a compromise?" he offered.

"You being here at all is already a compromise. Don't push your luck, buddy."

"One question apiece. Only one. Then it's back to the orgasms."

She gave him a baleful look but her body settled down on top of his. The warm, sexy weight of her and the kiss of her pussy against his belly made him throb and burn.

"One question?" she said suspiciously. "No funny stuff."

"No funny stuff."

Demi sighed. She crossed her arms over his chest, sliding her fingers into his chest hair and resting her chin on her forearms. "Go for it, then. You first."

Eric's mind went stupidly blank, dazzled by the challenge in her bright green eyes.

She waited, eyebrows tilting up, faintly amused. "So?"

"Give me a second," he protested. "I don't want to waste my question. It's like a genie's wish. You have to think about it. Make it count."

He realized that this was the first genuine smile he'd seen on her face since he'd arrived. He'd seen her only at Otis's funeral and graveside, and then at the reception with her glaring dad looming over her. Then their brief meeting at the café. Then the bar fight, then the fraught conversation in the car. All those grim situations had precluded smiling.

"I figured you had some big question burning in your mind," she said. "But no, you don't. Here you are, fishing and stammering."

He seized on the first thing that came to him. "Why did you come back to Shaw's Crossing? I thought you hated it here. And your dad…well, never mind. I just thought you'd be far away from here by now. In New York, Paris, Hong Kong."

Demi's smile faded. "That was the plan," she admitted. "I had every intention of leaving. Then my dad caught me in his trap. But I already told you about that."

"I'm sorry about that," he offered.

Demi waved that away. "You had nothing to do with it. That's between me and Dad. You were just a pretext."

"That's generous of you."

"Moving on," she said briskly. "Anyhow. When Mom died, she left me the restaurant property, and Ricky, who rented it and ran the diner, wanted to retire. If my dad could have stopped me, he would have, but Ricky offered to sell me all the equipment dirt cheap. I had to buy some equipment and do some renovation, but it was minimal. I figured, this was my last, best chance to get back to something vaguely resembling my original plan, before Dad laid down the law about Shaw Paper Products."

"Culinary school, right?"

"Yes. You don't have to feel guilty about that. Even without you as leverage, Dad would have found some way to scuttle that. But when this chance came around, it was different. I was older, stronger. I knew for a fact how much I hated working at Shaw's Paper Products, in any capacity. And the property was legally mine, thanks to Mom. He couldn't stop me anymore. So I went for it."

"Oath-breaker," he murmured.

She laughed under her breath. "It was too late for him to punish you for my sins," she said. "Besides, that was a dirty trick on his part. A promise that was immorally extracted. So in the end, I didn't really feel that guilty about breaking it."

"I'm glad you feel that way. So you like running a

145

restaurant?"

"That's technically another question, but I'll let it pass. Yes, I do like it. It's a crap-ton of work, but it's all mine, and there's lots of scope for creativity. I make yummy, good quality food. And I don't compromise."

"Yeah," he said. "I'd call that your defining personality trait."

She frowned. "What the hell is that supposed to mean?"

"It's a compliment," he assured her quickly.

"It's been seven years since you saw me." Her voice had gone as sharp as crystal. "What the hell would you know about my defining personality traits?"

"You show them whenever you open your mouth. You don't hide anything. That's another defining personality trait. It's all out there. What you see is what you get."

Demi's brows came together, suspicious. "Should I be offended?"

"If you want, I guess, but that would be a big waste of our precious time."

She let out a short bark of laughter. "Okay, I'll skip it. So, moving right along. Time for my question."

Eric braced himself. This could go any goddamn direction at all.

"Okay, this one's risky," she said. "But here goes. Why were you so twitchy and angry that last night when you came to my folks' house? That fight we had...it came out of nowhere. I will never understand why we crashed and burned so hard."

That took him by surprise, and his mind locked up. "Ahhhh..." He shook his head. "I, ah...I guess must have been pissed off about being fired."

She drew in a startled breath and sat up on her elbow. "You never told me you were fired."

"I didn't want you to know," he said. "It was embarrassing. It happened right before I came to your house. First the construction job, then the care home. Suddenly I was unemployed, and I knew I'd have to leave Shaw's Crossing to get more work. I bought that bottle of tequila and the limes with my last twenty bucks. I was flat broke. But I wanted to just forget it all and lose myself in a hot Demi fantasy, at least for one night. I figured I'd tell you the truth in the morning. But I never had a chance. We fought, you threw me out, and then all hell broke loose."

"Flat broke?" Her voice was sharp. "You weren't broke. You'd been working like a bastard all summer. Saving every penny for months, ever since you got back from Afghanistan. Saving up for your app launch, as I recall."

Here was a dilemma. A truthful answer could torpedo this whole night. But Demi would smell a lie from a mile away. And he sucked at lying anyhow.

"I'd just spent all my money," he admitted. "That very day."

She looked confused. "On what?"

He hesitated for several seconds before answering. "A ring."

He could feel the tension rise up, like a force field leaping to life. She pulled away from him. "Excuse me?"

"Yeah. You heard me. I blew every last cent I had on a ring." He rolled onto his back and stared up at the ceiling. "I put it on layaway. Didn't have quite enough to buy it outright, but I found the perfect one at Steigler's Fine Jewelry. Then right after I spent all that money, I got fired from the construction job. Then the care home. A one-two punch."

"Oh my God," she whispered.

"I didn't mean to give you the ring right away. I knew it was too soon. That it would freak you out. I just wanted to be ready whenever the perfect moment presented itself. I had no doubts. I was one-hundred-fucking-percent convinced about you. I thought, with a girl like you, I should really go for it. You know. The grand gesture."

Demi sat up, turning her back to him.

Fuck. He shouldn't have told her. He'd miscalculated. Too heavy, too much. The night was already top-loaded with trauma. Put the fucking cherry on top, why didn't he.

But he'd gone too far to turn back. "I got the idea from Otis."

That brought her head around, eyes wide. "You talked about us to Otis?"

"He knew about us being involved, yeah, but that's not what I meant. I'm talking about when he adopted me and Mace and Anton. He said that we'd be on our own soon, so it wasn't like we needed raising, but he didn't want us to carry the Prophet's name around our whole lives, not after everything that happened. He thought we deserved for someone to make a grand gesture. It was up to him to show us how it was done. So he gave us his name."

Demi wiped her eyes. "You should have said that in his eulogy."

He shook his head. "It's nobody's else's business. Besides, everybody in this town urged him not to take us in. It would have come across like a big scolding fuck-you."

"So? They deserved it. Why not make them all suffer?"

"No point. Anyhow, back to us. You deserved a grand gesture, too. I just wish I'd been able to follow through on it before everything blew up in my face."

Demi rolled off his body, and stared up at the ceiling. The silence was absolute.

"It really messed me up, you know," she said finally.

He braced himself. "Yeah? How so?"

"It was so confusing, comparing every man I was ever with to you. It wasn't fair to any of them. And we only had that brief moment. Like a flash of lightning."

He seized her hand, pressing his lips against her knuckles. "I'll shut up now."

She smiled, but she wouldn't meet his eyes. "You better," she said. "I asked you an innocent question, and you just took it and ran me right over a damn cliff with it."

"Sorry," he said. "I guess you'd call that one of my defining personality traits."

"Smart-ass," she muttered.

"That's another one."

Laughter broke the tension, but his big-ass emotional revelation had killed that conversation stone dead. The moments that followed were so quiet, the sound of his stomach grumbling made them both laugh, grateful for the distraction.

"Whoa. That was loud," she commented. "Hungry?"

"I'm okay," he said. "I had way too much to think about. Food didn't make the cut."

"I've got food here," she informed him. "Leftovers from the reception. Awesome food, in great abundance. I just stacked up trays and put them in a bag, and it's all down in the fridge, so it would be quick and easy. If you want to eat something."

"What about your rigorous, focused all-sex agenda? No sleep, no talk?"

"Food's fine." There was a smile in her voice. "I advise

that you fortify yourself. You have seven years of scorching sexual fantasies to live up to, so fuel up, buddy."

He realized, surprised, that he was grinning. "Lay it on me."

13

It was distracting, having Eric Trask lounging in the kitchen half dressed.

Demi had found a pair of striped cotton men's pajamas in the drawer and divided it between them. She took the buttoned top, which hung down to the tops of her thighs, and he took the loose drawstring pants. They hung low on his hips, showing off the deep, enticing vee of his abs muscles, his taut six-pack, his cut pecs. His tight, flat dark nipples were taut from the chill. But pajama pants were better that than having him walk around naked with that thick, gorgeous dick bobbing and bouncing.

It wouldn't stay down. It tented out the pants. That level of relentless sexual enthusiasm boded well for the rest of the night.

Damn, girl. Concentrate. Forks…napkins…plates.

The kitchen was chilly, but she felt hot, like she'd just stepped out of a sauna. She could have taken a dip in the frigid lake water right now and liked it. Not that she was going to waste one single second of this night swimming.

The trays were out, the covers off. She laid out honey-glazed ham, peppery roast beef, grilled veggies, a red potato dill salad, an assortment of cheeses, puff pastries filled with spiced sausage, big juicy fruit chunks and grapes, freshly baked rolls, fat gleaming Greek olives, smoky cheese-and-artichoke fritters.

She handed him a paper plate. "There you go. Knock yourself out."

Eric went for it without hesitation. As she took the first bite, she realized that she was ravenous, too. Eric was well into his second plate of food before it occurred to her to pull the beer out of the fridge.

Eric popped the tops of the bottles for her with a spoon and took a deep swallow. "Ahhh. That's good."

"Local beer," she told him. "Artisanal brewer. Right here in Shaw's Crossing."

"Nice to see somebody around this place actually getting it right."

"I'm getting it right," she informed him. "Very right."

He stopped chewing. "Of course you are. I didn't mean you. The food's amazing, by the way."

"Don't sweat it," she murmured, trying not to smile. "But thanks."

The food tasted even better here in her chilly kitchen in the middle of the night than it had yesterday. Mind-blowing sex was hungry work. And she anticipated more of the same, with the stunning, half-naked man smoldering at her across the kitchen table.

She finished first and left him to it, taking her beer into the living room to check on the fire. She opened the glass door of the stove and loaded the largest log onto the glowing coals, enjoying the heat against her flushed face and the boneless relaxation in her body.

She felt a dizzy glow of anticipation for the pleasure still to come. And she could feel the weight of his eyes on her from the kitchen as he finished his beer.

When she stood up, she looked over her shoulder. Their eyes met. The air charged.

Demi shook her hair back and loosened the button that held the loose pajama top closed. She let it fall open, just slightly, so it showed a long, shadowy glimpse of her bare body. The little swatch of dark hair on her mound, trimmed up just how she liked it.

She drained her beer, and set the bottle down on the coffee table. Then faced him, trailing her fingertips slowly down the narrow band of exposed skin. Over her heart, over her belly. Then lower.

She stared him directly in the eyes as she put her hand between her legs. Pulling her vulva up, making her clit pop out between her fingers. Petting it with her other hand. Slowly, with a murmuring sigh of pleasure.

She was no stranger to touching herself, but doing it with Eric Trask's blazing silver gray eyes on her was a new world of arousal. She put her foot onto the hassock, and slid her fingers inside her pussy lips, spreading around slick, shining lube.

"While you finish your meal, preview the next course," she said.

Eric's throat worked as he watched. She pushed the shirt open just a little more. Enough to show her nipples.

He put the fork and knife down. "I want more."

"Good. I've got plenty for you." She threw her head back, thrust her chest out. Her nipples had gone taut in the chilly room. His lustful gaze made them tingle. She slid her fingers deeper inside.

He got up, pacing toward her. The glow of the firelight reflected in his eyes. When he was right in front of her, he sank down to his knees and flicked the pajama shirt wide open, gripping her hips.

"Stop," she said.

He glanced up. "Why?"

"Stay where you are. Just watch me get myself off. You'll get your turn."

"Go for it." His hands dropped to his sides, fists clenched. "Let the torture begin."

She made a big thing of it, showing him every detail as she caressed herself, opening her pussy lips, flaunting her clit in his face as she rolled her thumb around it. That look in his eyes was the ultimate magic ingredient, sharpening her self-pleasure into something terrifyingly good. It swelled into agony…and then shattered her.

She cried out as pleasure wrenched her. She almost lost her balance, grabbing his shoulders to steady herself.

When the orgasm had subsided to a delicious, shimmering glow, she looked down at his face. The naked hunger in his eyes made her heart speed up again.

"Great show," he said. "My turn."

She nodded, too shaky to speak.

Eric grabbed her hand and positioned it over her vulva again. "Hold your pussy up like you just did before. I love the way your clit sticks out. Makes me want to suck on it."

She did as he asked, putting her hand against him. But his big shoulder was too broad and hard to get much of a grip.

He pressed his face to her. She cried out at the first unbearably delicious wet lash of his tongue, then slid her fingers into his short, sweat-dampened hair, gasping with need. His skillful hand slid up, caressing her pussy lips while he flicked his tongue over her clit, then sucked it into his mouth.

Demi moved over him, pressing herself to his face. He brought her achingly close to coming...and he slowed down, dropping flirtatious kisses against her inner thigh, looking up with a devilish glint in his eye.

His dimples betrayed him. She grabbed his face. "You're messing with me."

"Ferociously. Wait for it. Suffer. Your words to me, remember? I want to make you feel so good, you pass out. I want you to come so hard you forget your own name."

"Do it," she demanded. "Now. Or I'll hit you."

His big chest vibrated with laughter as he grabbed her hips again, loving on the taut bud of her clit with lavish strokes of his tongue, and pushed her right over the edge.

Pleasure exploded through her. She unraveled completely. Lost herself in it.

When she came to her senses, she was afraid to look down. Her eyes were wet.

No, no, no. That wasn't the vibe she was going for. She wiped the tears away with the back of her hand. Mascara smears, damn. She tried to breathe like a normal person, not those helpless, desperate gulping sounds.

Eric rose up, and up. Towering over her. "Condoms upstairs. Let's go."

She gave up trying to speak and reached into the breast pocket of the nightshirt, pulled out the condom and presented it to him.

He seized it without hesitation. "I love a woman who thinks ahead," he said, tearing it open. He pressed the ring of latex into her hand. "Put it on."

She felt so clumsy, after that mind-shattering orgasm, but he seemed happy to wait while she slowly got the condom over him. She took her time, getting into the whole routine. Tight, squeezing, swirling strokes that made his breath get rough and ragged. Milking him from root to tip. Over and over. Making sure it was properly smoothed down.

He trapped both her hands there, tugging her until she fell forward, into another wild, no-holds-barred kiss. Devouring each other, while she gripped this stiff, thick shaft. She felt his heartbeat pulsing against her hand.

She tugged him closer. "Now," she said.

"All yours." He pushed the nightshirt off her shoulders. She tugged the pajama pants down over his hips. He kicked them off, and turned her around, cupping her ass appreciatively as he pushed her toward the couch.

She fell forward, knees perched on the couch, bracing herself against the back. Letting him pet and stroke and admire her from behind. His big, warm hands, stroking and caressing all the tender, sensitive spots, making her shiver with arousal. He nudged her thighs apart and stroked her labia with a teasing fingertip before sliding inside.

"It's so good with you," he said, his voice rough. "So good it's killing me."

No smart comeback this time. She was in no condition to speak. She rocked back against his thrusting, sliding fingers, and then against the slow, heavy intrusion of his thick cock. She loved that moment as he pushed inside. That slow, tight shove.

He fucked her, slowly and deliberately from behind. She took him in completely, molten and yielding. Gasping and panting. In this moment she didn't care about anything but getting more of him. He woke up parts of her that were asleep, freed parts that were trapped. She had no idea that she'd feel so helpless and desperate and needy.

Too late. She was too frenzied to care. He pushed her someplace deep and bright and new, a part of herself that she'd never known until he discovered it.

And then claimed it forever as his.

It was happening again. The plan was to get her off, preferably multiple times, before he let himself come again. But once again, it was not up to him. In no way did he control anything about this. He was crazed with need. Completely owned.

He gave himself up to it, not that he could have stopped himself, and thank God, she was with him completely in that pounding frenzy. Clutching, yelling …until the world split open…

And another blast of wild, primal energy went through him.

Afterwards, he pressed his hot face against the fine skin of her back, kissing her spine. His heart galloped onward, terrified of something he couldn't put a name to.

A point of no return. It could destroy him. Maybe it already had.

The world settled back into place around him. A log shifted in the fire, crackling and sighing. The lake lapped against the dock outside. He was still afraid to move or speak. Demi was just as still, her face pressed against the back of the couch.

He'd never experienced anything remotely like sex

with Demi. Not before, not after. He liked sex fine, pursued it regularly and enjoyed it always. But he kept it casual.

No strings. It was his iron-clad rule, and up to now, it had worked for him. He just kept on moving ahead, passing for normal. Living his life. Day followed day, and he was doing all right. Better than a lot of people were, from what he could tell.

Until Demi broke him open and showed him, without mercy or quarter, just exactly how empty and barren his life was without her in it.

And he'd begged her to do it.

He couldn't bear to pull out. Everything about her drew him in. Her smooth skin and luscious curves. Her skin, her hair, her scent, it defied description. He'd never felt anything so smooth and soft. He wasn't the type to sniff flowers or pet kittens.

Flowers were delicate, fragile. Not Demi. She was a fucking force of nature.

Her long silence was making him nervous. "You good?" he asked.

Her laugh sounded bitter. "Why wouldn't I be?"

Eric hesitated, sensing a pitfall. "Just checking."

She shifted, pulling away. "Afraid you overwhelmed me with your erotic mojo?"

He was chilled by her tone. "Not exactly."

"I'm not," Demi said. "I'm not crushed or shattered. Rest easy, Eric. Sex with you is spectacular. You're freaking amazing. I've never come like that in my life. Kudos."

"Good, then." He studied her, bemused. "Glad to hear it."

She slid off the couch. So beautiful in the flickering firelight, all those naked shadowy curves. She caught his helpless gawking, and lifted her arms, turning around in a slow three-sixty. "Go ahead, look your fill. Now's your chance, right? Make it count."

"If you're so fine, why do you sound pissed?"

She shrugged. "Chalk it up to our complicated history. It's been a strange day. You expect me to be bouncy and smiling at three in the morning?"

"I don't expect anything," he said. "I'm taking this one second at a time. Let's go back upstairs and get you back under the covers."

"I'm not cold," she said.

"I know," he said. "You're on fire. Upstairs."

He led the way. Demi took over the bathroom once he'd gotten rid of the condom, and she took her own sweet time washing up, leaving him to lie alone in the bed, fidgeting in the silence. He studied the moonlight shining through the boughs outside the window. Listened to the hollow, rhythmic slop of water against the dock.

The sex had been explosive, yes. But this time, it had shifted something inside her. He was walking a tightrope now. No fucking idea what might knock him off it.

When Demi finally came out, she avoided his gaze and immediately snapped the glowing night lamp off, veiling them in darkness. Not a good sign.

He got it, though. They both needed a moment to detach from this overwhelming power source. He wasn't used to this kind of raw voltage and he suspected she wasn't either. Not that he wanted it to stop.

She slid right back into the bed with no hesitation, thank God. Eric scooted into a cold-sheets zone and tugged her into the warm spot that he'd just vacated.

"I don't have to leave tomorrow." He blurted the

159

words, and instantly regretted them when he felt her body stiffen.

"What?" she said.

"I can stay longer," he went on. "I'll need to talk to the police again, after what happened last night. And there's Terry's funeral. I'll want to stay for that, if I can."

"What are you trying to say to me?"

He tried to make out her expression, but it was too dark. "I'm not sure," he hedged. "Just that it doesn't have to be only one night."

She jerked up onto her elbow. "Eric," she said. "Don't."

"It can be whatever it is," he persisted. "Let's relax. See where it goes."

"It doesn't have anywhere to go," she said. "Shaw's Crossing sucks for you. The only thing that held you to it was Otis. Whatever life you've built for yourself, it's not here."

"Maybe not, but that doesn't mean—"

"Hold it right there." Demi sat up. "The deal was one night to settle accounts, and nobody gets any ideas. Remember? You promised."

"I've had those ideas for years," he said. "One night isn't enough."

"Tough shit. I can't afford more than that."

He stared at the shadows of her face. "Always the hard-ass," he said. "At all costs. No compromise. Not for one second."

"It's my defining personality trait," she said. "Deal with it."

"I would," he said. "Gladly. If you'd give me a fucking break."

"If you push this, we'll end up someplace bad really fast," she warned. "And that'll be it, Eric. Fun's over.

Everybody out of the pool."

He wanted to bellow his frustration. "Damn it. This is special, Demi. What happens between us is magic. What's wrong with wanting more?"

"We knew it would be like that," she said. "So what? Don't get attached. We've been wondering for years if it was really as good as we remembered, or if maybe we were embroidering it with our imaginations. Am I right?"

"Yeah," he admitted. "Pretty much."

"So now we know. We weren't embroidering. It really is that good. Big fucking surprise, huh? Now leave it at that. Burning question answered. Moving on."

"I don't want to leave it at that," he said, rebellious. Damn this woman. He just needed a chance to show her he was for real. But she wouldn't give an inch.

She shrugged. "Not your call. You promised."

"Demi—"

"Shhhh." Demi put her finger to his lips and gently pushed him down onto his back. "Do not fuck this up for me," she whispered. "I want it."

He opened his mouth to reply. She kissed him before he could speak.

A kiss of such sensual sweetness, it made his heart throb and his dick jerk freshly to attention.

He gasped with need as she rose up over him, tossing the covers back. She swung her leg over his, straddling him. His swollen dick ached at her sinuous swaying, the sexy shadows between her slender open thighs driving him to madness.

"We have one more in the three-pack," she told him. "Gimme. On the double."

Eric pawed blindly in the direction of the bedside table.

161

His hand landed on the foil pack. He couldn't drag his eyes away from the sight of her undulating over him, tits swaying as she gripped his rod. Squeezing and stroking.

He jerked, moaning, as she bent to lick him. Slow, wet strokes, up the length of his shaft, then circling around and around until his back arched in mute pleading.

She lifted her head. "Are you going to open the damn thing or what?"

He did his duty, sheathing himself with shaking hands, then dropped back down to enjoy the erotic spectacle. That long dark hair swinging around her, first tossed back and swinging free, now falling forward to coil over his thighs. She cupped his balls and her gaze flicked up, ruthless seduction. One slow, final stroke of her hand and she clambered up to straddle him. Shimmied forward, gripping his cock.

She pressed his penis flat and high against his belly, settling herself so that her wet, slick divide was a full-length wet kiss of contact. Then she rocked back and forth. Caressing his stiff, broad red penis head with her fingers. Using it to pleasure herself.

She took her time, using the tip of his cock to caress her clit. Sliding it in her own slick juice. Sexual torment, and he fucking loved it. She closed her eyes, swaying. Driving him crazy on purpose.

"Let me put it inside," he begged. "Or else sit on my face. Let me lick you again."

"No, not yet," she murmured. "It's perfect just like this. Be patient."

A bark of laughter jerked his chest. "I want to make you wet."

"Oh, I am," she assured him. She rose up higher on her knees and grabbed his hand, pulling it down between her legs. "Feel me," she whispered. "Inside my pussy lips...see? Feel how wet I am."

His fingers were kissed, bathed by the hot well of her arousal. A slick, luscious glide, up, down, around...inside. So ready.

He caressed the slick furled folds. Thrust his finger inside her. Finger-fucking her as she danced over him with sensual abandon. Hair swinging, tits swaying. So hot.

He'd never get enough of this.

"Demi," he muttered. "Please."

Her mysterious smile almost brought him off right then. "Hold yourself up for me."

Anything. He held his stiff rod up and gasped as she settled over him, shuddering and arching backwards as he eased inside. All the way. Her snug pussy hugged his length.

So...good. She leaned forward, hands wound into his chest hair, nails digging into his skin and rocked against him, riding him. He gripped her waist, and their eyes locked.

And they were off. Carried away again. They couldn't look away from each other, and the frightened look on her face was mirrored in his own.

Her defenses were crumbling. His own had been rubble from the start. She moved over him, whimpering at each deep, plunging stroke.

He sat up, shifting her so that he could wrap his arms around her shoulders. She sat on his lap facing him, clasping him with her legs, which was a perfect angle for nuzzling her tits and nibbling her throat. He wanted to make her come again just like this, face to face, wrapped around each other. Nowhere to hide.

He sought out her secret hot spots, petting her clit until she writhed and moaned. Dragged the edge of his teeth tenderly along her throat and pressed hot kisses to the top of her shoulder, keeping the thrusting rhythm deep and slow, the angle just right to hit her inside sweet spots. Rubbing over them, and over them…again…and again.

The climax was thundering toward them. He had to get her off first. He tongue-kissed her as they fucked, as his thumb worked delicately over her clit, feeling his way. Her breath got shorter and her moans choked off, and she came, deep and hard, shivering with every delicious jolt of pleasure. Her pussy clenched his cock. Pulsing, deep and strong. She hid her face against his shoulder, chest heaving.

He couldn't wait any longer. He pushed her down onto her back, grabbed her knees and lifted them high. His penis shone with her juice as they surged, moving together.

Not for long. The power lifted him. Stormed through him.

Afterwards, lying close to her, he sensed that he'd messed up somehow. Pushed too hard. Gotten too close. Every action had an equal and opposite reaction, and now she was going to push back.

He clenched his jaw and braced himself for it.

Right on cue, she pulled away. Sat up with her back to him. Rigid.

Words just fell out of him with no filter, no thought of pride. A desperate bid to hang onto her for as long as he could. Preferably forever. "Come away with me," he said.

Her head whipped around. "What? Where? To do what?"

"Wherever you want. We could start in San Francisco. It's a great city. I have a big house there. Plenty of room for you. Or we could go to any other city you like better."

"To do what? Be your sex toy?"

"To be my lover. My lady," he said patiently. "We'll figure it out as we go along."

He saw her answer on her face, but the words still hurt like a knife.

"No," she said flatly. "And you're breaking faith with me by asking."

"You were ready to leave before—"

"Seven years ago! I was twenty-two years old, for fuck's sake!"

"You could follow your original dream," he said. "You could follow it more easily if you were further away from your dad."

She gazed at him, mouth half open. "You're insane, Eric."

"Maybe. I'm also dead serious," he told her. "I want you. Always have."

"It's been seven years since you last saw me," she said. "On the basis of what? One amazing roll in the hay, and you're sold? All is forgiven?"

"Technically, it's more like three amazing rolls in the hay—"

"Don't you dare get cute with me."

"Didn't mean to," he said swiftly. "It just came out."

Demi turned away. Her back was shaking. He realized, horrified, that she was crying. He reached to touch her shoulder. "Demi—"

"Don't." She pulled away swiftly. "Just...stop. Just shut up."

"What's happening? Why are you freaking out on me?"

"You can't just spout bullshit like that! Out of nowhere!"

"It's not nowhere. I'm dead serious. It's just my timing

that's crap. As usual."

"You have no idea what it took for me to get over what happened. What it took for me to shake off my dad's control and build something for myself. A little restaurant in Shaw's Crossing might not look like much to you, but it's everything to me."

"I never meant to belittle what you've done," he said.

"But you think I should ditch it and run off to your place in the city to be your concubine? Wow. That's living the dream, Eric!"

"Pursue any dream you want," he urged. "Open a restaurant in San Francisco. I could help you. I have plenty of money."

"Don't you dare wave your money at me," she said sharply. "This was never about money."

"I never said it was. I wasn't implying—"

"I don't do crazy dreams, Eric. I do concrete, realistic plans. You're not in any of mine. Not after what happened."

"You mean the Porsche, right?"

She tossed her hands up. "Well, yeah. Duh."

He swallowed, hard. "So you're never going to believe me."

"It's too late for me to make that call anymore," she told him. "Maybe it's true. Maybe not. I certainly don't trust my dad to tell me the truth. But I won't gamble my whole life on the basis of your word alone. Not with our history. Sorry, but no."

He couldn't make a sound. There was too much pressure in his throat.

"I'm sorry," Demi said. "I can't go that far. I've given you what I could. I gave you the fantasy tryst on the island. I fed you. I fucked you. It was incredible. I'm glad we finally

166

dispelled the mystery. But look." She gestured at the window. "It's almost dawn. Reality time. We knew it would come, and I'm not going to get suckered into daydreams about some fantasy future with you. I've heard that song before."

"I meant to propose to you, Demi!"

"So you said. But you didn't. Reality prevailed. In a big fucking way." She seized a terry-cloth bathrobe from a hook on the wall and put it on. "Now it's prevailing again."

Eric hadn't been this angry since after the Porsche episode. He wanted to howl and rage. Rip doors off hinges. Knock holes into walls.

No. That wasn't him. He clenched his fists and hung onto his self-control.

"We're done here," she said. "I'm taking my shower. Be gone when I get out."

"Damn it, Demi—"

"This thing has run its course. Goodbye."

She marched into the bathroom, coming back with his muddy clothes and boots. She laid them down outside the door without looking at him, then pulled the bathroom door shut.

The click of the lock was very loud in the silence.

14

You accepted her terms. Don't be a whiny little bitch.

The stern self-talk was not working. Eric pulled on his clammy, mud-caked clothing and made his way down the steps, no longer even trying to avoid leaving a trail of dirt behind himself. The damage was done, the mess was made. Fuck it.

He'd fallen at her feet like an asshole only to get thrown out once again.

Kick me please.

He had to get out of here before he went crazier than he already was. And the bar was set high, for a guy raised by the mad Prophet. Marked by fire and death.

Demi's shower was running now. He put on his jacket, trying not to picture her in there, naked and wet and furious. Convinced that he was a liar and a thief.

This was the Curse at work. It repelled her, like it had repelled everyone else. Everyone but Otis. But Otis was special.

He was also in a box in the ground.

Who knew? Maybe that was the Curse at work, too. It ate everything in the end.

He should have followed Anton and Mace's example, and fucked off. Sorted everything out from a safe distance, via third parties.

Right. Like Terry.

The memory of Terry's dead, startled eyes and bloodied face ran him down like a fucking train. He felt a lurch of nausea. Had to stop and bend over for a second.

Go-go-go. *Now.*

He pushed his way out the door from the stairway to the foyer. The remains of their feast still cluttered the kitchen. In the living room the coals glowed a sullen red in the pre-dawn gloom. The couch cushions were still askew, some scattered on the floor.

He opened the door and stood there, staring out for a moment as the clean, sweet cold air of dawn hit his nose. The sky was heavy and dark. Eerie tendrils of vapor rose like wavering ghosts up over the mirror-smooth surface of the lake.

The smell stopped him as he leaned forward to take that step outside.

Sour cigarette breath. Old armpit stench.

He jerked back as a blackjack whipped down. It grazed his forehead and cheekbone. He lunged for the attacker's wrist, yanking him inside. Smashed the wrist against the door jamb. *Crunch.* A punch to the throat choked off the attacker's howl.

Eric hurled the first guy into the second guy, who sprang from a hiding place on the other side of the door. Guy

Two stumbled back, hitting the porch post with a grunt. Guy One bounced off him and tumbled off the porch stairs, arms pin-wheeling.

Big guys. Black ski masks. More were coming at him. A third came darting from the other end of the porch. The second charged back at him again with a yell.

He blocked the kicks, and a roundhouse punch. Caught the punching arm—twist and flip—and hurled the attacker straight into the porch railing.

The railing splintered, and the man pitched head over ass into the shaggy greenery beyond as the third guy barreled down on him.

Eric whipped to the side to save his head. Took the club on his shoulder, fucking *ouch.* Caught the guy's arm. He shrieked as Eric twisted it. Tendons tore and popped.

He smashed the bastard headfirst into the wall siding, and jabbed a savage side-kick to his knee and another to his head when he hit the ground. *Stay down, prick.*

Smash. Picture window. One of them was inside. With Demi upstairs, naked in the shower. No fucking way.

Blood trickled into his eyes as he darted back inside. The guy was in the living room. Eric charged him. They toppled onto the coffee table and it caved, snapping in two.

They wrestled on the floor, rolling in shards of glass. This guy was bigger. Heavier and stronger than the others. His pale blue eyes in the holes of the ski mask were gleeful. Crazy fucker was actually enjoying this.

The guy was snake quick, jabbing a knee to his Eric's balls that stole his breath. Suddenly he found himself rolled underneath, the guy's huge hands around his throat.

The woodstove to the side of him radiated heat. Eric lunged out toward the wood box, struggling to breathe, groping wildly until his fingers closed around a twisted chunk of scrub-oak.

Whack, he bashed the blue-eyed maniac in the head with it.

The guy's strangling grip faltered. He tottered and swayed. Eric shoved him off, wheezing for air through his bruised, swollen throat. He saw the flickering shadow behind, and spun around—

Bzzzzzzzzzz. Jolting agony burning against his chest. "Not so fast, prick."

A stun baton. Taking him down. Tearing him apart. A furious stare through the holes of the ski mask hanging down over him. Dark eyes. *Bzzzzzzzzzzzzzz.*

Fuck. He couldn't move, couldn't see. *Demi.*

The asshole laughed, his foul breath hot in Eric's face as he leaned forward to gloat. He pressed the electrodes against Eric's throat again with crushing force. "Lights out, asshole," he taunted.

Thunk.

The man jerked—and toppled forward heavily, right down on top of Eric.

Eric struggled beneath the man's smothering weight. He could barely make his body move, or make his chest expand for air. He shifted the guy's weight with huge effort.

Demi stood behind the man, barefoot, dark hair dripping over her terrycloth robe. Her eyes were huge and shocked.

The white marble pastry rolling pin she held was splotched with blood.

Demi dropped the rolling pin and hurried to help him flop the man off of Eric, and onto his back.

Eric sat up slowly, rubbing his throat. "You okay?" His

voice was a rasping croak.

"Me?" Her voice cracked. "You're the one who just fought five big guys in ski masks and then got zapped with a stun baton. And you're asking me if I'm okay?"

"You just saved my ass," he told her.

She rolled her eyes. "Right. After you saved mine ten times over first."

Eric tried to put the stun baton into his coat, but he was still too clumsy and disoriented. His whole body felt shaky and numb.

Still, he looked her over with a frown. "You're wet," he said. "And barefoot. It's freezing in here and there's broken glass everywhere. Are your feet okay? Did you get cut?"

Demi suddenly saw all the shards of glass from the broken window and tried not to shiver in the chilly breeze that swept inside. "My feet are fine, Eric."

He got to his feet, still staggering, and looked out the door, monitoring the felled attackers. "Go get dressed," he told her. "But first tell me where I can find something to tie these scumbags up."

"Ah...there should be duct tape in the pantry cabinet. Let me go look for it. I'll be quicker." She backed away. "You're, um...watching them?"

"I'm not taking my eyes off these fuckheads until they're behind bars," he assured her.

The low vibration of a phone sounded loud in the quiet morning. It was the last guy, the one who'd stunned him. Eric leaned over, and felt inside the man's pockets.

He pulled out a burner phone. It buzzed insistently in his hand. He locked eyes with Demi as he opened it up, held it to his ear and waited.

"So?" a rough male voice said. "What the fuck's taking

so goddamn long?"

Eric hesitated, trying to remember the voice his attacker had, and then gave it his best shot. A low, gravely rasp. "Done."

The other guy grunted. "Good. There in ten."

The call ended. Eric flipped the phone shut and crouched down next to the fallen men. He unzipped his big black jacket, tugging it off.

"Eric? What the hell are you doing?" Demi's voice was sharp with alarm.

"I'm going to talk to their ride." He stripped off his leather jacket and pulled on the attacker's coat. "Should be interesting."

"But you don't even have a weapon! You need a gun!"

"I'll take one of their blackjacks. I'll be fine."

"Eric, you can't just—"

"No time to argue." Eric crouched down and yanked the ski mask off the head of the other unconscious man, looking with distaste at the blood on his fingers before he pulled it over his own head. The man was young, with a fleshy, freckled face and gingery hair. Blood dripped from a wound on his temple. "Get the duct tape. Let's secure these guys before the boatman gets here. Move!"

The edge in his voice made her jump to it. She brought duct tape, and Eric got to work with brutal efficiency, fastening the attackers' arms behind their backs, then their ankles. Then he bound the guys who were lying outside.

He glanced up at her. "That'll do for now. Get dressed. I don't know what's coming our way." He picked up the bloody rolling pin and handed it to her, along with the stun baton. "Keep these. Get your phone, call the cops and get outside, ready to slip out back into the trees and disappear."

"But I can't just—"

"Go, goddamnit! Move!"

Demi ran upstairs and yanked on her clothes, searching feverishly for her purse, her phone. She called the local police and stammered out the situation as best she could to Holly, the operator. Holly put her on hold while she held the phone in place with her shoulder and tied her boot laces with numb, ice-cold fingers.

"Demi? You there?" Wade Bristol's voice came on the line.

Tears welled into her eyes at the sound of his voice. "Chief Bristol?"

"They told me you were attacked? Are you okay? Do you need an ambulance?"

"I'm out at Dad's cabin on Spruce Tip Island," she told him. "Eric fought them all off, but he—"

"Eric Trask? He's out there with you?"

"Yes. He took them all down."

"Is he injured?"

"He got zapped with a stun baton, but he seems okay from what I can tell," she said, peering out the window.

She jerked behind the curtain as she saw a boat approaching swiftly, pushing through the glassy surface of the water to create a triangle of ripples. "Oh, shit."

"What? What's happening?" Chief Bristol demanded.

"The boat's here. The one that brought the guys who just attacked us. Eric is going out to meet whoever's on it."

"Demi, run out back and hide. Now."

"Gotta go, Chief. I'll call after and tell you how it

went."

She thumbed off the sound and crept down the stairs, stun baton in one hand and rolling pin in the other.

Two bound intruders lay there on the floor. The redhead was awake now and squirming, face empurpled. He looked up at her, wild-eyed, and made garbled sounds in his throat from behind the tape Eric had stuck over his mouth.

"Save your breath," she told him. "Not interested."

The kitchen window had the best view of the lake, so she sidled up to it and peered out the curtain.

That bastard weighed a fuckton. Eric sweated in the guy's heavy coat as he dragged the unconscious man down toward the dock. He'd picked the attacker who was closest to his own height and build to drag toward the boat, which happened to be the dude who stank the worst. And the ski mask he was wearing was slimed with sweat and blood.

The coat pulled tight at the shoulders. No time to plan something smarter. This had to go down fast. He couldn't overthink it. Strike like lightning. Shock and awe.

The hum of the approaching boat's motor got louder, and then cut out as the guy maneuvered next to the dock. He too wore a ski mask. Eric kept his back to the boat, dragging the unconscious man by his armpits and careful to keep his body between the boatman and the bloodied, bearded face of the guy he was dragging.

"Where are the others?" the boatman asked as he tied up.

Eric grunted with effort. The man's boot heels bumped over the planks. "Inside," he mumbled under his breath.

"Getting the girl ready for transport, huh?" The boat guy let out an ugly laugh. "I wouldn't mind guarding that bitch's cage. Nice rack. Sweet ass, too."

Eric stepped into the boat, heaving the man over the side, and flung him down onto the deck. The man's head made a loud, hollow *thunk* against the wooden deck.

The boatman looked down. His eyes widened—and Eric whipped the blackjack down, *whack*.

The boatman dropped like a rock, right on top of his colleague.

A sound behind him spun him around, but it was just Demi running lightly up the dock toward the boat. "I told you to hide!" he scolded.

"You need duct tape to secure him, right?"

Couldn't argue with that. He grabbed the tape and mummified the ever-loving fuck out of both those scumbags. Wrists, elbows, ankles, knees, around and around. Total overkill. They weren't going to so much as twitch until someone cut them free.

It was sweaty work, taping and dragging the other four bound men down to the boat. Demi tried to help, but he pushed her aside. He worked faster alone.

His mind was buzzing with adrenaline, speculating on the ramifications of what had just happened. What he had just heard. Hating every single goddamn one of them.

Soon he and Demi were heading across the water in the attackers' boat. It rode low in the water and went slow, overloaded with assholes as it was. They could have used Demi's boat and distributed them, but he didn't like having her out of his reach and with any of those fuckheads, even if they were bound hand and foot.

Demi had arranged for the police meet them at the

marina. Soon they'd be able to turn over their cargo to the law. But he kept on hearing words of the boatman before he copped to Eric's ploy, playing on repeat in his head.

Getting the girl ready for transport, huh? I wouldn't mind guarding that bitch's cage. Nice rack. Sweet ass, too.

The boatman had expected an unconscious man, plus Demi. The guys were there purposely to abduct Demi, but his own presence was no surprise to them. What the *fuck?*

Eric had been targeted before in Shaw's Crossing. He'd been forced to defend himself more than once. Many people had strong feelings about the Prophet and the Curse.

But why would anyone hurt Demi? And who the fuck knew that he'd be at Spruce Tip? He hadn't even known himself until late last night, and he had not told a living soul. Nor had he been seen getting into the boat at the Avery boat ramp. He'd bet money on it.

He couldn't figure out where these facts pointed, but it was nowhere good.

The town sparkled on the distant lakeshore. Police flashers pulsed red and blue at the marina. They gave him déjà vu. His hike down the canyon for Terry seemed like a lifetime ago, but it was only a few hours.

The big, heavy guy whose coat he had taken had regained consciousness. He stared up at them through puffy, hate-filled eyes.

Eric nudged him with his foot. "Who hired you, asshole?"

The guy spat blood, and let out a wheezy snort of laughter. He leered at Demi, who was now huddled in her winter jacket, as far away from the heap of trussed men as the boat would allow.

"Hey, bitch," he crooned. "You know what? I'm almost

sorry for you. You musta been a real bad girl for Daddy to hate you so goddamn much."

Demi stood, took a moment to steady herself and then hauled off and kicked him in the balls. The man jackknifed with a sharp grunt of pain. "Fucking cunt," he hissed.

"Tell it to the cops," Demi said.

Tough talk, but her face was ashen. But that scum would spout anything that came into his head to get under her skin. It was an unthinkable lie. It had to be.

Not even an asshole like Benedict Vaughan could do that to his own daughter.

15

The morning was a blur. Eric gave his report, and Demi must have done the same in some other room, but he didn't see her, or Benedict Vaughan either. At one point, he saw old man Shaw through the glass, talking to Chief Bristol and looking worried and agitated.

Eric had declined a medical examination. It was just bruises and his shoulder was the worst of it, badly bruised and throbbing hard. But it wasn't bad enough to spend hours tied up in a time-sucking hospital bureaucracy while someone was out there gunning for Demi.

When the cop wrapped up her report, Eric refilled his cup from a coffee machine and walked out to find Demi arguing with her grandfather in the corridor.

"...kidnapping attempt?" Henry Shaw bawled. "What the hell is going on around here, and where the hell is your father? Did you call him again?"

"Six times at last count, Granddad. No response. Chief Bristol said that Dad told him he was out of town, but that he'd hurry back as fast as he could."

"Out of town? What in God's name possessed him to go out of town?"

"Don't know, Granddad. I saw him last night before I went to Spruce Tip, and he didn't say anything to me about leaving town. Maybe he just took a drive. Got an itch."

"He's been an itch since the day I met him," Shaw growled.

Then Demi caught sight of him. Her smile was so startlingly beautiful, the rush of it lifted him right up off his feet.

"There he is," she said. "The man of the hour. All hail the conquering hero."

"Please," he muttered. "Don't even."

"Why not? It's true. You kicked ass."

"You!" Henry Shaw scowled at him beneath his bushy white brows.

Eric sipped the stale coffee, raising his eyebrows. "What about me?"

"He saved my ass, Granddad," Demi said in a warning tone. "Be nice."

"He shouldn't have been out there with you in the first place!"

"But isn't it incredibly, fabulously lucky that he was? Come on. Admit it."

"You shouldn't have been there either! You are coming home with me, young lady!"

"No, Granddad." Demi's voice had the flat, weary tone of someone who'd already repeated herself many times. "I can't do that right now."

"You're heading off to your townhouse, where you live all alone? At least I have a decent security system!"

"She can stay with me," Eric announced.

Demi sputtered something, but Shaw talked right over her. "Excuse me? You?"

"At Otis's place. Otis's gun is there if I need it. I was a Marine, sir. Like Otis, like you. I'll be her security system. Like I was on the island."

"Thanks, Eric, but it's not up to you, either," Demi said. "I live in a townhouse on a busy street with my neighbors crowded up on either side of me. No one is going to try to abduct me this morning in broad daylight. We'll talk later, Granddad. Please, go home."

"Goddamn stubborn female. Always have been. From day one." He frowned at Eric. "I wanted to kick your ass, but now I suppose I have to thank you," he added gruffly.

"Not necessary," Eric said. "But I don't recommend the ass-kicking. It never ends well."

"Well now," Shaw growled. "Aren't you the uppity young bastard."

"Eric, stop it. Granddad, go home." Demi's low voice had an edge.

Shaw reached out and seized a lock of Demi's hair, giving it a gentle tug. "Call me, sweet pea," he said. "I want to hear from you real soon. Dinner tonight?"

"Let's play it by ear, Granddad. I'm pretty wiped out."

Shaw walked out, still grumbling. They watched him get into his pickup.

"Wow," Eric said. "He's a piece of work."

"That he is," she agreed. "But he showed up for me. At least he gives a shit."

An awkward silence followed while he fished for the words. "Demi," he said. "What that guy said, on the boat. He was just fucking with you. No way could your father—"

"Let's not go there right now," Demi said. "Let it wait. One awful thing at a time."

Chief Bristol came out of his office and looked around. "Your dad still not here?"

Demi shook her head. "Still not answering his phone."

"Strange. I got him only that one time. Seems odd he'd stop answering his phone after news like this." Wade dug into his pants pockets, pulled out car keys and handed them to Eric. "Here, take these. Holly sent her boys out to the Avery boat ramp to get the pickup for you. It's parked right out front."

Eric took the keys. "Thank you, Chief."

"Thank Holly before you leave." Wade turned to Demi. "Do you have someone to stay with you?"

"I'm heading home," she said. "I need time to myself."

"I'd very much rather you weren't alone," Wade said. "Not until we know exactly what happened out there."

"She can stay with me," Eric said again.

The Chief and Demi exchanged eloquent glances.

"I appreciate the concern," Demi said. "But I am one hundred percent sure that nobody else is going to attack me this morning. And I need some goddamn privacy."

"I still want to keep watch," Eric pleaded. "Just indulge me. Your place, my place, I don't care. I just need Otis's gun and I'm good to go. You don't have to talk to me. Go into a bedroom and shut the door. Ignore me. Pretend I'm not there."

Wade cleared his throat. "To be honest, I would feel better if someone was watching your back today, Demi. But I'll leave you young folks to work this out on your own." His gaze shifted to Demi. "Unless you'd prefer that I stay, of course."

"It's fine, Chief," she assured him. "I can handle him."

They waited while he walked away.

"Handle me?" Eric murmured. "Like an unbroken horse?"

She snorted under her breath. "More like a frisky hound."

He held up his keys. "Please, Demi." His voice was low and intense. "Please."

"Eric." Her voice shook. "You don't want to see me fall apart. It won't be pretty."

"I don't need you to be pretty. I just want to stand guard while you rest. Otherwise, I'll have park outside your house, which is embarrassing and makes me looks like a fucking stalker. But whatever you do, I'm not taking my eyes off you until we know exactly what happened today."

Probably not even then.

He swallowed the words back. Pronouncements like that always got him into trouble.

Demi blew out a weary sigh. "Oh, fine," she snapped. "Watch my back if it makes you feel better. Just don't expect conversation or civility. That part of my brain is fried. I might be unsociable. As in, a bitch from the bowels of hell. Be warned."

"Not scared," he told her.

She lifted her eyebrows. "You should be."

16

emi regretted giving into pressure as they drove out Vensel Road. She was a hair away from total meltdown. Anywhere near Eric Trask was already meltdown central for her. His very presence was an intense stimulant. Not optimal for calming down.

Yet here she was, driving off to be alone in the woods with him.

She'd be better off huddled in the dark at home. The original plan had been to bash herself on the head with a shot of bourbon or three and burrow down into her bed with a pillow over her head, aiming for unconsciousness. Trying not think about what that guy said to her on the boat. At least until Chief Bristol told her what they'd learned.

Or rather, when Chief Bristol removed all doubt about what she already knew.

She wasn't confused about what those men were after. She knew perfectly well who had sent them.

She was just miserable about it.

Eric pulled in, parking the pickup right behind his Porsche. She slid out on wobbly legs, teeth chattering in the icy wind. Shaking. Too much bad coffee.

"You're cold," Eric said. "Let's get inside. I'll build a fire."

A few minutes later, she was curled up in a faded wingback chair by a pot-bellied stove. Eric crouched next to her, feeding a crackling fire with small sticks of kindling. He performed that task with the same absolute focus that he brought to everything he did.

When the fire was going to his satisfaction, he rummaged in a drawer in the wooden credenza for a plaid wool blanket and draped it around her shoulders.

"This is backwards, you know," Demi told him. "You're the one who engaged in mortal combat and kicked the crap out of a pack of big guys. You're treating me like the wounded soldier. Nobody even hit me, Eric. I don't have a scratch or a bruise. Thanks to you."

"I'm glad," he said. "That's a good outcome."

"I saw you rubbing your shoulder. Is it hurt?"

"I'll be fine."

"That's not what I asked," she said. "I see blood on your shirt. Let me see."

He sighed. "Demi, I'm fine. Don't—"

"Let me fucking see it, Eric."

Eric clenched his teeth, and lifted the grimy shirt, wincing.

Demi gasped at the spectacular bruise and scrape on top of his shoulder. "That looks awful. You have to get that looked at."

"It's okay," he said, covering it up. "Nothing broken or torn."

"How do you know?"

"Vast experience." Eric peeled off the shirt with a few swift gestures and wadded it up into his hands. "I'm going to take a quick shower and get some fresh clothes. Do you know how to use a gun?"

"I've done some hunting with Granddad. But I'd rather not—"

"Just while I'm in the shower. Please." He opened another drawer and pulled out a handgun. "Use this. He kept the others in the safe, but he kept this out for home defense. A Glock 19." He pulled out the magazine to check, and slid it back inside. "Full magazine, one in the chamber. Point and shoot."

"Eric, I highly doubt that—"

"Just until I'm out of the shower. Don't give me a hard time. I'll be quick."

She sighed. "Whatever."

Demi held the gun on her lap and listened to the fire crackle in the stove and the wind moan in the eaves. The pane in the door that she'd broken when she'd seen Otis on the floor was still missing. Someone had taped a small square of cardboard over it, but the wind had torn it loose, making it flap in the wind.

The desolate flapping and moaning underscored all the craziness. So did the gun in her hand, heavy and cold. Otis's death. Terry's accident. The attack this morning.

And more to come. Lots more misery still in store.

She had to face the truth about Dad's part in this. She'd heard the fights between him and mom years ago. She knew about the mysterious phone calls. She'd heard stories about massive debt. Whispers about embezzlement.

Things had blown over after Dad been transferred as

GM to the Granger Valley Distribution Center, when she was in high school. Her folks had pretended that things were fine. But Mom couldn't hide the worry in her eyes.

Things hadn't been fine for her father, or for Mom. Not for a long time. And there was that odd conversation that Eric had spied upon, too. Those thugs, shaking Dad down.

Dad had been in trouble. Scared and desperate. The kidnapping insurance that her grandfather had taken out on her all those years ago had been too much of a temptation.

Eric came in a few minutes later, hair damp, wearing a fresh gray waffle-weave shirt and jeans. She held the gun out to him.

"Hang onto it," he said. "I'll use one of the others."

"I'm not in danger anymore," she told him. "It's unnecessary."

"You don't know that. After what just happened—"

"I know it, Eric. For a fucking fact."

Eric looked almost afraid to speak.

"No," he said. "Not possible. He couldn't have done that to you. He's your father."

At least Eric wasn't playing dumb, which was a relief of sorts. "Dad was the only one who knew I was going to the island," she said. "I told him. No one else knew."

"You left from the public marina," he argued. "Anyone could have seen you go."

"And organized a six-man team on the spot to abduct me?"

Eric paced restlessly around the room. "It's still an incredibly short lead-in time. No more than what, six hours? Maybe it was me they were after."

"Do you have a rich grandfather who took out a crapton of kidnapping insurance on you when you were a kid? I remember Dad joking about kidnapping me himself when I was little. As I recall, I didn't think it was funny even then."

"I don't have a rich granddad, no. But I am the Prophet's spawn, so there are many people out there in this town who hate my guts for no good reason. I'm the usual trouble magnet. It makes more sense that this is about me, not you."

Demi shook her head. "Not this time, Eric. It's a generous thought, but I doubt it. Anyway, Chief Bristol will get it out of them eventually." She twisted her hands together. "The awful thing is, he probably felt justified." Her voice shook no matter how she tried to steady it. "He probably thought I deserved this. I've always bothered him, and this is my punishment." The lump in her throat was choking her. "I knew he was mad at me. I just didn't know he was *that* mad."

"I just can't see it." Eric said vehemently. "I can't see him doing that to you."

"Unfortunately, I can. So you see? There's no need to go to all these lengths to protect me. I appreciate what you did out at the island, but it's over. The danger has passed. Dad can't organize another abduction now. Not now that he's been discovered."

"It might not be what you think," Eric said. "It's too soon to relax."

"I'd rather face reality all at once and get it over with," Demi said. "It would really help me if you would do the same."

Eric stared down at the gun in his hand. He laid it, slowly and deliberately, in the open drawer, and pushed it closed.

"Okay," he said. "Let's just say, for the sake of

argument, that you've faced reality. Let's say there's no more danger. Let's just presuppose that for a minute. Just for kicks."

She eyed him, apprehensive. "Eric, don't start."

"Bear with me. So tell me, Demi. Why did you come out here?"

Demi felt suddenly on the defensive. "I was too tired for another battle," she said. "You, Chief Bristol, my granddad, throwing your weight around. It's fucking exhausting."

"I don't buy it. You've never backed down from a fight in your life. It's one of your defining characteristics."

Demi stood up, letting the blanket drop. "I'm not in the mood for games," she said. "Tell me what you want and I'll tell you if you can have it."

His silvery eyes bored into hers. The grandfather clock on the mantle ticked loudly in the charged silence.

"I want it all," Eric said.

Demi let out a sharp laugh. "Wow. Ambitious much?"

"Very," he agreed.

"I might have known you had an agenda, you sneaky bastard," she said. "I thought you wanted to keep me company while I sipped tea and shivered pathetically by the fire."

"You've got plenty of other people in this town who could do that for you."

"I suppose so. But what's your point?"

"I can give you a hell of a lot more than tea and company," he said.

The hot smolder of his eyes was hypnotizing. The sensual shape of his lips, curving in that faint smile. He knew the effect he had on her. He could feel her react.

Sexual awareness ignited, and suddenly she was hot

for him. Weak in the knees. Short of breath. Wet. Goddamn that man. It infuriated her, when her body betrayed her.

"You brought me here on false pretenses," she said. "You said you were going to guard me while I rested. Not come on to me and make eyes at me and jerk me around." She looked around for her coat. "Where's my damn phone? I'll call a car."

Her coat was on the back of a chair at a dining room table, but Eric stepped in front of her as she reached for it. "Don't call," he said. "Don't go, Demi."

She blinked back furious tears. "Crap," she muttered, digging for tissue. "You are such an opportunist. You want to have this conversation now? For real?"

"I have to take my opportunities where I find them. I didn't get to say it seven years ago. You didn't answer my letters. You blocked me online. This is my only chance, so I'm goddamn well taking it."

"Eric, don't do this."

"We belong together, Demi. We always have. I made myself forget it, because I had to. Until last night. Last night made me remember all of it. I can't forget again."

"That's not what last night was about," Demi said.

Eric made a frustrated sound. "So what the fuck was it about?"

"Sex," she said. "I wanted it. You delivered. It was awesome. Then you saved me from the kidnappers. Also awesome. I owe you infinite gratitude, Eric, and nothing else. Until the end of time. End of story."

"Stories can start again," he said.

"Oh, for God's sake—"

"We're good together. I'm not just talking about sex. Face reality all at once, Demi. Get it over with."

She held up her hand. "Don't you throw my words back at me. My world is crashing down today, just like it did the last time I got close to you. Now is not the time. And you are all up in my face. So back...the fuck...*off*."

Eric let out a slow breath, and stepped back. "Sorry," he said. "Let me walk this back a little."

"Yeah? How might you accomplish that? I'm already massively pissed."

She flinched back as he reached to stroke her cheek with his fingertips. "You said to tell you what I want."

"And?"

"You know what I want," he said. "What can I have?"

The sound of the fire swelled in the foreground as Demi contemplated his invitation to step back into his sexual spell. To give in to that raging hunger once again. One more time, to just let pleasure burn every coherent thought out of her head.

At least for a while.

His erection was already visible. And of course, he saw her look.

As a distraction, he was a lot better than bourbon, that was for sure. But everything had its price. "You want more than I can give," she whispered.

"I'll take what I can get."

She stood there, speechless, as Eric moved toward her, enveloping her in his heat. His arms slid around her waist, drawing her close. "Just sex. Great sex. No strings."

"You said no strings last night, too. I'm not falling for that bullshit again."

He nuzzled her hair. "I learned my lesson." His deep voice vibrated next to her ear, making delicious shivers race down her back. "I'll be good. Just red-hot, fabulous fucking.

As much as you want. As long as you want."

"And after all that's happened, you're still up for sex? You're not tired?"

"No," he said.

Sex throbbed off him in waves, making her giddy and unsteady on her feet. "You bad boy," she whispered. "Tempting me."

"Can't help it," he said. "It just happens."

She felt it, too. Like some physical force inside her that pulled her toward him. She laid her hand on his hot chest, her fingertips digging in, feeling that sleek, hard muscle.

She slid her hand slowly downward. "It doesn't seem right to take you up on it. Not after you declared yourself to me like that. It makes me feel like I'm using you."

"Use me," he said. "I'm fine with that."

It was a terrible idea. So stupid. She couldn't fall for this a second time.

"There's a bedroom with a double bed upstairs," he said. "I just put on fresh sheets."

"You did? When did you have time to do that?"

"After my shower. In case I got lucky."

She found herself laughing. "Calculating much?"

Eric's grin was unapologetic. "I have to deliver on all my seductive hype, right?" he said. "That takes foresight. Planning. Come upstairs and I'll make you forget all your troubles. For as long as you let me." He scooped her hair over to the side, pressing slow, hot kisses against her throat. "Just pleasure," he whispered. "No guilt."

She shivered, clutching his shoulder for balance. "I've heard that before."

"Let me try again. I'll be so good."

They looked at each other. This was the moment to say

no, if she was going to say it. And mean it.

She dug her fingers deeper into his densely muscled shoulder.

"Yes," she said.

17

Eric reached up to his shoulder, covering Demi's hand with his own. He lifted it to his lips and kissed it, reverently.

The contact made his heart speed. It pounded in his ears.

But it was still his job to keep them safe, whether she'd dismissed the danger or not. He opened the drawer and took Otis's Glock. "This goes upstairs with us," he told her. "I'm not completely convinced that you're in the clear. Not yet."

Her smile made his face heat up. "Whatever makes you feel better."

She was humoring him. He was fine with that.

He led her up the creaking farmhouse stairs and into the bedroom he used whenever he was in this house. It was a small, white-painted room with a dormer window. Dim light filtered through the boughs of a big oak tree that swayed and knocked the siding in the wind outside, making the room a cave of shifting green shadows. Not much in the room, just a bed, a straight-back chair, and his suitcase. A dresser was cluttered with his toothbrush and shaving gear, wallet, change and car keys. Otis had been a widower for decades, and he'd never been much of a decorator.

But the bed was comfortable. Eric laid the gun on the nightstand and turned the comforter back. Demi paced toward him, her eyes full of teasing challenge. She pried off one shoe, then the other, kicking them aside. "Your turn now."

Shoes seemed as good a place as any to start, so he followed suit.

Demi started in on her sweatshirt, making a slow, sexy thing out of it. She tossed it onto the chair, shaking out her hair into a sexy, tousled mop over her face and shoulders. She was wearing a peach-colored satin bra that propped her stunning tits up. The chill in the room made her nipples taut, poking against the soft fabric.

Her eyes pierced him with their intensity. Daring him. He realized it was his turn.

She was keeping it playful. He had to do the same. Iron control. No sweeping declarations. No staring at her with the eyes of his soul. None of it. It was all off limits.

He had to be careful, calculated. Keep her close, for as long as he could manage it, until she got used to him. Used to the idea of them together.

Right. When hell froze over. Who was he trying to fool?

There was nothing playful about the feeling raging inside him. His hands shook, his heart pounded, his cock an ache of need. He hadn't known how numb he was before, but there was a big fucking downside to not being numb. And he was feeling it all.

He started to pull off his sweatshirt but stopped

partway with a hiss as his shoulder blazed white-hot.

Demi moved closer, pushing up the hem of his shirt, her cool fingers stroking his belly. "Let me," she murmured.

Sensual torture, the way she slid her hands gently up his chest, taking the sweatshirt up with it. Splaying her fingers over his pecs, circling her hands over his nipples. Sliding her fingers into his chest hair, giving it a tug. Just to the edge of pain.

She lifted the shirt gently over his head and tossed it in the direction of the chair. She was inches from him now, staring him down. She undid the front clasp of her bra.

She leaned down to drop a soft, careful kiss on the bruise on his shoulder, then looked up again, swaying forward until her tight brown nipples were just barely touching his chest. The contact burned sweetly, like a kiss.

Their embrace felt so inevitable, like a trap springing. One he never wanted to escape from. There could be no playing it cool with Demi. Not if he was kissing her, tasting her, feeling her. The pain in his shoulder was already a distant memory. Every cell of him was electrified at the contact. There was nothing playful about the way he grabbed her hips and pulled her against the bulge of his erection, nothing playful about his devouring kiss. He struggled feverishly with her jeans, and she did the same, his mouth moving hungrily over hers. Pleading, demanding, insisting, he couldn't tell and didn't care. He just needed more, more, more.

All his. Forever.

Pants and underwear kicked away and forgotten. One hand grabbing his ass, her nails digging in. The other cupping his balls, a seductive caress before she gripped his shaft and squeezed, stroking...ah, God. Oh please.

Chill. He had to slow this...way...the fuck...*down*.

It took everything he had not to just throw her down and fall on her, but he broke away from that kiss, panting. Counting slowly. Down from ten, then once again.

He slid his hand up between her hot, smooth thighs, into that secret paradise between, teasing that swatch of silky fuzz that decorated her pussy. Caressing the whole length of her folds, his fingertip dipping into that hot silken well. Up...down...and in. Stroking, sliding. Tenderly thrusting inside. Slick, hot heaven.

She moaned, writhing. Her body clenching eagerly around his hand. Her fingers tightening around his cock. An expert, swiveling stroke that almost made him come.

He blocked her hands and breathed it down. "Not yet," he whispered. "You first."

She pressed her face against his shoulders. "If you insist."

"I do," he murmured.

He took his time about it, making her wait, but when she got to the point where she was digging in her nails and sobbing with need, he insisted, and pushed her over the top and into a shattering orgasm.

She was rigid in his arms, making breathless keening sounds, her pussy squeezing his fingers as pleasure wracked her. So sweet.

And it was that perfect sensation that reminded him of something that could wreck his world. "Damn," he muttered. "Condoms. Don't have any. This is going to kill me."

Demi lifted her face. Her cheeks were blushed deep pink, eyes bright and dazzled from pleasure. "I can't wait for you to go buy some. I'll explode with lust."

He just stared at her, bewildered. "Uh...but I can't..."

"I have a contraceptive implant. Got it a few years ago,

but it's still good. And I've had bloodwork done since I was last with anyone. You?"

The implications of that news for his hard, pulsing dick wiped out his powers of speech for a few moments. "Ah…ah, yeah, I have. Same. Clean bill of health."

"Well then," she said briskly. "So? Proceed."

"Just like that?"

She frowned. "Don't mess with my head. Why not? Don't you trust me?"

"Of course I trust you! I just assumed that you wouldn't trust me."

Demi laughed under her breath. "Well, it's complicated. You have a problematic habit of completely pulverizing my life, yes, but I really don't think you'd lie about something like that. So for what it's worth…feel free. If you want to, that is."

That left him wordless, staggered. Demi pressed a kiss against this jaw. "Don't sweat it," she murmured. "Remember? No past, no future, just your thick fabulous cock moving inside me. So deep. Nothing between us. Just heat…and wet." She cupped his face in her hands and pulled it down to hers, dropping soft, lingering kisses against his jaw, his mouth. "Don't overthink this. Or I'll change my mind."

"Oh no. I'm in." That snapped him right out of his daze and he kissed her again. Putting everything he was afraid to put into words into the kiss.

She rocked back, her breath unsteady. "Um, Eric. One thing."

"Hmm?"

"Did I thank you for saving my ass last night?"

"I don't need to be thanked. I'm glad I got the message out, loud and clear."

She frowned at him, puzzled. "Message?"

"Anyone tries to hurt you, I will fuck them up so hard I'll make them wish they'd never been born. Let the world know it. Let the message spread far and wide."

The flash in her eyes made his breath stop. Her gaze slid away, almost shyly. Time started up again. "Um, thanks," she whispered. "For caring, I mean. It means a lot to me. Particularly right now."

"Anytime."

Eric backed her up until her legs hit the bed. She sat down suddenly, and he lifted up her legs, pushing her onto her back against the cool sheets. He wanted a good long look at that her like that, thighs spread wide. Her beautiful, shining pink pussy on display.

He tugged her ass to the edge of the bed, taking in every tiny detail as he stroked her with his fingers. Opening her wide, stroking that puff of silky dark curls that decorated her mound. He wanted another go at her with his tongue, but first things first. He had to get inside her or he was going to pass out.

Demi propped herself up, her direct gaze burning him alive.

The bed was high, the perfect height for him on his feet, her at the edge. He seized his dick at the root and petted her pussy with it until she was squirming, biting her lip, gasping for air. His penis head gleamed with their juice.

She locked eyes with him. "Now," she said. "Do it."

He drove inside her, one long, slow stroke, and oh. *Fuck,* it was beautiful.

So tight, so hot. The snug perfection of her. His whole length, stroked by her clinging hole. He drove inside all the way. Eased himself out, riveted by the sight of her tender flushed pussy lips kissing and caressing his flushed shaft on the slow outstroke.

He clamped his hand into her thighs and pumped his cock into her as slowly as he could. Best feeling ever. Deep, hot, juicy fucking. Eyes locked. Her red lips were parted, her lush tits bounced as the jolting rhythm got more intense. Deeper, harder. His flushed, swollen red cock shone. A fresh slick of balm with each slamming stroke.

The bed rocked with them. They panted for air. Demi arched and writhed beneath him, clutching his shoulders, her pussy squeezing him as she climaxed again, clenching wildly around him.

That was the end of his self-control. He hadn't meant to come inside her, but he didn't have a hope of stopping it. He let out a hoarse shout as his orgasm crashed down like a landslide.

After, he found himself hunched over her, staring into her eyes. Naked and exposed. Everything he felt, written on his face. Blazing out of him in fucking neon.

Feelings she didn't want him to have. Hopes she didn't want to encourage. He was hers. Body and soul, whether she wanted him or not. It was a done deal. On his part.

But he couldn't say it. Couldn't offer it. He'd promised.

He pulled out of her and turned away, to hide his face. This was the danger spot, the no-go zone, every damn time. After they had sex, he just couldn't fake it anymore.

He grabbed his jeans, pulled them on. "Bathroom's down the hall," he muttered, without looking at her. "Towels in the cabinet. Help yourself."

"Eric?" She sounded worried.

He gritted his teeth through the pain in his shoulder as he tugged his shirt back on and grabbed the Glock off the nightstand. "I'll go downstairs. Make some coffee."

"Hey!" Her voice was sharp. "Eric! What the hell is the matter with you?"

He stopped, his hand on the doorframe. He started to say something stupid and ill-considered and true, but swallowed the dangerous words back. Then tried again.

"Just trying to play by the rules," he said. "I suck at it, that's all. See you downstairs."

He splashed his face and hands, but what he saw in the mirror over the bathroom sink was too much for him. Soap and water wouldn't wash that look off his face.

Coffee. That made sense, at least. He headed downstairs barefoot. Laid the gun on the dining room table before heading into the kitchen.

Not much in the way of food in Otis's kitchen. Best he could find was a sleeve of chocolate-dipped butter cookies. Better than nothing.

He heard the stairs creaking a few minutes later. He poured out two cups of coffee and brought them and the cookies into the dining room.

"I don't have milk or cream," he said. "Hope it's okay for you black." He stopped short at the sight of Demi at the table with Otis's gun in her hand, a strangely abstracted look on her face.

He set down the coffee. "What is it?"

She glanced up. "You said this gun is a Glock 19?"

"Yeah. What of it?"

"I was just thinking of those minutes in the ICU when Otis was awake and lucid. He kept repeating 'lock, lock, lock.' It just occurred to me that maybe he wasn't saying lock at all. Maybe he was saying something else. Like...Glock."

The loud, discordant clang of the grandfather clock

over the fireplace striking the hour made them both jump.

They looked over at it, and then at each other. Her eyes widened, and she laid the gun carefully down.

"Clock," he said softly.

Eric went over to the grandfather clock and pulled open the small glass door over the pendulum, decorated with a fading pattern of gold-painted curlicues. He pushed gently against the corner of the back.

It popped loose. He fished the panel out. Behind it was a recessed area with a square, silvery object tightly lodged inside.

Demi appeared next to him. "Did you know that the clock had a false back?"

Eric shook his head as he pried out the object. It proved to be a small digital camera. He turned it over in his hands. "Mace and Anton and I got this for him a few years ago when his old Pentax bit the dust," he said. "For his bird-watching."

They gazed down at the camera in Eric's hands.

"He didn't tell you about what was going on with him?" she asked.

Eric turned back to the table and laid the camera down, picking up his smartphone. "He sent us a voicemail the night before he died. At five AM. He was anxious to tell us something, but he didn't spell it out in the message. Listen to this."

He set it to play. The sound of Otis's rough, halting voice made his throat clench.

Hey. Otis here. You boys need to come home. Soon as possible. All of you. Got things to tell you about GodsAcre. Can't say it on the phone. I'll explain when you get here. Bye now."

"He sent the exact same message for Anton and Mace," Eric told her. "Then he hid this camera in the clock. Maybe he

202

fell while he was going for his gun."

Demi made a noncommittal sound. "He just had a stroke, Eric."

Eric made a doubtful sound in his throat. "Maybe. Let's see the pictures he took."

The display screen on the camera was large enough to see the pictures clearly, but the images themselves were baffling. The camera's memory was full of generic pictures of parked cars, trucks, heavy equipment. There were some shots of a mass of deeply rutted tracks in the mud. Other shots of large piles of building materials. Big heaps of dirt.

"What the fuck is all this?" he murmured. "Come on, Otis. A little help, here."

Demi peered over his shoulder as he scrolled through more and more. Dozens of them. All more of the same. Muddy vehicles, parked outdoors.

Then one of the pictures blindsided him. The distinctive shape of the tall chimney in the distance, looming up behind a back-hoe. The chimney of the Great Hall at GodsAcre.

The hall was a heap of ashes and blackened bricks on a block of cement, but that chimney still stuck up into the sky like a burned bone.

It was like a kick to the gut. His hand jerked. He suddenly felt waves of blazing heat billowing in his face, saw showers of sparks in the dark. Heard the screaming, echoing in his head against the sound of his own thudding heart—

"Eric? You okay?"

Demi's worried voice came from far away. She clutched his arm, squeezing it.

The fog of darkness receded. He found himself collapsed over the dining room table on his elbows, gasping for breath. His forehead was chilly and wet.

Demi held Otis's camera. She held it out to him. "You, ah...dropped this," she said, her voice wary. "I caught it. Just in time."

"Thanks," he forced out. "Sorry."

"You looked like you were having a seizure."

"Just a bad moment," he said.

"Bad how? Was it the picture? I saw it, too. But I didn't see anything but a big dirty backhoe in the mud."

Classic Demi. She wouldn't let it go. He exhaled, very slowly, and held up the camera, showing her the image again. "These pictures were taken at GodsAcre," he said. "I recognized the chimney of the Great Hall. That's where they all died. Someone had bolted it shut from the inside, and padlocked the bolt. They found the padlocks afterward. Still intact. They never managed to get them open before...before the smoke got them."

"Oh, God, Eric," she whispered.

"The three of us sneaked out that night, to take care of some stuff. By the time we got back and figured out what was going on the door was red hot. We couldn't get it open. The flames were so high." He showed her the burn scars on the heels of his hands. "I passed out. Anton dragged me away. Mace has burn scars all the way up his arms. Some on his chest."

She pressed her face against his back. "I'm so sorry," she said. "I didn't know."

"I didn't want you to know. I wish I didn't know myself. I don't like to talk about it. Or think about it." He shook himself, like he was trying to fling something off. "I didn't want that in your head. I wish it wasn't in mine."

She pressed her lips against the back of his neck.

"Anyway," he said. "I saw the chimney. It got to me. Sorry I scared you."

Her arms slid around his waist, her face pressed against his neck. He stiffened, but after a moment, the contact with her somehow let air inside. His clenched fists relaxed.

He turned around, grabbed her and held her breathlessly tight.

After a couple minutes of that, Demi made a low noise in the back of her throat and gave his back an encouraging pat-pat-pat. He was squeezing her too hard, arms shaking. A thank-God-you-weren't-killed-in-the-earthquake hug. So much for the no-guilt, no-strings scenario. He couldn't keep up the act for any length of time.

For once, she was letting it slide. The stress flashback had earned him a pity pass.

He let go and turned away. "It's starting to make sense, if these pictures were taken at GodsAcre. Something's happening up there. Otis tried to document it. And he was stopped."

"Is that all of the photos?"

He scrolled through them again, hoping the chimney wouldn't set him off if he was braced for it. "Couple more shots. Gotta get these onto my laptop and blow them up."

"The police could run the plates on those cars," she said. "Otis was careful to get the license plates. I bet that's the purpose of these pictures. Recording license plates."

"Could be, but I don't want to involve the cops yet."

Demi looked startled. "The hell? Of course you have to involve them!"

"Not yet," he repeated. "I don't want anyone else near the place until I know what's up there."

"And you think you can figure that out better than the

local law enforcement, with all their resources? Alone and unassisted? Jesus, Eric! That's insane!"

"Maybe," he admitted. "But I still have to check it out first."

"Okay, fine. Let's go take a look right now. Just you and me."

"Fuck, no!"

Demi crossed her arms over her chest. "Oh? So it's dangerous, you think?"

He was irritated to have been trapped in his own reasoning. "Yes, it is fucking dangerous," he said. "Otis went up there, and died that next day. I sent Terry up and he never even made it back down."

"That could just be a —"

"It's not a coincidence. Not in context, with all the other weird shit that's happening. Plus the ancient history. You're not getting anywhere near GodsAcre, Demi."

She gave him a long, level look. "I don't do stupid or dangerous things as a rule, Eric. And I won't do them just to spite you. But I do hope that you understand the futility of laying down the law with me. That shit will never fly."

Aw fuck. "Demi. Please."

"I get your reasoning," she went on. "I shouldn't go near it. The cops shouldn't go near it. It's mysteriously toxic. By that token, you shouldn't go near it either."

"I own it," he said through his teeth.

"So? What does that change?"

"No, I mean...not just in the sense of holding the title to the land. I mean, in terms of final responsibility. Me and Mace and Anton—we're bound to that place. By blood. Whatever's going on up there, we're the ones who should take care of it."

Demi's eyes were thoughtful. "I'm hearing echoes of

the hardcore survivalist doctrine of your youth, Eric. That line of thinking is arrogant and dangerous. And pretty fucking stupid, too, if we're being brutally honest."

Eric looked down at the photo still up on the camera's display screen. That blackened spike, sticking up out of the tumbled ruins like a horrible monument.

"I still have to do this," he said. "Please, keep this to yourself. At least for now. Let me talk to Anton and Mace, and check out the scene up there—"

"You can't take this on alone! The cops have weapons, training—"

"I have weapons and training, Demi," he said grimly. "A lifetime of it."

"The cops have access to a huge national database to identify those vehicles parked up there," she continued stubbornly. "That you do not have."

"Otis was a tough son of a bitch. He drove up there to take his pictures, and within hours, he was dead. Same with Terry. I don't want to go to Bristol's funeral, Demi. Or any of the other officers. I've got too much on my conscience already."

Demi gave him a thoughtful frown. "You blame yourself for what happened at GodsAcre? You were a child, Eric!"

"A teenager," he said. "I should have come back sooner. Found a way to get those doors open. I should have gotten them all out somehow."

"Eric—"

"No one else dies from whatever took Otis and Terry. The tally stops here."

"You really think these deaths aren't natural? You're back in Prophet's Curse territory again, Eric. That's where you lose me."

"I'm sorry," he said. "Just let me deal with it my own way first. Nobody gets near GodsAcre until I have a look. Then I call Mace and Anton, and we come up with a plan."

"So because it's so deadly dangerous, you're going to run straight into its jaws alone? Because you're Eric Trask, the only man tough enough take the risk. You macho jerk. You infuriate me."

"No one will see me," he said stubbornly. "I'm a Marine, Demi. I was trained by the Prophet. I'll wear Otis's bird-watching forest camo and hike up the draw so I can come down over the ridge from behind GodsAcre. I'll bring a long-range camera lens. Whatever's going on out there, I'll take pictures of it from a distance. That's all I mean to do. I swear. I'm not going in there with guns blazing all by myself. I'm not stupid."

Demi shook her head furiously. "I hate it."

"I can't let anyone else get hurt," he said. "Especially not you." He caught the look that flashed over her face. "Yeah, I know, that boat has sailed, I already hurt you and I can never fix it, yada yada. Be that as it may, I don't want to go to your funeral, Demi. I prefer you alive and mortally pissed off at me."

She looked like she was trying not to smile. "Actually, I wasn't going there," she said. "The you-already-hurt-me routine, I mean. I think we've, ah, moved past that. I'm kind of bored with it, to be honest."

His breathing just about stopped, but he didn't dare let himself float up off the ground on the basis of such a guarded, careful, cagey statement. "Well, good. Progress."

"I suppose. I'm still pissed as hell, though."

The silence was so charged with terror and hope, he

had to break it or he'd snap.

"How pissed?" he asked. "I want to touch you. Are you going to smack me?"

Demi's shoulders lifted. "I can't tell you how I'm going to feel until I get there," she said airily. "Risk it if you have the balls."

Ahhh, nice. Fucking with his head again. An excellent sign. Eric slid his arms around her waist, and pulled her close.

Her arms went around his neck and squeezed, aggressively. "You make me angrier than anyone in the world, Eric Trask."

He squeezed her back and kissed her fiercely. "I know," he said. "Get your coat. I'll drive you home."

18

The drive back to town was deathly quiet. Demi didn't break the silence. She had plenty to think about already. When they reached the Narrows Bridge, Eric finally spoke.

"I'll take you to your Granddad's house. You can't be alone right now."

"No," she said. "Take me to Dad's house."

He glanced at her, startled. "Why?"

"I want to check on him. I have a couple of hard questions for him. And I need to look him in the eyes while he answers them."

"He's not there," Eric said. "He told the chief he was leaving town. He's not answering the phone."

"Maybe he lied. He often does. If he's not there, I can see if his passport is in the file, and if his suitcase is in the closet. That would tell me a whole lot."

Eric looked pained. "It's been a hell of a night. You want to pile it on right now?"

"Why drag it out?"

Eric shook his head, but he took the turn that led them up to Osborn Grade. The pickup climbed up to the Heights. He stopped right in front of the Vaughan family home, on Cedar Crest Drive.

"Well, well," she said flatly. "Dad's car's still there. Fancy that."

"I don't like this," Eric muttered.

Too bad. She liked it a hell of a lot less than he did. Demi got out of the car and started up the driveway.

Eric loped after her. "Does he have any other cars?"

"Mom's BMW is inside the garage, but he mostly drives the Volvo."

The front door was locked, but Demi had a key in her purse. Eric followed close on her heels as she went inside.

It had been a long time since she'd been inside the family home, and the change in it was a jolt to her sensibilities. The house had been her mother's pride, and she'd kept it sparkling. Dad must have let the housekeeping service go. The shelves, furniture and knickknacks were fuzzed with a heavy coat of dust. There were cobwebs on the closed curtains and the air was stale and heavy.

"Dad?" she called.

No response. They walked slowly through the house where she had spent her childhood. Down the corridor along the staircase that led back into the huge kitchen, which was a mess of smelly, festering take-out containers. Dishes were piled up high, in the sink and on the counters.

"Dad?" she called.

Dread kept deepening inside her. A sense that she was missing something crucial.

She turned around and forced herself to move. One

foot after the other. "Upstairs."

The printer was blinking in Dad's office. She went to the file cabinet by the desk and looked inside one of the files. "His passport is gone," she said.

"Maybe he left it in a different place," Eric said.

"Maybe." She headed back out into the hall and toward the master bedroom.

It had been turned upside down. The closet hung open, the drawers pulled out. Clothes were piled on the unmade bed and scattered all over the floor.

She looked into the closet. "His travel case is gone. And he packed really fast." Demi shivered, wrapping her arms across her chest. "But why the hell is the car still here? Could he have taken a taxi?"

"Demi," Eric said. "Let's get the fuck out of here. Please."

"I'll take a look out back first. The lawn. The garage. To make sure Mom's car is in there and see if he took one of the bigger suitcases."

Eric shadowed her down the stairs and back into the kitchen, but she was the first to see Dad's hand stretched out on the floor as she went around the bar. The high barrier of the bar had hidden it the first time they came into the kitchen.

"Dad!" She dropped down to the floor next to him. He lay on the floor, sprawled on his side, clutching his chest. His mouth was open, his eyes wide and empty.

She shook him, calling to him and feeling for a pulse with hands that trembled.

Eric kneeled beside her and touched her father's throat. He shook his head. "He's cold," he said gently. "He's been gone for hours by now. Babe, I'm so sorry."

She thudded onto the floor on her butt, vaguely

surprised to realize that she was crying.

Eric made the necessary phone calls. When he was finished with that, he got down on the floor, wrapped his arms around her shoulders and just held her.

She finally pulled away, wiping her eyes, and noticed the suitcase by the door. She stared at it for a moment, and then reached around her dad's body, sliding her hand carefully into his deep coat pocket.

She found his passport and boarding passes and wiped at her eyes until she could read them. "He was going to Australia," she said. "A layover in Hawaii. Then Sydney."

The ambulance arrived, along with Chief Bristol and the ambulance crew. Once her father's body had been loaded up and the ambulance had pulled away, Chief Bristol lingered on the side porch, patting her shoulder.

"I am so sorry, honey," he said sadly. "Also that you had to be the one to find him."

"He was terrified," Demi said. "Running away from something. Or someone."

"Maybe those guys I saw," Eric said.

"What guys are those?" Chief Bristol asked sharply.

"At Otis's funeral," Demi told him. "Remember those two guys that nobody knew? They were associated with my dad. I'm not sure exactly how, but it was in a way that was not healthy for him. Eric overheard them threatening him."

Chief Bristol scowled. "And I'm just hearing about this now?"

"Sorry, Chief," Demi said wearily. "We had no idea how bad it was."

"But there's no sign of breaking and entering," Eric said. "He was inside a locked door the whole time. All of the doors in the house were still locked. I checked."

Demi and Eric looked at each other. She saw in his eyes that he was thinking exactly what she was thinking.

"The security cameras," he said. "Are they still running?"

"Can't imagine why they wouldn't be," she said. "Chief Bristol, what time did you call Dad this morning?"

"About six," he said. "Maybe a little after."

She went back inside, the two men following close after. The security monitors were set up in the breakfast nook, which had annoyed Mom no end when she was alive. Mom had thought that breakfast nooks were for breakfast, but that time around, Dad had prevailed.

She sat in front of the computer, squeezing her memory for the password. Dad had been comically lazy about passwords, a fact that she'd taken advantage of more than once back in her teenage years. It used to be Demetra1234. Now it was Demetra4321.

She ran the footage back to 5:45 AM and fast forwarded from there. Chief Bristol hunched forward, peering at the screen. Eric watched from over her other shoulder.

At 7:21 there was a flurry of activity. Demi ran it back and they watched the two funeral crashers march up to the side porch and pound on the door. They pounded for over a minute, then stopped while the smaller man talked to someone behind the door. The camera angle showed only the side of his face. They couldn't tell what he was saying.

The greasy-haired guy gave his larger companion a smug smile and pulled something from his pocket that they could not see, the big guy being in the way.

They held their breath, but nothing happened. The men just stood there, motionless, looking at the closed door.

The bigger guy finally went over to the window of the

mudroom and peered inside. He turned back to the other man, grinning. The two men high-fived and walked away, having never even gone inside the house. The door remained unopened.

Demi stopped the film once the men had disappeared out of the camera's frame. "What the hell?" she whispered. "What did they do to him?"

"Can we watch from another angle?" Eric asked. "How about the camera over the door to the pool house? It'll get them from the other side. Farther away, but worth a try."

Good idea. She ran that feed back to 7:21. They watched the same sequence of events again from the pool house angle. This time, when the smaller man pulled the object from his pocket, the hulking back of the bigger one didn't block their view.

He held a narrow, longish silver cylinder. It looked almost like a pen.

"What the hell…?" Chief Bristol leaned in, squinting.

The point of the object lit up, intensely bright. The man directed it at the door at chest level, holding it still for several seconds. The big guy peeked into the window and came back grinning. Again the high-five. Again they walked out of the camera frame.

Demi stopped the footage.

"What did we just see?" Chief Bristol said, after a tense silence.

"Could that thing have hurt Dad?" Demi whispered. "Through a closed door?"

"Or Otis," Eric said. "Or Terry."

"Slow down," Chief Bristol warned. "Let's not get ahead of ourselves. First we'll see what the coroner has to say."

"He'll say natural causes," Eric said. "Like he always does. Like he did thirteen years ago."

Chief Bristol gave him a quelling frown. "We'll see, Eric. Demetra, looks like I'm declaring this place a crime scene. I also need that footage, and all the archives."

Demi wrote down the password and laid it on the keyboard. "All yours, Chief."

She got up from the chair. The feeling came over her very fast. She had to sprint for the downstairs half-bath. She made it just in time before she threw up. Not that she had much inside her, just some coffee, but her belly wouldn't stop heaving.

Afterward, she splashed water on her face and patted it dry with her sleeve. Eric and Chief Bristol were on the front porch when she emerged, so she went out to join them.

She sank down onto the porch swing. Her legs wouldn't hold her up anymore.

Chief Bristol walked over to stand in front of her. "Demetra." He sounded wretched and apologetic. "I have, ah…even more bad news for you."

Demi let out a peal of bitter laughter before she could stop herself. "Really, Chief Bristol? You think you can top the morning I've already had?"

"No, I do not," he said quietly. "But I am very sorry to add to it."

Demi flapped her hand at him. "It's okay. I think I already know what you're going to tell me. Dad paid those guys to kidnap me. Is that what they told you?"

Chief Bristol looked miserable. "Honey, I am so, so sorry."

"Granddad was supposed to fork up a ransom. And Dad intended to steal it."

Bristol shoved his hands into his jacket pockets. "How do you know?"

"One of the kidnappers threw it in my face on the boat. It's true, right?"

His mouth tightened. "That's their story. We're still investigating. It'll take a while."

Her belly cramped again. Like it was a surprise. She'd taught herself not to let Dad hurt her, but he'd upped his game. He'd won this round. The ultimate burn.

He'd never been able to handle the fact that she saw through his games, his mask. He had charmed and manipulated most of the people in his life with ease, but not her. She'd somehow seen him for exactly what he was, even when she was little.

And he'd always hated her for it.

"One of them said that Ben had hired them to do this job before, about three years ago," Chief Bristol said. "That your dad called it off at the last minute. Lost his nerve."

"Three years," she said. "When Mom died. Just like this."

Eric kneeled beside her and seized her hand. "Your Mom died of a heart attack?"

"Yes," she said. "Also while packing for a trip no one knew about. Also while shoving things into a suitcase every which way. Oh God." She leaned over, her head whirling, stomach lurching. "Mom...must have found out what he meant to do."

Could Dad have...no. Not possible. Bad as he was, he couldn't have been that bad.

"Don't get yourself worked up," Chief Bristol urged. "What happened to Elaine was sad, but it was years ago, and it has nothing to do with what happened today."

"I found her, Wade," Demi said forcefully. "I saw her suitcase. She'd taken a framed photo of the two of us. From when I was a kid. That's not the kind of object that you take on a spontaneous weekend getaway."

"Demetra—"

"She found out that Dad was going to stage my kidnapping, and she objected. Then she died, right next to a hastily-packed suitcase. Maybe those guys pointed that thing at her chest, too." Demi pressed her hand to her mouth, rocking. "Oh God. Mom."

"Don't get yourself all worked up," Chief Bristol soothed. "You don't know that for a fact. You're just speculating."

Eric squeezed her hand. "I'm so sorry, baby."

She looked up into Eric's calm, resolute face, and realized something, in an intuitive flash of pure dismay.

With all this death raining down on her, that obstinate fool was still planning on sneaking up to GodsAcre today, all alone.

He winced when she grabbed his shoulder. She'd gripped the bruised one. "Come stay with me in my townhouse now." She tried to keep her voice calm, but it sounded shrill and desperate. "I've changed my mind about that. I need the company. Right now."

Eric looked straight into her eyes. "Soon," he said. "Just a couple things I need to take care of first. We talked about this already."

"Seriously?" Her voice cracked. "After *this*?"

"Especially after this."

No. Not possible. He wasn't walking into that goddamn death trap all alone. She couldn't lose him, too. Just couldn't.

"They can wait," she said wildly. "Or someone else can do them. You can't, Eric. You can't leave me alone today."

He pulled her into a hard embrace, kissed her and gave her that straight-on, unwavering look. When Eric Trask made up his mind about something, the sky could fall and the world shake apart into chunks and he would not budge one single fucking inch.

"Stay with me. Damn it, Eric." She knew it was useless. She was just hammering on him to no good purpose now, but she just couldn't help herself.

He pressed a hot kiss against her knuckles. "Soon," he repeated.

"Fine." Demi pulled away from him, her throat clenched like a fist, and got up onto her shaky feet. "Chief Bristol?" she said, her voice thick. "Would you give me a ride back to my house, please?"

"I'll give you a ride to the station," Chief Bristol said sternly. "Where you will wait until Henry comes to pick you up. I'm afraid I can't be budged on that. Not now."

"I see. Well, then. One second while I grab my coat and purse."

"It's just a few hours, Demi," Eric said. But she could read the rest in his eyes.

Don't tell Chief Bristol where I'm going.

Chief Bristol fixed him with a baleful look while they waited. "What the hell are you doing here, Eric?"

"Looking out for her," Eric replied.

"That remains to be seen. She needs someone to step up for real. Not some lightweight who'll let her down again, like everybody else. Too damn much bad luck for that girl. And you accounted for some of it yourself, if you recall."

Eric felt the wind bite against his suddenly hot face as he imagined stepping up.

Not letting Demi down. Forever. What that would look like. Feel like.

It would be incredible. It would change everything. Night and day.

"I'm not going anywhere," he said. "Not without her."

"A nice start would be to stand by her now," Bristol scolded. "She shouldn't be alone. She was just attacked, and bereaved, and betrayed. All at the same goddamn time."

He let out a mirthless laugh. "Sounds like one of Otis's lectures."

Bristol grunted. "Well, then. I'll take that as a compliment."

"You should," Eric told him. "And I will step up. I will stand by her. Until the end of time. I just have to take care of a couple things today. It won't take me long."

Demi slapped the screen door open, descended the porch steps and stalked past him, her face stiff.

"I'll come to you as soon as I'm done," he told her.

"Don't bother," she said coolly. "I'll be busy planning a funeral. I'll be at Granddad's anyway, so it would be better if you stayed away. You make him nervous."

"Demi—"

"Have a great day. Thanks for your help. Come to the funeral, if you're still in town. Watch the paper for the announcement. Chief, shall we go? I'm all done here."

Chief Bristol gave him a disappointed look. "Looks like it, hmm?"

Demi didn't look at him as the patrol car pulled away.

Fuck. He didn't blame her for being angry, but he couldn't make a plan of action if he didn't check GodsAcre out. And he couldn't delegate that task to anyone. The death tally was already growing.

And Vaughan? For fuck's sake. What a towering scumbag. Above and beyond Eric's worst expectations. But being angry at a dead man was an exercise in frustration.

The Prophet's Curse couldn't have laid its spectral finger on a shittier guy. If only the Curse had struck a couple of days earlier, before Vaughan got around to his crowning achievement in selfishness and cruelty.

Demi deserved better. From everyone, including himself. But he couldn't start something important with her after weaseling out of his responsibilities.

She was in danger. All of them were. The whole town, maybe even beyond it.

If the Prophet's Curse was anybody's mess to deal with, it was his. And Mace's and Anton's, of course, but they weren't here, and this couldn't wait another second.

People were dropping dead, for fuck's sake.

He drove back out to Otis's house, and started to prepare. He rummaged in the hall closet until he found the forest camo coat they'd gotten Otis for bird-watching with its many deep pockets. It was too narrow in the shoulders, but the extra concealment was worth the discomfort. He found a faded olive drab hoodie to cover his head and put the small digital camera with Otis's GodsAcre photos into one of the coat pockets. He hung another of Otis's cameras around his neck, and a pair of Otis's powerful bird-watching binoculars. The Glock and some full magazines went into one of the pockets. He filled a water bottle, grabbed the keys to the four-by-four and his silenced phone, and took off.

He stopped at the turn-off to Kettle Canyon Road for the second time in less than twenty-four hours, and looked at it for a moment, thinking of Otis. And Terry.

He was doing this for Demi. For the hope of a future with her. He wished he could make her understand that. He could barely explain it to himself, but he knew it would never work between them unless he broke the Curse somehow. Whatever the fuck it was.

She was mad and scared and grieving, but time was short, and shit was getting weird really fast. He put the truck in gear, and surged forward.

He was between a rock and a hard place, just like always. Braced for pain.

Bring it on. He wouldn't let himself flinch this time.

19

emi didn't remember much about the ride. She just realized, at a certain point, that they were parked outside the police station, and that Chief Bristol was patting her arm. Timidly. Like she was a bomb that might explode in his face.

She got out of the car and had to hang onto it for a second while that sickening, ice-cold sucking feeling pulled at her, making her vision dim.

"...okay? Demetra? Should I take you to the ER?" Chief Bristol's anxious voice.

She managed a wan smile. "Fine," she said. "Just a little head rush."

"Come on in and have some coffee while you wait for your grandfather to get here. He's already on his way."

Oh, yikes. She loved Granddad with all her heart, but he'd been agitated already after the attack. This fresh shocker about Dad's betrayal and death was going to throw him into full-on rant mode. Granddad had never liked Dad. God knows, she understood why like never before. But today was not the day to hear his list of grievances again.

She had her own list to ponder.

Demi stumbled into someone at the door. She mumbled an apology but her words cut off when she looked up and she met Boyd Nevins's startled eyes.

Blackened eyes. His face was puffy and discolored, and his nose was bruised and swollen like a potato. Butterfly bandages covered a cut on his cheekbone. He looked awful.

He deserved it, the jerk. "Boyd," she said. "Hey."

Boyd's eyes darted around frantically. He looked hunted.

She stood squarely in the middle of the door, leaving him no easy way to slide by.

"Hi, Demi," he said.

"What are you doing here?" she demanded. It was none of her damn business, of course, but who cared? She didn't give a shit about manners today, and she wanted to know.

"I just came down to see if, ah, the rumor was true," Boyd said nervously.

"You mean, about my dad being dead? Not a rumor. It's a fact. I saw his body."

Wow. Her words sounded cold and uncaring. But that was where she was right now, and she sure as hell wasn't going to fake it for this clown.

"So Holly told me. Um, my condolences, then," Boyd said awkwardly.

Demi stared intently at his battered face as he tried to sidle past her. She shifted smoothly to block him. "Wait," she said. "Tell me something, Boyd."

He looked alarmed. "Ah, not today, Demi. I gotta go–"

She grabbed his wrist. "This won't take long. Just tell me. Were you really driving my dad's Porsche that day seven years ago? Did you pick Eric up and drive him to Peyton State Park?"

Boyd's mouth twisted. "Jesus, Demi! Is that all you can think about? Today, of all days? With your dad lying in the morgue?"

Icy clarity settled over her. "Well, I'll be damned," she said. "Look at you. You're trying to make me feel guilty for asking you that. Today, of all days."

"This is not the time or place to—"

"So it's true," she said. "Eric really was set up. By my dad. And you helped him do it. You lying, cheating shithead."

Boyd pressed past her more urgently. She snagged his wrist and hung on.

"I am not having this conversation with you right now, Demi," he said stiffly. "You're upset and irrational, and I don't blame you. I'm sorry for your loss, but I—"

"Dad organized it, right? Gave you the Porsche? Told you exactly what to do? Did he pay you? Or offer favors? That job with Shaw Paper Products, in Spokane? Was that a payment for services rendered? And the Granger Valley job, later on?"

"Demi, it's over! He's gone! It's ancient history! What's the point of this now?"

"I just couldn't believe it," she said. "I couldn't believe Dad was capable of that. But he was. All along, he was."

Boyd broke away and hurried out just as her grandfather was coming in. He slammed right into Granddad, almost knocking the elderly man over.

"Watch your step, for God's sake!" Granddad snarled. "Damn idiot."

"Sorry, Mr. Shaw. My condolences for your—"

"Do not condole me for that no-good, lying, thieving piece of shit," Granddad snarled. "I'm glad he's dead! He can burn screaming in the flames of hell and good goddamn riddance to him!"

Boyd backed up, bewildered. He turned tail and fled, in a stiff, limping trot.

Demi met Granddad's eyes, and the two of them both shook with a burst of nervous, stifled laughter.

Granddad was the first to recover his self-consciousness. "Stop it," he muttered, his gaze darting around. "People are looking at us. It's unseemly."

"It's cool, Granddad. You can be as nuts as you want if you're as unlucky as me."

"Oh, honey." He pulled her into a tight hug. "It's just not right. You're such a fine girl. You didn't deserve any of this."

"I know." She pulled away, wiping her eyes. Hugs were dangerous right now. The Shaw's Crossing Police Station was no place for a fit of wild sobbing. "Let's get home, okay? I could use some privacy."

Predictably, Granddad started ranting as soon as they pulled out of the parking lot. Demi tuned it out as they drove through the town, sorting through the painful jumble of her thoughts. She watched the stores on the downtown shopping strip go by with odd, crystal-sharp clarity. Her restaurant, the bookstore, sporting goods, jewelry—

"Stop!" she said.

Granddad jerked to a halt. "What is it? Are you sick?"

"I just need to do something, real quick. Wait for me. Just a sec."

"What the hell? Where?"

226

"The jewelry store. Wait here for me, Granddad."

"Does this seem like the time to shop for trinkets? For God's sake!"

The thud of the car door closing muffled the rest of Granddad's scolding.

She ran across the street and pushed open the door of the jewelry store. Marlee Steigler was at the front counter, Arthur and Trudi Steigler's daughter. She'd been a few years ahead of Demi at school. Her eyes widened when Demi came in, her mouth forming a nervous little O. "Demi! I was so sorry to hear about—"

"Thanks, Marlee. Look, can I ask you something?"

"Ah, sure." Marlee looked doubtful.

"Seven years ago, did Eric Trask put an engagement ring on layaway here?"

Marlee blinked, puzzled. "Ah...I wouldn't know. I wasn't working here back then. I was living with my boyfriend up in Bozeman. Mom's in the back, though. You want me to ask her?"

"Please do," Demi urged her. "I'd appreciate it."

Marlee disappeared in the back. Demi waited for a couple of minutes, staring at the glittering trinkets in the glass cases.

Trudi Steigler came out from the back, a big, heavy lady with a ruddy face. Her white eyebrows were knit with puzzlement. "Demi. I'm sorry to hear about your father."

"Thanks, Mrs. Steigler. Please, I know this is an odd question, and not really my business, but I just need to know if it's true that Eric Trask had a ring on layaway here."

Trudi Steigler hesitated, studying Demi's face with a worried frown. She let out a sharp sigh. "Ah, well...yes," she said heavily. "He did. One moment."

She disappeared again into the back, and soon came back with a small paper bag, stapled closed with a receipt. She ripped the bag open, shook out a ring box and held it out to Demi. "I suppose I really shouldn't show you this. But I felt bad about it ever since. He only had two hundred and seventy-five dollars left to pay on it, but he never came back, after his troubles. So I kept it, in case he ever returned. It's a boulder opal."

Demi moved in closer to look. The ring that the jeweler held up was a slim band of white gold. The stone was an irregularly shaped blue-green opal ringed with tiny diamonds. She picked it up, watching the fire in the opal flash that intense, unearthly pale blue. The exact color of the glacial water in the streams where they had made love.

That was why he'd chosen it.

Demi stared down at the glowing point of blue. It all hit her, full force. Dad, lying dead on the floor, after lying to her and selling her out. So fucking awful. It burned her heart. All the love and hope and effort that Eric's ring represented. All the lies and hate and ugliness that had crashed into it head-on, trying so hard to kill it.

Never quite succeeding.

Demi passed the ring back to Trudi, muttering incoherent thanks and ran out of the store, sprinting across the street. A station wagon skidded to a shuddering halt in front of her, horn blaring angrily.

"Good God, Demi! Do you want to get yourself killed?" Granddad yelled, once she was back into the pickup. "What's got into you?"

"The truth," Demi blurted, her voice unsteady.

Granddad looked uneasy. He harrumphed. "Well, go easy on the truth," he advised gruffly. "Dole it out a little bit at a time. Truth is strong stuff. Especially if you're not used to it."

"I have to start somewhere," she said.

The tears started, to Granddad's dismay. "Oh, honey," he begged. "Please. Don't."

"I can't stop," she quavered. "Drive the car and leave me the hell alone, please."

Grandad did as she asked. Demi covered her face with her hands and sobbed silently all the way back to his house. The sobbing had the extra bonus effect of silencing Granddad's angry rants. It also intimidated him straight into his den once they got to his house, leaving her to lick her wounds alone at the kitchen table in blessed solitude.

Demi stared blankly at the cup of tea she'd made for herself until the steam stopped rising. She'd forgotten that she was supposed to drink it. After her sob-fest she felt numb and distant, but she kept seeing her father on the floor, by the door. The shame in Boyd's shifty eyes. The beautiful ring that cost Eric so much more than he could afford.

His grand gesture.

Oh, crap. If she thought about it, she'd start to cry again.

She closed her eyes, rubbing them hard, and saw Eric in her mind's eye in Otis's camouflage coat, moving through the woods like a shadow.

The feelings flared up, fighting it out inside her. Stubborn macho idiot. Always had to be the man. She wanted to bash him over his head, but what a waste that would be when she could leap on him instead and tear his clothes off. Run her hands over that fabulous hard body. Stare into those hypnotic eyes. Listen to that deep, scratchy voice. Pin him down. Make him stay. Hers, for-fucking-ever.

This was no time to be thinking of sex. But oh, she'd so much rather dwell on someone who wanted her and valued her. Someone who would fight for her.

Her whole life, her father had only pretended to care. He'd sold her out to save his own skin. On some level, she'd always known it.

Her mind flinched away. She turned her thoughts back to Eric, wondering if he'd seen anything up at GodsAcre. Or, more to the point, if he'd been seen by anyone else.

She sipped her tea with a grimace. It was cold and bitter from steeping so long.

The alarm system chimed. Someone was coming up Granddad's long driveway. She went to the monitor to check.

Well, look at that. Eric's Porsche. Her heart jumped. She couldn't see him through the shadows of the thick, overgrown pines that lined Granddad's driveway, but she'd know that car anywhere.

But it had only been a couple of hours. Nowhere near long enough to have completed the hike he'd proposed, and get himself back down to town.

Strange, too, that he was driving the Porsche when Otis's pickup was so much more practical for those rough country roads. Maybe he'd started up that hill and come to his senses. Changed his mind.

But Eric Trask didn't change his mind. It was one of his defining characteristics.

Well, he'd explain himself soon enough. The Porsche pulled up alongside the kitchen, slowing to a stop when she leaned forward, tapping the glass and waving.

She threw on her jacket. She really ought to tell Granddad they had a visitor, but she preferred to have this conversation in private, especially if it involved any mention of the Prophet's Curse. That was a subject best avoided in public.

Eric had pulled into the shady corner of the car park right beside Granddad's pickup, but he didn't get out. He just tapped the horn, a short blip of sound.

Like he was summoning her. The hell?

She hurried over to the passenger's side and knocked on the window. She leaned in as it buzzed down, her eyes still adjusting to the dark from the bright light outside.

His face was shadowed in a hooded sweatshirt. He turned to her, and she realized as his arm whipped up. That wasn't—

Pffffftt. Vaporized spray hit her face, eyes, nose. Ice cold, burning.

Couldn't see. Couldn't breathe. Eyes watering, stinging. Nose on fire.

Her face was numb. She couldn't get enough air to yell. Only gasp and choke.

Darkness dragged her from below, sucking her down.

20

Eric peered down from his perch on the rock tower above the ruins of the GodsAcre compound through the binoculars. It was getting dark, but he'd walked over every part of the place and hadn't seen any vehicles. He'd seen huge rutted tire tracks from the big earth-moving rigs everywhere, and piles of excavated rock, mostly down the hill toward the entrance to the caverns. Which was now a huge, hollowed out crater in the ground where part of the cavern had evidently collapsed.

That labyrinth of rough caverns had been the feature that had attracted Jeremiah Paley to this land in the first place. Jeremiah had liked the idea of an underground refuge for the dark days that would surely come after the fall of civilization. Over the years, those caverns had been extensively built up. Ceilings and passageways had been reinforced, paths had been smoothed out, electricity and water and ventilation and drainage had been installed. There had been huge storerooms packed full of supplies. Bottles and cans, potable water, freeze-dried food, MREs, fuel, weapons, explosives, electronics, an enormous technical and medical library. Kimball's large and well-equipped med lab.

He and Mace and Anton had blown it all to hell on the night the fire broke out.

The crater was right at the level where Mace had set the charges. Mace was the pyrotechnics guy. He'd always loved blowing shit up. Anton and Eric had the necessary technical expertise, but they didn't take quite the same unholy pleasure in it that Mace did.

After that filthy perv Kimball had gotten Anton flogged, they had all decided that they'd had enough. GodsAcre was a living hell. It had to end, and the three of them were the only ones with the nerve to get the job done.

Fiona got away clean, thank God. But the rest of them had paid. In blood and skin.

They had blasted the caverns because GodsAcre was nothing without the caverns and their contents. That was its reason to exist. But they particularly wanted to bury Kimball's precious lab, if only because all Kimball's own personal money had been sunk into it, if the rumors were true. So fuck Kimball and his needle-sticks. Sliming on a fifteen-year-old girl. Pedophile prick asshole could watch all his expensive equipment get blown all to shit and then go fuck himself. That had been the plan. Fuck the consequences.

They knew damn well that Jeremiah and Kimball might kill them. They were too angry to care.

Then, they saw the smoke from the building complex up the hill. Flames, glowing a lurid orange above the trees. By the time they ran back, the Great Hall was an inferno.

Everyone had been trapped inside. Someone fastened bolts in place on the armored doors with the big heavy locks...from the inside. Whoever had done that had committed both murder and suicide. The building had no windows to jump out of. It had been built to be an impregnable defense. Those steel doors had been massive.

And now the memories were fucking with him. Rattling him.

So ghostly, the shapes of those familiar buildings, now blackened ruins. Trees he remembered were now dead stumps or else much taller. The Great Hall was a big rectangular block, just the towering, lonely chimney jutting up. Its concrete foundation and heaps of fire-blackened bricks were overgrown with climbing vines, ferns, thick moss.

The place was strewn with garbage. Cans, fast food wrappers, Styrofoam, cigarette butts and plastic bags everywhere. The stench of piss. A lot of men must have been working here for some time now.

But why? There was nothing here worth excavating. Anything in the cavern's storerooms below would have been buried in broken rock for thirteen years. It would be trashed, crushed, molded, rusted out. And even if there was something, who would want it? Who could be looking for it? Anyone besides the three of them who might have known what was in those caverns was long dead.

Not all of the bodies inside the Great Hall had been positively identified, but Jeremiah and Kimball and most of the adults, the ones with dental records, had been. Eric and his brothers had refused to let Kimball's name be carved on that monument with Jeremiah and the rest. Kimball's ashes were probably in a box on in the police station storage closet. Eric didn't care where that bastard's ashes were as long as he wasn't buried along with the GodsAcre people.

Eric heard a car motor down the hill. He crouched,

234

peering between a cleft in the rocks. Headlights strobed through the tree trunks on their way up the hill on the old road. They jogged and jolted past the ruined Great Hall, and on down the newer, muddy tracks that had recently been carved through the hillside in the direction of the collapsed caverns.

Another set of headlights appeared. Then another. A convoy. A big four-by-four truck emerged from the trees, mud spattered. A black SUV. Followed by — what the *fuck?*

Alarm buzzed inside him. That was his own Porsche, rattling and thudding over the rough terrain, scraping over rocks and ruts. Past the ruins down toward the first plateau. It stopped behind the other two trucks, in a muddy open space near the huge open crater where they had been excavating.

Eric peered through the binoculars as men spilled out of the pickup and the SUV. Two men got out of each. The back of the big SUV popped open. A man got out of his Porsche and walked around to the back of the SUV, gesturing to one of the others.

The two men stared into the car for a moment before reaching inside together and hauling out what looked like a bulky burlap bag.

The bag twitched, jerked. Someone was inside it. One of the men holding it elbowed it savagely.

They hauled the twisting, struggling bag over to where the other three men stood, grouped near the excavated pit. He heard the hum of a generator starting up, and then a bright light shone out. They had switched on a lantern that was strung up on a pole.

A man stepped forward. The one who had driven his Porsche. He was the guy with the black receding hair in a deep widow's peak and the spotted, fish belly skin, from the funeral, the reception, Benedict Vaughan's house. The other guy had called him Felix.

Felix looked up into the darkness in Eric's direction.

"Eric Trask!" he bawled out.

The relative silence of the forest and the natural amphitheater shape of the land on that mountainside amplified his voice. "I know you're up there!" the guy yelled. "We saw you through the surveillance cameras, you big dumb fuck. You've been poking around in our shit for hours."

Eric crouched, motionless, his hand on the Glock. Waiting for Felix to finish grandstanding and get to the point.

"I suggest you focus your long range camera lens right down here at what I have to show you," he called out.

Oh fuck. He braced himself. Bad times ahead.

"Poke your head out of the hole. Look at what we've got in the bag."

Eric trained his lens through the cleft in the rock on the struggling figure in the canvas bag. They hoisted the bag upright. He recognized another of the funeral crashers. The slab-faced, beefy, bearded guy who always accompanied Felix. Rocco.

Felix whipped the hood off the figure's head, releasing a mass of dark, tousled hair. He yanked a cloth out of her mouth. She coughed, gasping for air.

Demi.

Demi's shriek of rage choked into a racking cough as they dragged the gag out of her mouth. Her head throbbed with whatever they'd drugged her with. The bag over her head had muffled what was said, but she'd caught the gist of

236

it.

They were going to use her to control Eric.

If she could just stop coughing. The black-haired guy patted her on the back. His breath smelled like death.

"Dry mouth?" he asked solicitously. "Something cold to drink?" He looked around at the garbage scattered around them and reached down for a filthy, crushed Styrofoam cup, the kind fast food joints sold coffee in. He scooped up some filthy brown water from a puddle with it. "Here you go, beautiful." He heaved the contents straight into her face.

Demi sputtered as the filthy water dripped down her face. "Asshole," she spat.

"You're in a canvas bag, you dumb bitch. Be more polite." He grabbed her face, sealing her mouth and nose shut. Her lungs bucked desperately for air.

Her struggles were weakening. The black wave swept up, rolled over her again...

Consciousness came back. She choked in a little air, coughing and gasping—and the hand clamped over mouth again, so hard she cut her lip with her teeth and tasted blood. He grinned down, and the harsh glare of the lantern cast grotesque shadows over his face. His twinkling dark eyes looked gleeful and crazed. Her vision dimmed again...

"...be more polite?" *Whack*, he slapped her again. "Pay attention, bitch!"

She spat blood into his face. "Fuck you," she gasped out.

He wiped his face. "You are a rude, dumb cunt," he said. "But tonight, you'll learn manners. You'll be so eager to please by the time I'm done with you. You'll do fucking anything to make it stop."

He grabbed the back of her head, winding her hair

through his fingers and called out in Eric's direction again. "I'm asking one more time. Are you going to be good?" He waited, cocking his head as if listening to her speak, and then forced her head to nod violently. Her hair flopped and swung in front of her with the movement.

"That's better," he called. "See? The bitch can be reasonable! She just needs a strong hand. You were too soft on her, Trask. She likes hard discipline."

She inhaled to speak, and found his hand on her mouth and nose again.

"Trask! I'm going to teach your cunt girlfriend manners now. Think I'll start by slicing off an ear." He wrenched her head up, yanking her ear so hard she yelped.

She stared up at a hole in the clouds. A star glinted through it. A bright one, glowing against the blue. Out of nowhere, she thought of the ring he'd gotten her. The love he'd shown. The grand gesture.

"Eric!" she shrieked. "I love you! Run!"

Whack. He rapped the side of her head with his knuckles. "Eric, don't!" he mimicked, in a taunting singsong tone. "After the ear, we strip her down and take turns picking what tender pink part to cut off next. Waste of a sweet piece of ass, but business is business. And I'll make it entertaining. Say goodbye to your ear, beautiful."

She sucked in air, feeling the pressure of the blade —

"Don't cut her."

Eric's voice. Low and calm, and startlingly close.

He emerged like a ghost from the shadows. The gleam of his intense silvery eyes came into focus first, reflecting the lantern-light, and then the shadows around his hooded face took on shape as he moved toward them with soundless grace.

"Hold it right there!" the dark man yelled. "Hands in the air!"

Eric stopped and raised his hands. He tossed the hood back.

Demi felt a blade's edge against her throat. "I've got a razor blade at her jugular," her captor said. "And it's your own razor blade, asshole. I took it from the bathroom, down at Otis Trask's house. It's all covered with your DNA. Your hair, your skin. Just so we're clear about how this is going to play out."

"We're clear," Eric said.

"We know you've got a gun," the guy said. "Pull it out. Real slow. Toss it on the ground in front of you. Real slow."

Eric reached into the coat pocket and pulled out the gun, holding it out so that it dangled from between his thumb and forefinger. "Let it drop!" the dark guy bawled out. "Two steps back!"

The gun thudded softly to the ground. Eric took a step back. Another.

"Are you carrying any other weapons?"

"No." Still that quiet, utterly calm voice.

The dark guy jerked his chin at the huge giant with the beard. "Search him," he said. "And get that gun."

The big bearded guy marched stolidly over and picked up the gun, tucking it into his coat. He moved around behind Eric, who never took his eyes off her, and started removing things from his pockets. Otis's camera, the one that they had found in the clock. The big camera that hung around Eric's neck. The magazines for the gun. Binoculars.

"You killed Otis," Eric said. "Because he saw your operation?"

"Shut up. You're wasting my time. Take off your coat.

Throw it on the ground."

Eric did so. No weapons. He was as helpless as she was, but he didn't look even remotely afraid.

"Take the memory card out of the cameras," her captor ordered. "Destroy them. Throw both cameras into the pit."

The bearded behemoth swiftly, mechanically did as he was told, and hurled the two cameras, one after the other, into the excavated pit.

They hit the bottom with a splash.

"What do you want with this place?" Eric asked. "There's nothing here for anyone."

"Not your business, punk."

"Why kill Otis?" Eric asked.

"Kill who? I never hurt anybody. Otis was an old man. He didn't have a mark on him. Natural causes, fuck-face. I build the narrative. And that's what the narrative says."

"My father, too," Demi croaked it out, against the choking pressure of the man's arm against her throat. "You killed him, too."

"Your father was a dumb fuck. He got what was coming to him. Years late, but he got it."

"But why?" she demanded.

"Why do you care? Selfish prick tried to have you kidnapped to get the money to blow us off. Not happening. The boss would never allow that."

"But how did—"

"Natural causes, bitch." He chuckled, his foul breath making her gag. "No muss, no fuss. Just like your mom. Big shame. Nice lady. Cute, too, for an old broad."

Demi flinched as he jerked her chin up, running a latex-covered finger along her lower lip. "Mom?" she faltered, fresh horror yawning inside her. "You killed Mom?"

"Heart attack," he taunted. "No foul play. So sad. And now it's your turn, thanks to dear old Daddy. You know way too much now. Even if you hadn't fucked a Trask." He leaned down, and licked the side of her face. She shuddered in revulsion. "But it won't be natural causes for you, sweet cheeks. Your narrative is different."

"What…what do you mean, narrative?"

"The story. The one where he kills you." He gestured at Eric. "That filthy animal. He's going to cut you into fucking pieces with his own razor, the sick sonofabitch. Then he'll have a crisis of conscience, too late, and kill himself. Murder-suicide. Not surprising after all the childhood trauma. But what the fuck do you expect from trash like that?"

He tilted Demi's chin up again. "You deserve to be punished, just for being such a dumb slut. Fucking the Prophet's spawn, eh? Not smart, beautiful. That boy is damaged goods. I hope he was a good lay, at least. Did he make you scream?"

"Let go of me!" Demi struggled madly in his grip.

The dark man let out an oily laugh. "I'm gonna make you scream, bitch. Until your throat cracks."

"What do you want with this place?" Eric asked.

"You're not here to get questions answered. Your time's up."

He looked down at Demi. "You know what? I was going to kill you clean. Something boring and generic, like snapping your neck or shooting you in the face. I was going to pack your body into his Porsche and shove the two of you off a cliff in it. But you turned out to be such an annoying little cunt, I changed my mind. I'm going to make it interesting. Blood and guts. And your boyfriend gets a front row seat. He'll be soaked in your blood. And when we're done, he gets all the credit for my artistry. Lucky boy."

"You don't have to do this," Eric said.

Demi bit down on the man's hand. Tasted the powdery, perfumed bitterness of his latex glove, his sweat, his blood.

Crack, he smacked her again. The world disappeared in a hot red flash.

"Be good," he snarled. "Bitch."

Pain made it hard to see or hear for a moment, but his taunting tone came slowly back into focus in her mind. "...bad thing about the natural-causes-scenario is the same as the good thing, see? It's too easy. The death pen is clean and quick, but it's no fun. Not if you like to see blood squirt and bones break and hear them squeal and beg. I kind of miss that. But today, I get to have my fun."

"Death pen?" Demi gasped out. "What the hell is a—"

He yanked her hair brutally back. "Shut up. You lived in this town thirteen years ago, right?"

"I—I, ah..." She was baffled by the question. "Uh, yeah, I—"

"Did you check her in the database?" he rapped out to someone over his shoulder.

"Yeah, I looked her up. She was in ninth grade, at the high school," one of the men answered. "She was in the database. She was definitely exposed."

"Exposed?" Eric's voice sharpened. "To what?"

Crack. The dark guy rapped at her head with his knuckles. "One more question, and I cut her face right down to the bone. Rocco, bring him over here and hold his arms behind his back. I can't have rope burns on him. Randall!" He jerked his chin at another guy. "Hold her up while I get her arms out of the bag. Move!"

242

Demi started fighting as soon as he pried her arms loose of the strangling fabric, flopping and flailing. He caught her wrists, twisting until she shrieked. "Save it for him, bitch. You're going to scratch his face now. I need skin and blood under your nails for the evidence techs."

Demi looked at Eric's grim face, horrified. "No!"

The dark-haired guy punched her in the stomach, knocking out her air. Light fading out. Sound distorting. The blade pressed against her throat.

"...try anything, you sneaky bastard, and I'll slice her throat right now. That works for my narrative, too. It's up to you."

"Demi," Eric said softly. "Demi? Baby? Do it. Just do whatever he says."

"Sensible advice, bitch." Her tormentor gave her another head-ringing slap. "I suggest you take it."

"Don't hit her," Eric said softly.

"Oh, I'm gonna do so much more than hit her," the dark man crooned. "I'm going to fuck her up so hard, when I'm done with her, you might just want to kill yourself without any help from me. Come on. Let's get those fingernails bloody!"

Two big guys muscled Eric forward. The one called Randall hoisted her up. His huge arms squeezed agonizingly tight around her ribs, making her gasp.

Eric winced. "Don't hurt her!"

"She's paying for her smart mouth. Closer. Let's get on with it."

Demi's eyes met Eric's gaze. That piercing intensity, charged with emotion.

It electrified her. That sadistic piece of shit was not going to cut her to pieces to hurt Eric. Having her throat slit was a much better death. They could all go fuck themselves.

Randall lifted her. The blade against her throat shifted. *Now.*

Demi jerked her legs up, using Randall's crushing grip as ballast. She shot her feet out explosively, kicking Eric in the chest.

Knocking him away from herself.

21

Eric wrenched his arm free and rammed his elbow into a guy's throat. He was airborne, kicking Felix in the face.

Felix stumbled backwards. Randall struggled with Demi. He'd clamped his arm around her neck, choking off her screaming, but her throat wasn't cut. She was fighting for breath, mouth open, gasping and mute. Scratching at Randall's face.

He aimed a flying side kick to Randall's face. *Crack,* dead on the nose.

Randall reeled backward, taking Demi with him. Careening right down to the edge of that fucking crater. Eric dodged a club swinging at his head, and the other guy aimed a gun —

"Don't shoot! Asshole!" Felix bellowed. "That fucks up everything! Just take him down!"

The gunman faltered, casting a panicked eye at his boss.

Yes. That was all he needed. Eric leaped, jerked the

guy's gun arm down—

Boom. The gunman screamed, and clutched his thigh. Blood squirted between his fingers. He hit the ground. Eric landed on top of him, scrabbling for the gun—

Whump, something huge hit him in the back, knocking him forward.

He scrambled around, and blocked Rocco's club, this time with his forearm. Pain blazed up into him, but he still snagged Rocco's arm, yanked and twisted it, making the man stumble and howl.

He used Rocco's own momentum to hurl him headfirst off the edge of the pit. Scrambled back himself just in time as the wet ground began to give way, then spun to face the attacker behind him, blocking a knife slash. He took the knife, wrenching the attacker's arm around until the bone popped from its socket, then stabbed his fingers into the man's eyes.

The guy screamed, stumbling to his knees. Eric aimed a flying kick to the side of the guy's head, then left him and ran toward Demi, still struggling to wiggle out of that sack. Her arms were free, but her legs were bound.

"Stay down!" he yelled, groping for a weapon. Rocks, sticks. His fingers closed around a largish, bolt-shaped stone.

"Fuck you." Felix howled. "You pain in the ass. I'll just kill you now and stage it later." He pulled out a silver cylinder. Bigger and blunter than a pen, seen at closer range. "Ladies first, eh?" he snarled at Demi. "Die, you dumb bitch."

Eric hurled his rock as the guy pointed the silver rod at Demi. It struck Felix in the face and he stumbled back with a grunt. "Fuck!"

Eric dove for Demi, who lay right the edge of the crater, and pushed her over the edge. At this point, the edge of the crater had collapsed, and had a gentler slope of muddy earth, so instead of falling, she bounced and rolled.

He had to block that thing Felix was pointing at her. Instant death. It had killed Otis, Ben, Elaine, Terry and God knows who else. He couldn't let them point it at Demi.

"Die first, then, if you want it so fucking bad!" Felix yelled. "Go to hell, shithead." He brandished it at Eric. Two bright, colored lights glowed intensely at the end of it.

Eric froze, braced for anything. Pain, burning, paralysis, convulsions.

Nothing happened. He looked down at himself, then looked at Felix. The guy looked shocked and betrayed. He rattled a button on the side of the pen, and brandished it again. Once again, the lights at the end of it blazed. Pale yellow. Poisonous green.

"Forget to change the batteries?" Eric asked. "Whoops. Asshole."

He charged Felix like a bull. They crashed together and hit the mud rolling. Eric rolled up into guard, blocking a kick, a punch. Felix was fast and strong. He got in a punch to the other man's jaw—

Crack, the death pen smacked him hard in the head. Eric scrambled back, cursing. Felix tried for another whack, but Eric ducked, seized his arm, and ran them both straight toward the crater, swinging the guy over the edge—

Felix flew out into free-fall. Eric went over the side along with him. He landed almost on his feet on the muddy slope, sliding to the bottom with an avalanche of rocks and mud. Finishing with a dramatic belly-splash into the slimy mud.

He dragged himself up, looked frantically around until he saw the back of his opponent's body poking out of the wind-ruffled, rippling brown water.

Eric trudged through the knee-deep water and feet-sucking mud. He used his foot to roll the man over onto his back.

Felix shrieked. His leg was broken, his knee bent at a grotesque angle. He didn't have his death pen. It could be fucking anywhere, buried in this slop.

He was neutralized.

"Demi!" Eric looked around frantically. "Where are you?"

He caught a flash of movement in the corner of his eye. Demi appeared, among some tumbled rocks at the side of the pit. She was so completely slimed with mud, she'd disappeared from view. She rose from a huddled crouch, and staggered his way.

Alive.

He dragged in a grateful breath, jerked his feet up out of the mud and launched himself toward her, slogging as fast as he could. "Are you okay?"

"Ah...yes," she said through chattering teeth. "I think so. You?"

"I'm good." He grabbed her, holding her shivering body tight. "I'm great. Now."

"Thank God," she said, through lips that shook. "What about him?" She jerked her hand toward Felix.

"He's done. Leg broken. Want me to kill him?"

Demi's eyes widened. In her mask of smeared mud, they seemed weirdly brilliant.

"Jesus, Eric," she murmured. "Are you serious?"

"He was going to hurt you. Kill you. He's killed others before." He looked around until he saw Rocco, who had tumbled into the pit earlier. He was face down in the water, and his back did not rise or fall. "I think that guy's already dead. Don't know about the others."

"It's one thing if he dies while we're fighting for our lives," Demi said doubtfully. "It's another thing entirely if you finish him off in cold blood. When he's helpless."

"Helpless, my ass. He'll be a threat to us, and to others, as long as he breathes. He's like a rabid dog." Eric looked down at the shivering injured man lying in the mud and contemplated the rage that still burned in him. "And my blood is not cold."

But Demi shook her head.

Aw, hell. Whatever. He wanted this woman. If she didn't want to watch him execute an injured man, he'd grit his teeth and back down. The things he did for love.

With luck, the cold night and the icy mud would finish the job. Felix was probably in shock already. A cold, lonely death, in the dark, in pain…it would do the job.

It was a better death than that bastard deserved.

He turned his attention to the side of the pit, searching for the best route back up. "I'm sorry I threw you down," he told her. "I was scared of the death pen. I figured if it killed Otis and Terry and your folks, it might kill you, too, and your chances were better down here. Even if you got knocked around some."

"So you ran straight at the pen yourself. Your usual stellar reasoning, Eric."

"What can I say." He shrugged. "I panicked."

"That's not panic, Trask, that's heroism. Get your fucking labels straight."

"Whatever," he said absently, scanning the walls. "Let's climb out of here while there's still some light." His teeth were rattling in his head now. Adrenaline aftermath.

"What about those other guys?" Demi asked.

"I think I took them all down. I'll check on them before you climb out."

"There you go again, Eric," she said. "Watch out. Your heroism is showing."

"It's not a matter of being heroic." Eric sounded impatient. "He pointed that pen right at me, and it didn't hurt me, which surprised the shit out of him. They might have more of those death pens, but it looks like I'm not subject to whatever damage they inflict. So that means that until further notice, I'm always up first. Are we clear on that?"

"Fine, Eric," she said soothingly. "We're clear on that. Calm down."

It was a long and frustrating slog up the sloppy, rain-soaked, and constantly collapsing side of the crater. Several times they both slipped and slid almost back down to the bottom. When they reached a relatively solid perch not far from the edge of the pit, he gestured emphatically for her to wait, and climbed over the top alone.

The light was almost gone, but he still could make out the still forms of the other three men sprawled on the muddy ground. The one who had shot himself in the thigh was dead. His femoral artery had emptied out all over the ground. Another, the one he'd elbowed, had a shattered trachea. He was gasping for air around a throat that appeared to be swelling shut. His face was blue.

That would do fine. Choke away, shithead. See you in hell.

The guy who'd disarmed him was face down, still unconscious, his head a sticky mess of mud and blood and hair. He found Otis's gun in the man's pockets, the magazines and his own cell phone, which amazingly was not shattered. He dug around in the other men's pockets for clues. He found nothing. He found some burner phones and pocketed them, not that they would be much use. Whoever financed this was watching on the cameras that Felix had taunted him about. These guys weren't in the same league as the feckless kidnapping crew at the island. No one was ever going to call those phones again.

He retrieved his own coat, which was slimed with mud but relatively dry on the inside, and went over to the pit. He reached down to Demi to help her the rest of the way out. Rain pattered down, beginning to rinse some of the film of mud from her face.

Demi looked around at the carnage. "Wow. Should we, uh…"

"Let them lie," he said. "We're getting the fuck out of here."

"But they're still alive. The police could interrogate them, right?"

"And get slammed by the Prophet's Curse while they're at it? Shall we start another big death cluster? How many more funerals do you want to go to?"

Demi bit her shaking lip. "What, so we just let those murdering, torturing assholes walk on back to whoever hired them?"

"They won't be walking anytime soon." He nudged the choking guy with his muddy boot. "I could just take care of them right now. Say the word."

"Me?" Her voice cracked. "I'm the one who has to say the word?"

"They'd already be dead if it was up to me," he said. "So yeah. You."

They stared at each other. The man's face was empurpled. Blood vessels had broken around his eyes. His gasps were getting shorter. His eyes were going dim.

Another asshole almost down. That left two still breathing. Barely.

She shook her head. "No. No more killing." Her voice rang out, suddenly strong. "Except in self-defense. Let's be better than them."

Fuck. Eric let out a sigh of resignation. He wrapped Otis's heavy coat around her shoulders and nudged her along. "We're done. Let's get out of here."

"Eric," she said. "We can't deal with this alone. Whoever's doing this...it cost a lot of money. Someone has a huge agenda."

"You saw that death pen," Eric replied. "We don't know how many they have, or by what mechanism they kill. And we're being watched as we speak. They saw me sneaking around before they arrived, so this place is under surveillance. If we bring police and ambulances up here and try to take them into custody, more innocent people will die."

Demi looked around at the bodies, her mouth tight and worried.

"And if we hang around up here and waste too much time arguing, they'll send up reinforcements and trap us, like they did to Terry," he went on mercilessly. "There's only one road down to Kettle Canyon from GodsAcre. It's a sheer drop off that mountainside for miles."

That finally convinced her to move, thank God.

22

Demi's legs felt like lead. She hung on grimly to Eric's arm until they reached the Porsche, which had the keys in the ignition, to Eric's relief. The car spun and struggled for traction out of the heavy slop, but after a few false starts and some very colorful profanity from Eric, they started to move, the low undercarriage scraping on the rocks and ruts.

He cranked the heat to full bore and opened the windows to air out the stench of cigarettes and body odor as they started a long, grinding, thumping ride out of GodsAcre and up onto the main road. Once they passed the ruins of the Great Hall, their muddy track connected with driveway, and from that, the only slightly smoother Kettle Canyon Road. Windshield wipers swished in the gloom, which had curdled into pitch darkness as soon as he turned on the headlights.

"We're telling Chief Bristol everything," Demi said. "We can't carry this alone."

"And my brothers," he agreed, accepting the inevitable.

"But that's all for now."

"For now. This is bigger than just you and your brothers, you know. This involves everyone in Shaw's Crossing. All of us are in danger."

"I know that." He reached into the coat pocket, and handed her his phone. "Call Bristol. Tell him to meet us at Otis's—no, have him come to your townhouse. They'll be less likely to move on us there with all your neighbors around. At least I hope so. And Bristol won't want the whole town in a panic. He'll be discreet. I hope to God."

Demi's thoughts raced feverishly on to the rhythmic squeak of the windshield wipers, taking her to terrifying places. "That guy...he said I was exposed. In high school."

"Yeah," he said grimly. "I heard that."

"Sounds like he's talking about some sort of...pathogen."

"Sounds like it."

"That is terrifying," she whispered.

"Maybe the death pen only works on people who were exposed," he said. "Maybe that's why they have that database they talked about. People who were in this area at that time."

"Except for you," she said.

"Right. The Prophet's Curse, explained. Someone's been using this thing to kill people in this town for over thirteen years. Now, they're using it to kill anyone who makes trouble for whatever in the unholy fuck they've got going on up at GodsAcre."

"Otis made trouble when they saw him taking pictures," Demi said. "And my dad must have been involved. Until he disappointed them somehow. Then he panicked, so they punished him. Mom must have found out about his involvement, or the kidnapping plot, or both, so they killed her, too. Poor Terry was just in the wrong place at the wrong time. All of them were in Shaw's Crossing thirteen years ago, just like the guy said."

"But who is doing this?" He pounded the dashboard. "There's nothing up at GodsAcre. What in the fuck could they possibly be digging for?"

They were silent, staring at the small part of muddy, narrow road the headlights illuminated, through the pounding rain.

"It's messed up," Demi whispered.

"Yeah." He reached across the center console and placed his hand on her arm, clasping it through the sodden jacket. "But you're alive. And that's so fucking great."

She wiped away a rush of tears and squeezed his hand. "Yes. Both of us are. Thanks to you. Again."

"I never wanted you to be touched by this. I'm so sorry, baby."

"You're not the one who dragged me into it," she told him. "But you sure as hell are the one who keeps dragging me out."

He smiled at her. "Call Bristol now."

She ended up on the phone with Chief Bristol for most of the way back to town. It was late, so none of her neighbors saw their mud-slimed state when they got out of the car.

Demi had no keys, but she reached into a hanging flower basket on the corner of her porch for a spare, to Eric's horror.

"Holy shit," he said. "A fucking flower pot? Seriously?"

"I thought I could afford to," she said sheepishly. "Sleepy little town, and all that."

"A sleepy little town that's under a fucking curse,

Demi!"

"Okay, okay. I'm convinced. I promise. Never again." She pushed the door open.

Eric followed her in and waited while she dead-bolted it. He poked his head into the living room, then the kitchen, admiring it. "Pretty," he said. "Colorful. I like it."

"Come on in. Don't just lurk in the entrance hall."

"I'm all muddy," he said. "I'll make a godawful mess. As usual."

"So am I," she pointed out. "We're a matched pair."

"You're gorgeous even when you've been dipped in mud. Go on up and take your shower and I'll watch for Chief Bristol from outside, on the porch."

"Come up with me," she offered on impulse. "We can shower together."

His gorgeous teeth flashed in his mud-smeared face. "You're breaking my heart, but I have to keep watch now. No distractions."

Of course. Duty called, and Eric Trask always answered. Hero to a fault.

She hoped the mud hid the embarrassed flush on her face as she ran up the stairs, leaving a trail of dirt clods behind her.

There was no place for Eric to put himself, in this condition. It was just his luck that Demi decorated with bright, light colors. Her floors were blond hardwood planks, her carpets were pale beige woven wool. He'd destroy anything he touched. He couldn't even sit down on her floor without leaving a dirt stain on the peach-toned walls.

He headed back out the front entrance and sat down on the porch steps to wait.

First order of business, Mace and Anton. Both of their phones went straight to voicemail so he encrypted a text message and sent it to both of them.

This place is fucked up. Prophet's Curse is a physical weapon. They killed Otis with it. Tried to kill me and Demi. Whole town in danger. Get back here asap. Bring backup. I need someone trained in close protection to help me cover Demi 24-7. Call me.

Bristol's police cruiser pulled up behind the mud spattered Porsche, and the chief got out and stopped as he came through the small iron gate. Taking in the mud, the blood.

The older man looked impressed. "Damn, Eric. You look like shit."

"Rough night," Eric said.

"Tell me all about it. How about Demi? Her grandfather keeps calling. She has to tell that man to calm the hell down. Henry saw your Porsche on his security camera footage and now he's convinced you abducted her."

"Not me," Eric said. "She was abducted by a different guy, one who stole my Porsche. The ones you saw in that video at Vaughan's house. Demi's upstairs taking a shower. She's fine. She got smacked around and scared half to death, but she's tough."

"Smacked around by whom?" Chief Bristol crossed his arms over his chest. "I confess, I didn't understand a goddamn thing she told me on the phone."

Eric rubbed his stinging eyes. "Long story. Let's wait for Demi. That way we tell it only once."

"Fair enough." Chief Bristol creakily let himself down onto the porch steps to sit next to Eric. "Speaking of long stories, I've got a story for you."

"Oh, yeah? What's yours about?"

"Boyd Nevins came by the station a while earlier."

"Ah. That story." It seemed so far away now. Hardly even important anymore.

"He wanted to confess," Bristol went on. "Seems like he told us a big lie seven years ago. And he feels real bad about it."

"I'm familiar with that lie," Eric said.

"He said Benedict Vaughan promised him a big contract for his roofing company for his dad and a plum job for him in Shaw Paper Productions in Spokane if he would pick you up in his Porsche, drive you out to the Peyton State Park and leave you there with the car. And then never say a word about it. No matter what happened afterward."

"As I told you all," Eric couldn't keep himself from saying. "Repeatedly."

"One of the kidnappers said that Vaughan arranged for you to be forced off the road back then."

"Yeah," Eric said. "But I'm hard to kill. Bummer for him."

"Hey, Chief Bristol." Demi stood in the doorway behind them, wrapped in a pink fleece robe, hair hanging down in long, damp curls. She smelled of honey and flowers.

"Demi." Wade's eyes ran over her, looking for damage. "You're okay?"

"Thanks to Eric. Like I said on the phone. Kidnapped. Eric saved my ass, again. But this time it was much worse. These guys would have hurt me for real."

Chief Bristol nodded. "I was just telling Eric about how Boyd came in—"

"I heard. Come on inside. I put on some coffee. We

have a lot to talk about."

It took hours to make a full accounting of everything that had happened. And even longer to dissuade Chief Bristol from rushing right up to GodsAcre himself.

They were still arguing at three in the morning.

"It's too dangerous," Eric said, for what felt like the hundredth time. "The Prophet's Curse is real, Chief, and it sounds like a pathogen is involved. Everyone in town could have been exposed, including you. They can kill you with this thing from a distance. Through a door, like Demi's folks and Otis. In a car, like Terry. Don't go near the place, at least not until we know what the hell is going on up there. Please. Go slow."

"I have to do something! I can't just sit on my hands! It's my responsibility to investigate the—"

"It's your responsibility to protect people as best you can. To keep people alive."

"How can I do that, if I can't investigate the crimes these bastards are committing?"

"For one, keep this quiet," Eric said. "Don't tell your wife. Don't tell anyone at the station. At least not yet. And two…deputize me."

Demi jumped up to her feet. "You've got to be joking."

"You got a better idea? I'm the only one who can't be hurt by that thing."

"You just won't be happy until they kill you," Demi said. "You won't be satisfied until you're, what, crushed, shot, strangled, stabbed, dismembered? The gorier your ultimate martyrdom, the better you'll like it."

Eric sighed. "I don't want to die. I've never had more to live for than I do right now. I'm just trying to—"

"Prove your worth to everyone in this town, and the

whole world while you're at it. Prove yourself to the ghosts of all the people who died at GodsAcre. Ransom yourself from your stupid misplaced guilt. But you won't succeed. It'll never be enough for you."

"Demi—"

"I've had enough of your grandiose bullshit. I'm grateful to you for saving my ass, but your hero complex is exhausting me. I'm going to bed. The couch is comfortable, if you dare to close your eyes with the weight of the whole world on your shoulders. 'Night, Chief. Sorry I'm being such a cranky bitch. It's been a hell of a night."

"I should say so," Chief Bristol agreed. "Take care, honey. I'll check on you tomorrow."

Demi stalked out. They listened to her bare feet, running lightly up the stairs.

Bristol grunted thoughtfully. "Looks like you have more problems than just the Prophet's Curse, son. Good luck with that one."

"I'll need it," Eric said bleakly.

"Well then, goodnight. I'm going to head home to get some sleep, if I can. I suppose there isn't much we can do to protect ourselves from whatever those people have going on. At least not tonight. But I'm not going to sit on this for long. We need to call the Feds, the CDC. Everyone. And soon. This could be a general public health crisis."

"Please, Chief," he said wearily. "Take it easy. Wait until my brothers get here. Don't turn this into a media feeding frenzy until we know what we're dealing with."

Chief Bristol harrumphed. "We'll see." He studied the younger man, frowning. "Try to get some rest. You look like crap."

"Will do," he said. Like he could sleep, as jacked up as

260

he was tonight.

After Bristol left, Eric poked around the ground floor and found a bathroom off the kitchen with a washer-dryer, a utility sink and a shower. Perfect, since he didn't want to disturb Demi by making noise in the upstairs bathroom. He didn't like being naked and blind in a shower with their mysterious enemies floating around out there, but Wade had a point. There was no stopping those bastards if they wanted to attack. They weren't likely to make a move so soon after losing that last battle so decisively. He hoped.

He risked a shower, just long enough to scrub the mud off. As soon as the water ran clear, he wrapped a big towel around his waist, shoved his filthy clothes into Demi's washing machine, glugged in lots of soap and set it to wash. Tomorrow, they went to Otis's for a suitcase, guns and ammo. He hated being naked, but that clammy mud was nasty. At least he had the Glock, even if his balls were flapping free in the breeze.

After that, he used his phone to buy a long-range drone, and a home security and surveillance system for Demi's house from his favorite Seattle-based security company, SafeGuard. Those guys had the best security gear anywhere, and it would arrive by private courier tomorrow. That done, he went up to Demi's bedroom. Her bay window overlooked the lake, which glimmered with the lights of the town. She slept on a king-sized bed under a fluffy comforter, her hair fanning wildly over the pillows.

He'd walked away from her once by necessity. It had almost killed him. He couldn't do it again. Not now that he finally understood what he had to live for.

He settled down in the wingback chair near the window, gun in hand. Keeping an eye on the street outside.

Demi might have banished him to the downstairs couch tonight, but he wanted her in his unbroken line of sight. Forever.

23

The hours dragged by. Eric struggled to stay focused. He was a one-man army whose sole objective was protecting Demi Vaughan. No other thought should be allowed in his head. But images kept stabbing through his mind.

Felix, holding Eric's razor blade to Demi's ear.

Demi, disappearing over the edge of the crater and out of his sight.

Demi, shouting at him from that monster's grip. *Eric! I love you! Run!*

That was on auto-repeat. Those spasms of wild hope were messing him up. Hope was a dangerous ingredient to combine with the rest of this toxic garbage.

Hope could take him down if he gave into it. If he let it in, even for a second.

Come on. Of course she would say that. At that point, she'd figured she was already dead and she'd been trying to save his ass. Like the boss that she was. Selfless. Fearless. She probably didn't even remember she'd said it. It was a heroic reflex.

His pissed off, prickly goddess. He'd never get enough of that.

He was glad that the issue of his past sins had been finally put to rest, but at this point, who gave a fuck? It seemed very far away and not particularly relevant anymore. Their real, current problems were so huge and baffling, the past could get no air time.

One thing was for sure. Until he figured out who was behind this shitstorm, he was not leaving Demi's side, not unless they dragged him away from her in cuffs. And there was only one true way to make her safe for good.

He had to lift that fucking Curse. Once and for all.

The phone buzzed in his hand. A text from Anton.

Outside Demi's house. U in there?

He got up, startled, and looked around for something more substantial than a towel, since his clothes were still rattling in the dryer downstairs. His brother must have driven at top speed from Seattle the second he got Eric's message.

He grabbed the first thing he saw, which happened to be Demi's fluffy pink fleece bathrobe, and went downstairs to peer out the peephole. Anton's black Mercedes was parked right behind Eric's mud-slimed Porsche, with another silver SUV pulling up behind it.

He opened the door as Anton flung open the gate. His brother's dark eyes had that intense, burning look he got when he was wound up. The one emotional tell-tale in his tough guy mask.

Anton's gaze swept him, taking in the cuts, scrapes and bruises as he strode forward. Eric put his finger to his lips before his brother could speak. "Shhh," he said. "Demi's sleeping."

"Eric," his brother hissed. "For the love of *fuck?*"

"She's exhausted," Eric explained. "I don't want to wake her until—"

"No, not that. I mean, what the fuck are you wearing?"

"Ahhh…" Eric glanced down at the puffy pink robe, his bare legs and feet. "My clothes are in the—"

"Never mind." Anton's eyes fastened onto the spreading bruise, partially visible along the top of his shoulder. "I don't care. Let me look at you."

Eric pulled away. "I'm fine."

"Let me see." Anton wrenched the bathrobe open.

"Hey!" Eric yanked it shut and gave his brother a baleful look. "Jesus, Anton. All of Shaw's Crossing does not need to see my dick! Let's take it inside, for fuck's sake."

Anton scowled. "That bruise looks like shit. You got more? You get cut? Shot?"

"I'm fine," he said, with savage emphasis. His gaze went to the guy who had emerged from the second SUV and was following Anton up the walk. He was big and dark with gleaming black hair and lots of beard scruff. He wore a battered leather jacket and carried a large box. His knuckles, clutching the box, were heavily tattooed.

He looked at the pink robe. White teeth flashed in his dark beard. "Great color for you, man," he said. "Brings out your eyes."

"This is Nate," Anton said. "He was in Force Recon with Mace, back in the day. He's my head of security. He'll cover you and Demi for a few days, until I can work out something more long-term. Plus, I wanted another set of eyes and ears to listen to all this crazy shit. Someone who's not from this place. We're too steeped in it to see it straight."

"Great," Eric said. "Sounds good. Come on in."

Anton hesitated. "You said that Demi was asleep."

"Yeah, so be super quiet," Eric said.

"Wait," Anton said. "You sure it won't stress her out if she wakes up and finds two big guys she doesn't know inside her house? After what happened last night?"

His brother had a point, but Eric shook his head. "She's tough. She'll understand. I'm not leaving her alone here to go talk to you someplace else, that's for damn sure. I'll go upstairs and warn her before she comes down."

Anton and Nate followed him in, and Eric closed and locked the door behind them.

"Thanks for coming out at such short notice," he said to Nate.

"My pleasure," Nate said. "Anything for Mace's people."

"What's in the box?"

"A drone," Nate said. "This is a prototype that a friend of mine designed. Nothing like it on the market yet. A DTS-Ultra Gray Ghost. Very long range, extremely tough. Super lightweight, but it can face a stiff headwind and stay on course. Obstacle sensors on all sides. You can take it down real low and get great control."

"Thanks," Eric said gratefully. "I ordered one, but it won't be here until tomorrow, and this one sounds better anyhow. Let's send it up right now."

Nate pulled a pen drive out of his pocket. "I'll install the app."

While Nate got to work on the drone, Eric ran down a general overview of what had happened. It was harder than he'd thought it would be. He did a lot of backtracking, and repeating, answered a lot of baffled questions that only raised more questions. Nothing made sense. Nothing hung together.

They were so focused on Eric's adventures, the key in the front door lock took them by surprise. They leaped to action. Nate was closest to the door, gun in hand. No time to check the peephole before the door swung inward—

Elisa came in, a paper-wrapped tray in her arms. Her eyes fastened onto Nate and his gun.

She flung her tray at his face and leaped at him with a cry.

Eric saw a flash of steel. "Watch the blade! Don't hurt her!"

Just in time. Nate blocked the stabbing blow with his arm, catching Elisa's wrist in his huge hand. A box-cutter was clutched in her fingers.

Nate wrapped his arms around her struggling form and slid down along the wall, pulling her to the floor. Elisa kicked and writhed wildly, her eyes unseeing.

"Hey," Nate soothed, both arms holding her tight. "I'm not going to hurt you. Calm down. I just don't want to get cut. Relax. I'll let you go. Swear to God. Relax."

"Elisa." Eric crouched next to her. "You're safe. Sorry we scared you. Relax. It's okay."

Her tension broke. Elisa shuddered, blinked, and went limp in Nate's grip.

After a breathless moment, Nate took the boxcutter from her and passed it to Eric.

Elisa drew in a ragged breath. "You can let go of me," she said shakily. "I won't rip off your face. Promise."

Nate released his grip, and looked up at Anton. "You told me your hometown was screwy, but holy shit, man. This place is fucking tense."

Elisa lurched forward, crawling away from him. She sat

there for a minute, catching her breath. "Sorry," she said. "I saw the gun and I panicked."

"You're as quick as a rattlesnake," Nate said. "You almost got me."

"Glad I didn't."

"Me, too," he said forcefully.

Eric held out the boxcutter. Elisa took it without looking at it and slid it into the pocket of her long flounced skirt. Then she got to her feet, straightening her clothes.

"Well," she said stiffly. "This is awkward."

"My fault," Eric said. "I didn't know you had a key. I didn't have time to check before the door opened. And we're all on edge."

"Of course. From the kidnapping." Elisa shook her tousled hair back over her shoulders. "I should have called. I'm used to coming right in, but these are strange days. I thought Demi might be sleeping, so I thought I'd just slip in and out. Leave the tray."

As she mentioned the tray, she saw it on the ground upside down and crouched down, righting it.

"What is it?" Nate asked.

"Breakfast pastries. Sweet and savory. They'll be a little the worse for wear, but they'll still taste good. I'll leave them on the counter." Elisa hurried down the hall toward the kitchen.

The three men looked at each other. Anton shook his head at the look he saw on Eric's face.

"Don't," Anton said softly. "Keep it simple. One big scary problem at a time."

Elisa came back, heading straight for the door.

"Elisa," Eric said. "Is there something you want to, uh..." His voice trailed off, and he tried again. "Can we help

268

you out with some problem you might have?"

"No," she said forcefully, her hand on the door handle. "I'm fine, and you have problems of your own. I'll see you around later."

"Stress flashbacks are nothing to be ashamed of," Nate said baldly.

Elisa shot him a startled look. "Excuse me?"

"I've had them. It's just a thing your brain does in response to stress. I've never had one with a boxcutter in my hand, but that's just pure dumb luck."

Elisa opened her mouth—and closed it again with a snap. "I have to get back to the restaurant," she said, backing away. "Tell Demi I stopped by."

"I'll go back with you," Nate offered.

Elisa shrank back. "No, that's not necessary. I'll be fine."

"This place is not safe. Isn't that what you've all been telling me?"

"No. Thanks, but I'm fine." Elisa turned and ran down the porch steps, her shoulders high and hunched against the frosty wind.

When she was out of sight, Nate finally turned around. "Who is she?"

"Elisa Rinaldi," Eric said. "She waits tables. Helps out in Demi's restaurant."

"Somebody's after her," Nate said.

"You mean somebody other than you?" Anton murmured.

Nate looked outraged. He lifted his arm, and showed them the long slash in the thick leather of his jacket. "Get off my back. See that? Whatever her problems are, they are no joke."

"Nobody said they were," Eric said. "Just please, keep your eye on the ball. How's that drone doing?"

"It's fine." Nate turned his back to them and got to work, radiating annoyance.

Eric left him to it and turned to Anton. "Hey," he said. "Got a couple hundred bucks you could spot me?"

"Cash?" Anton looked baffled. "What for?"

"There's a thing I need to take care of. I have some money on me, but I need a couple hundred more. I'll drop by the bank later on and pay you back."

Anton dug into his wallet, looking bemused, and handed his brother a handful of bills. It was now business hours, so Eric looked up the number on his phone and called.

"Good morning, Steigler's Fine Jewelry. This is Trudi Steigler."

"Hi, Mrs. Steigler, this is Eric Trask. I'm not sure if you remember me, but I—"

"Of course I remember you. I was so sorry to hear about Otis."

"Yeah. Thanks. Anyhow, seven years ago, I put a ring on layaway, and I was wondering if—"

"Yes. I still have it. Whenever you're ready. Come on in."

"Thanks for hanging onto it for so long. I'd like to pay the balance, but I can't come in this morning. I'm at Demi Vaughan's house at 228 Lakeshore Drive, right up the street from the Marina. I'd give a generous tip to anyone who would deliver it to me here, and accept the final payment from me. I have the cash on me now."

Trudi Steigler seemed bewildered by the request, but after some persuading, she finally promised to have her daughter Marlee stop by that morning with the ring.

Nate was staring down at the drone and trying not to smile as Eric closed the call. He headed outside with the drone in his arms, shaking his head.

Anton just scowled, his big arms crossed over his broad chest.

"What?" Eric demanded.

"Don't mind us," Anton said. "Take all the time you need. Dinner reservations for two at the Lakeside Lounge? His-n-her massages and mani-pedis at Solaris Spring Spa? A honeymoon suite at the Five Oaks Inn, with the vibrating heart-shaped bed?"

"Anton, I'm just—"

"Dude," Anton said flatly. "You are under siege. Now is not the time to pick out china patterns and monogrammed pillowcases, for fuck's sake. Focus."

Nate walked back into the room. "She's airborne." He handed Eric the controller. "There's not much wind today. Let's get her up there and take a look around."

24

Demi woke with a gasp.

She'd been buried alive. Smothering darkness and terror, the taste of dirt in her mouth. She stared up at her own ceiling, heart galloping.

Just a dream. She was safe in her own bed. But yesterday it had been all too real.

She closed her eyes, remembering Eric emerging from the trees like a shadow, hands in the air. Offering himself up. *Don't hurt her.*

Everything that happens up at GodsAcre is my responsibility.

Deputize me.

God. It hurt just to think about it. She admired his selfless heroism, but she wanted to shred his ass for taking it all onto himself. The way he was wired up for self-sacrifice could drive her stark raving nuts. And at this point, she didn't have that far to go.

She could not enter that category. Things Eric Trask Was Responsible For.

She was responsible for her own goddamn self.

Say goodbye to your ear, beautiful.

She jolted upright, shivering. That memory stung like a lash.

Yeah, she was just doing a stellar job taking care of herself lately.

A sound intruded on her consciousness. A murmur of male voices. It sounded like it was coming from downstairs.

"Hey, there." Eric's voice. "Finally awake?"

She looked around. Eric leaned in the bedroom doorway, wearing only his jeans. His thick brown hair stuck up every which way from running his fingers through it. He held a cup of steaming coffee that she could smell from across the room.

He looked gorgeous.

He gave her a brief, blinding smile that made her heart trip over itself, like always. It hardly mattered that he looked exhausted, eyes shadowed, his face marked with scratches and bruises. The bruise on his shoulder from the fight at Spruce Tip had turned a violent blue and purple. Even so, he looked so freaking fine, she could hardly breathe.

"Good morning," she said. "If it's still morning."

"Yeah," he said. "Will be for a couple of hours yet. It's almost ten."

"Were you just on the phone downstairs? I thought I heard voices."

"No. I came up to tell you that you've got company. My brother Anton drove from Seattle like a bat out of hell, and he brought a friend with him to cover us."

"Cover...? Meaning?"

"You know," Eric said. "As in, guard us. So we can sleep from time to time."

"Ah." Demi pondered that for a silent moment. "I'd appreciate being informed of decisions like this. At least when they involve me."

"I would have," he assured her. "I just hadn't gotten around to it yet, and I wasn't expecting Anton to move that fast."

Demi flung the comforter back. "Guess I should get up, then. Be hospitable."

"There's no rush. Take your time. But, ah...I should tell you that Elisa came over, to bring you some breakfast pastries."

"Oh. That was so sweet of her."

"Yes, it was," Eric agreed. "Except that, um...she wasn't expecting to see us."

"Eric," Demi said in a warning tone, rifling through her sweater drawer. "Will you please stop waffling and just say whatever the hell it is you're afraid to say?"

"She panicked," Eric confessed. "Looked to me like she had a stress flashback. She attacked Nate. With a boxcutter."

Demi spun around with the sweater stretched over her arms. "Holy crap," she said. "Is he hurt?"

"He's fine," Eric said. "Intrigued, even. I guess he's like me. He goes for complicated femme fatale types with mysterious problems."

She narrowed her eyes. "You think this is funny, Eric?"

"Nope," he said swiftly. "Serious as hell."

Demi harrumphed, jerking the sweater over her head, and wrestled it down, then shoved her staticky hair out of her face to admire his bare chest. "If you met her at the door half naked like that, no wonder she had an attack."

"Actually, I was wearing your robe." He gestured at her fluffy coral fleece bathrobe, tossed over her reading chair. "I like it. It's soft."

"I'm sure you looked delicious in it," she murmured.

Now she was smiling, in spite of herself, but now was no time for flirtatious banter. She had to be tough. Face reality. And visitors. God help her.

She tugged on some battered jeans and slid on her house shoes.

"You could just keep resting," Eric said. "You don't have to come down."

"Nope. I'm ready to face the day. Is that cup of coffee for me, by the way?"

He held it out. "Yeah. I realized as soon as I poured it that in all the time we've known each other, we've never had a coffee moment. So I don't know how you take it."

She took the cup, sipped it and coughed. "Wow," she said. "Black death in a cup."

"Yeah, that's how I like it," he admitted.

"I'll tart it up with cream downstairs."

Eric followed her down into the kitchen, where two extremely large men sat at her kitchen table, hunched over a laptop. One she recognized as Eric's older brother.

Both men got to their feet as she approached them.

"Hey, Anton," she said, shaking his hand, then extending it to the other man. "And...?"

"Nate. Sorry to descend on you like this. We didn't want to stress you out."

"Not at all," she said. "Eric tells me you're here to help. I appreciate that." She smiled at them, and jerked her chin in the direction of the tray of goodies on the bar. "How's Elisa's breakfast buffet?"

Nate and Anton looked at each other, alarmed. "Ah...great," Nate said.

"Eric said you made a big impression on her." Demi tried to keep a straight face.

"All I can say is, do not mess with that girl," Nate said, with feeling. "Because she will fuck you up."

"Good to know." Demi grabbed the cream out of the fridge and made the coffee drinkable. "What are you guys looking at on that laptop?"

"We sent a drone up to GodsAcre," Anton said.

Demi choked and sputtered on her coffee and grabbed a napkin. "Really? What did you find up there?"

"Nothing," Eric said grimly. "So far."

Demi came around behind them to look into the screen. "Show me."

They did so, flying the drone slowly over the entire property, lingering finally over the scene of the mortal confrontation that had taken place the night before.

The bodies and the injured men were gone. There were just indistinct stains of blood on the earth where one of the men had shot himself in the thigh.

"All gone," she whispered. "But who moved them?"

"None of those men were in any condition to drive," Eric said. "Or walk. Somebody was watching what happened, and he moved fast. He had a team on call. The means to haul two bodies out of a deep muddy pit in pitch darkness."

"We saw Otis's pictures," Demi said. "There was a whole fleet of cars up there when he took them. Plus all those big earth-movers."

Eric nodded. "Whatever this is, it's big, and well-funded, and it's been going on for a long time."

"And then there's the death pen," Demi said. "They

killed my parents with it. And tried to kill me and Eric."

Eric stared at his brother, a look of challenge in his eyes. "Will you come back here and help me fight this thing?"

Anton nodded reluctantly. "I need a few days to wrap some stuff up. I have some shows left to do this week, one in Vegas, one in Portland, and one in Seattle, but I can reschedule all the ones that are farther out. Nate will stay with you guys until I find someone good to take over. Excuse me for a second. I'm going to try to get Mace on the phone again."

"I gotta bring the Ghost back down," Nate said. "She's got just enough juice now to make it home."

Nate followed Anton out, the remote in his hand, leaving her alone with Eric.

Demi leaned against the kitchen counter, sipping her coffee. "So," she said to him. "Things were so intense last night, I don't think I said thank you. Again."

"Don't thank me," he said. "I don't want thanks."

"But here you are, making like you have to save me. Protect me."

He shrugged. "Well, yes. Duh."

"You are not responsible for me, Eric," she said. "I can take it from here. You can go. Anton, too. Much as I appreciate the thought."

"No," he said. "Not gonna happen."

"This place is poison for you." Her voice had started to shake, to her dismay. "You should leave while you still can."

"I'm not going anywhere without you," Eric said.

"I'm not leaving here," she said. "I'm committed to this place. I have family here. Granddad, the diner, my employees. I still have to bury my father. This is my home, and I'm going to defend it."

"Good," he said. "I'll help you."

Her throat ached. "You did more than your share already, pulling my ass out of the fire. Twice. But it's not your job to save Shaw's Crossing. You owe this place absolutely nothing after the way you were treated. I might be stuck here, but you're not."

Eric paced over to her slowly and placed his hands on her shoulders. The warmth radiated straight into her core. His body heat already felt like an embrace.

"I am so stuck on you, Demi Vaughan," he said. "You have no fucking idea."

"You've just got to make this as hard as possible, right?" She brushed tears off her cheeks. "The Prophet's Curse hurt you, Eric. You live better away from it. So go. Be free. Don't make me be a heinous bitch to you. Please. It takes energy, and I'm tired."

His mouth twitched. "Nothing on earth could make me walk away from you now," he said. "Don't even try. It's just energy wasted."

Demi placed her hands on his hot chest with the vague notion of pushing him away, getting a little personal space so she could think straight, but the contact muddled her thoughts still more. That sweet throb of awareness rushed instantly into every part of her, bright and energizing. She looked down at his hand, which rested on her shoulder. It was battered and scraped and scabbed from yesterday's combat.

She placed hers over it, and squeezed. "Don't try to lay down the law. I've had enough of that from Dad. Granddad, too. I won't be dictated to. That doesn't work for me."

"So what does work for you? Spell it out for me."

"I don't know," she said impatiently. "If I knew, I'd be, I don't know. Happy. Fulfilled. In my dream job. Married with kids. But no. I'm a hot mess. My own father tried to sell me out for a bag of cash. Someone else tried to cut me to pieces. My parents were both killed by the Prophet's Curse. I thought you had it tough, but I just might have you beat. Don't take this on, Eric. Get into your fancy Porsche. Go back to your perfect life."

Eric stroked his hands tenderly down her arms, then back up over her shoulders.

"Marriage, kids, dream job, happiness, fulfillment," he said. "All doable, with hard work and some luck." He kissed her knuckles. "Our luck has sucked lately, but I can feel it starting to turn. I think we just might beat this. If we stick together."

The feeling of his lips against her hand was a shimmer of delight, and now it wasn't just her hands that were shaking. It was her face, her chest, her throat. She vibrated with emotion. As if she were about to do something deadly dangerous.

"Are you running us off another cliff?" she whispered.

"No. We're on solid ground now." He pressed more kisses to her hands. "Let's not waste any more time. We have things to do. A curse to break. A life to build. Together."

She didn't dare to speak. Just bit her shaking lip.

"I stopped fighting the way I feel about you a while ago," he admitted. "I can't pretend anymore. I love you, Demi. I'm yours. Forever."

The look in his eyes was too much to take. "But...I told you. I'm a mess."

"You're incredible," he said fiercely. "I've compared every woman I've ever seen to you. No one even comes close. Let me stay with you, Demi. For as long as we get. I will destroy anyone who fucks with that. I will grind them into paste."

"Aw," she murmured. "That's sweet, Eric. I'm, ah...touched."

"I'm serious." There was a hint of impatience in his voice.

"I know, but what about your company? Your jet-setting tech mogul life?"

"What about it? I'll work from here until we get this sorted out. Video conferencing works fine. I don't need to be physically there every day. Later on, I'll commute. When I'm sure you're safe. Everything in my life is negotiable except for you."

She pressed her hand to her mouth. The feeling was breaking over her like a huge wave. Terrified happiness. "I don't know what to say."

He sank down onto his knees. "So say yes."

"Oh, Eric," she whispered.

"This is the ring I told you about the other night." He pulled a small black velvet-covered box out of his pocket, opened it, and held it up. "But if you wanted something different, we could always—"

"No," she broke in.

Eric froze, looking guarded. "Uh...no to what, exactly?"

"Sorry," she said, gazing down at the flashing, back-lit aqua blue of the boulder opal with wet eyes. "What I mean is, I don't want any ring in the whole world except for that one."

"You like it?" His eyes lit up.

"It's perfect. That blue. It's the Kettle River, right? And the waterfall?"

His smile made tears well into her eyes. "Right."

"But...diamonds?" she said, laughing through her tears. "God, Eric. What were you thinking?"

"I was making a grand gesture," he said simply. "You're worth it."

"You're nuts, you know that?"

"For you, absolutely."

"Eric!" Anton came back into the kitchen, still staring at his phone. "I've got Mace's flight itinerary here, but he says it's going to take him at least three days to get back to Nairobi, so we'll have to—oh." He rocked back on his heels abruptly when he saw Eric on his knees in front of her, ring in hand. "Holy freaking *shit*."

Eric just lifted an eyebrow. "Remember to breathe," he advised.

"Oh, fuck me." Anton backed away so fast, he ran into Nate, who stood behind him, grinning widely. "You could have warned me, bro."

"Sorry." Eric sounded unrepentant. "Guys. Do you mind? We're in the middle of something here."

"We'll be outside," Anton said. "Let us know when it's safe to come back in."

The front door slammed a moment later, somewhat harder than it needed to.

"Poor guy," Demi murmured. "Such a shock."

"He'll live. Back to us. You like the ring. That's excellent. But I'm still waiting for that magic word that will change everything for me. I've waited seven years. I don't want to wait anymore. Please, Demi. Have mercy on me."

She slid her hands into the buzzed off hair at his nape. "Eric, are you for real?"

"It doesn't get any realer than this."

The love in his eyes made her throat close up. She couldn't speak, but she could sink down to her knees, wrap her arms around his neck and hang on, dragging him as close to herself as she possibly could.

"Yes," she whispered, as their lips met.

WANT MORE? The saga of the Trask Brothers rages on in Hellbent, The Hellbound Brotherhood Book Three, Anton's story! Now it's Anton's turn to grapple with the Prophet's Curse, along with a searing passion like he's never imagined...

Available for preorder now!

https://shannonmckenna.com/books/hellbent/

Turn the page for more...

HELLBENT
THE HELLBOUND BROTHERHOOD
BOOK THREE

She thought her tormenter was dead...
Find out why New York Times bestseller Maya Banks hails
McKenna's books as "A non-stop thrill ride..."

He couldn't forget her...

Famous bad boy DJ **Anton Trask** stays the hell out of other people's business. He learned that lesson long ago and paid for it in blood. But when the gorgeous, prickly Fiona Garrett shows up at one of his nightclubs asking for his help, he can't say no, and it throws his inner world into chaos. He and Fiona grew up together at GodsAcre, a remote doomsday cult in the mountains. She was only fifteen when he helped her escape that hellhole, but she's all grown up now. Anton hates to lose control, but Fiona's direct gray gaze, her soft red lips and her gorgeous body make his heart race and his temperature rise.

Pursued by a ghost...

Fiona (Fi) Garrett is on the run. Brutal killers are looking for her, and she doesn't understand why. All she knows it that it must tie back to GodsAcre and the people who died there years ago. She hates asking Anton for protection once again—she owes him her life already—but he's the only person who might believe her. Still, Fiona is not prepared for the effect that Anton has on her senses. His big muscular body, the hypnotic glitter of his silvery eyes, the controlled, masterful power he exudes...it sparks a desire inside her that she'd never imagined—and she can't control the blaze.

Anton just wants to leave GodsAcre and its painful memories in the past, but they have to face it down to save Fiona—and as danger ignites all around them, all he can do is keep her close.

And the closer she gets, the less he ever wants to let her go...

Available for preorder now!
https://shannonmckenna.com/books/hellbent/

Turn the page for a peek at Hellbent...

HELLBENT

1

Hellbound Nightclub
Seattle, WA

The lightshow that accompanied the first set in the nightclub downstairs sliced like a razor straight into Anton's aching head, but he didn't allow himself to close his eyes or turn his head.

Don't flinch. Only pussies flinch from pain. Jeremiah's harsh, drill sergeant voice echoed in his mind.

Get the fuck out of my head, old man. You're dead and gone.

The past had no hold on him. He repeated that to himself often. Most of the time, it was true.

It didn't feel true today. Going back to Shaw's Crossing for his foster father Otis's funeral last week had stirred up all the old, toxic memories in his mind. He'd left the place at the first opportunity, right after the funeral. So had his youngest brother, Mace. But not Eric, his middle brother. Eric had lingered in town, all hung up on a woman there. He'd been madly in love with her seven years before, but things had ended badly. A total clusterfuck. Eric had barely survived it.

But had he learned his lesson? Nope, not Eric. He was drawn to Demi Vaughan like a moth to a flame. He just couldn't wait to self-immolate.

Eric had gotten himself all wound up with Demi again last week, and then he and Demi had proceeded to almost get themselves killed by a band of murderous thugs up at the moldering ruins of GodsAcre, the long-defunct doomsday cult in the mountains where they'd been raised. It was a miracle they were still alive at all.

None of it made any sense, but according to Eric, they had to go back to that godawful place and figure out what happened before more people died. According to Eric, GodsAcre was their responsibility. Their property. Their sacred charge.

Damn. Eric had always been afflicted with a pain-in-the-ass hero complex, but Anton was not so afflicted. Why the hell should saving the town of Shaw's Crossing be their job? What had that place ever done but relentlessly kick their asses?

He wouldn't abandon his brother, of course. He'd go back and offer what help he could. But the whole thing made him so fucking tense, his teeth were grinding.

He stood by the viewing window that covered the entire wall of his private office and stared down at the gyrating crowd below, and mused upon the young DJ on stage doing the opening set. The kid had talent. He was young and green, but he could instinctively manipulate a crowd. It was still early, but the dance floor was already packed.

A nearer source of light assaulted his eyes as the door to his office opened. Nate Murphy, his head of security, leaned inside. "Anton," he called. "The hot redhead's back at it again. She says—"

"I said to get rid of her," Anton snarled.

Icy silence followed his words. Anton turned and saw Nate lounging casually against the doorframe, just waiting. He appeared to be relaxed, but his eyes were hard.

"You get a free one today," Nate said. "One free one. Just because you've been bereaved, and it's been a weird week for you. But I am not your fucking butler."

Anton blew out a sharp sigh. "Yes," he said tightly. "Message received."

The two men gazed at each other. Anton lifted his hands. "So?" he said, with deliberate calm. "About the redhead? You were saying?"

"Yeah, her. She had a personal message for you."

"Don't they all."

Nate's face stayed impassive. "She says her name is Fiona Garrett. And she says that she's in trouble. Ring a bell?"

Anton stood there, mind totally blank. Shocked stupid.

Fiona.

The heavy beat from downstairs made the building throb dully. The way a wound did when the painkillers started wearing off. He couldn't seem to breathe.

Nat's eyes narrowed. "I guess that answers my question. Is everything OK?"

"Fiona?" Anton repeated, the name seeming to stick in his throat like a rock. "You're sure she said Fiona Garrett?"

"I'm sure. What's up with her? She pregnant? Do you owe her money? Does she want to break your kneecaps? Does she intend to sue you or shoot you or castrate you?"

Anton shook his head. "I haven't seen her in years."

Nate's puzzled frown deepened. "Dude. You do not

look OK. Is there something I need to know about this girl?"

"No," he said. "It's old stuff. Ancient history. We grew up together. In the mountains."

"You mean, she's from GodsAcre?" Nate's eyes widened. "Holy shit!"

"Yeah." Anton strode over to the bank of security monitors on the wall. "Where is she now?"

Nate pointed at one of them. "She's waiting by the staircase near the back bar."

Anton leaned toward the camera feed Nate had indicated. It was the girl they had told him about before. The hot one who'd asked for a private meeting with him earlier.

As his celebrity had grown, he'd gotten accustomed to the sex continually on offer. It got boring sometimes, but it was convenient. When he felt the urge, he barely had to reach out his hand. And with a minimum of mental acrobatics, he managed not to feel guilty about it. They came to him begging to be used. Sometimes he obliged them.

Two things he made sure of. One, any woman he fucked understood that it started and ended there. Two, any woman he fucked walked out of his presence weak-kneed with sexual satisfaction. He made it absolutely worth their while. It was a point of pride.

When he saw the redhead, he hadn't seen her face. He'd been tempted by the long legs, high-riding breasts with tight nipples poking out the stretchy fabric of her dress. In those spike-heeled boots, she'd only be a few inches shorter than his six-foot-five frame.

Plus. He liked that long red hair. And the freckles that usually came with it.

He'd thought about having her brought to him. Imagined fingering her into whimpering readiness. Making her come repeatedly before he bent her over the big desk in his soundproofed lair, her pussy hot and slick and utterly primed.

He'd have her keep those silver boots on while he put it to her from behind. Deep and hard.

But no. Shaw's Crossing and Otis's funeral and that vicious attack on Eric had left a lingering bitter taste in his mouth. He was bad-tempered and ugly and not in complete control of himself. Best not to fuck anyone in that mental state. Bad things could happen.

He was sick of drama.

The redhead's back was to him in the camera, offering an amazing view of a world-class ass. Her back was straight and upright. The long, wild mane of fiery hair looked right, but he couldn't see her face.

"Who's closest to her?" he asked.

Nate muttered into his Bluetooth. "Wong is close," he said, after a moment.

"Have him ask her to look up at the camera. I need to see if it's really her."

Nate's eyes widened, but he relayed the message without comment. Jim Wong, one of his security experts, entered the camera's view, a hulking Asian man, immensely tall and broad, with a thick neck, a goatee and a long ponytail hanging down the back of his leather jacket. He approached the redhead, spoke into her ear and politely gestured toward the video camera mounted on the wall.

The girl's long hair swung out around her like a cape as she turned to look at him. Her big, bright eyes were painted up with smudgy black, blazing and intense. He couldn't make out the color in the camera, but he remembered it perfectly. Stormy slate-gray on the outside of the iris, fading to light gray and then a sunburst of amber gold right around the pupil. Amber that matched her hair and her freckles. Fi had been covered with freckles.

He stared into her eyes. Their brightness sparked a restless, uneasy stirring inside him. Lust, fear, all mixed together, way down deep.

Yeah, that was Fi. There was no mistaking defensive, screw-you-too look in her eyes. The sexy shape of her full mouth. She was no longer the skinny waif with the thick red braid. She was taller now, still lean and slender, but filled out. She looked lithe and strong. Her lips were painted hot red.

She faced the camera head on, with an aggressive, wide-legged stance like a comic book gunslinger. A glittering belt of crystal studded links hung low on her hips. She stuck out her chest, hands on her hips, elbows out. Staring him down.

After a minute or two, she lifted her hand, fluttered her fingers at him, and blew him a kiss. Her straight dark eyebrows were arched high. As if she could see right through the camera, all the way to where he stood, frozen and dithering.

What are you waiting for? You scared? Of me? Awww.

What the *fuck* was she doing here? Tonight of all nights? He was still all wound up about what had happened to Eric in Shaw's Crossing. Dealing with Fiona would put him right over the top.

Besides Anton and his two brothers, Fiona was the only other survivor of the lethal shitstorm that was their childhood. Everyone developed his or her own fucked up coping mechanisms for dealing with massive trauma. Evidently Fiona's had been to morph into a drop dead gorgeous, man-killing femme fatale.

Damn. There were worse strategies.

"Tell Wong to bring her up," Anton said.

He turned to the viewing window, checking his own reflection before he could stop himself. Thirteen years had gone by. He'd changed. Last time Fiona saw him, he'd been seventeen. No tats. His hair a shaggy, dirt-blond mane. He'd looked very different.

His current bad boy DJ vibe was edgy and hard. Buzzed off hair, designer jacket hanging open to display the tattoo art all over his shirtless chest and flaunt the eight-pack abs. His professional look was carefully cultivated, and definitely not for everyone.

Nate didn't miss a trick, goddamn the man. He caught Anton checking his reflection and snorted under his breath as he turned to the door.

"Smile, loverboy," he said. "I'll tell you if you have spinach in your teeth."

"Fuck you, man." Anton slammed the door after him, cutting off Nate's laughter.

***

Fake it till you make it, Fi. That's what we all do. Don't think you're so damn special. Imagine they're all naked. Everyone feels scared and awkward. Not just you.

That was her cousin Patti's standard lecture from the old days, when she was teaching Fiona how to navigate the "normal" world after her escape from GodsAcre.

She'd tried to practice Patti's advice, but it hadn't been much comfort then.

Nor was it now. Every thought of Patti caused intense pain.

Focus, damn it. Fiona followed the burly Asian guy up the stairs to the lofted space above, grimly intent on keeping her ankles from wobbling in her ridiculous boots. She'd chosen them for the girls-gone-wild sexbot vibe, but they practically crippled her. If she needed to fight or run, she'd be fucked.

And if just staring into a video camera that might have Anton Trask at the other end made her knees turn to jelly, what would the real, flesh-and-blood Anton do to her?

Hoo, boy. Her mind could go absolutely anywhere with that notion, and keep itself happily entertained for hours on end.

It took nerve to get glammed up like this. Not something she did often. Or ever, really. Only when Patti insisted. Patti's pet project had always been Fiona beautification. Domestication might actually be a better word, come to think of it. Fiona had done her best to be a good sport, but she had to fight conflicting inhibitions.

Jeremiah Paley, the leader of the survivalist cult where she'd grown up, had insisted that women and girls dress in modest, feminine clothing. She'd dressed according to his dictates, but her modesty hadn't done her any good when Redd Kimball arrived up at GodsAcre. His hot, fixed gaze felt like ants crawling on her skin. Kimball had been lurking around every corner, rubbing up against her. Groping. Pinning her to the wall and whispering flesh-creeping filth into her ear.

She'd tried to just fade away, evade his notice. Hadn't worked worth a damn.

A deep hesitation to invite male attention had stuck with her ever since, long after her escape. And whenever she tried to push back against that fear, she ended up overcompensating. She overdid it, egregiously. Went all-out sexpot. Put out confusing messages and got into all kinds of embarrassing, sometimes dangerous trouble.

It was more hassle than it was worth.

Patti had despaired of her. She'd tried so hard to teach her clueless country mouse cousin to pass for a normal California girl. The hair, the make-up, the clothes, the laughter, the lightness. Hah. As if.

She pushed down the memories of bouncy, friendly, giggling Patti. Later. That pain would wait for her. Pain was endlessly patient.

Today's goal was to face Anton Trask and ask for help. There was no need for all this shivering and sighing. The guy's only sin was in being terrifyingly gorgeous, talented and charismatic. She had a crush on him, yes, but that was hardly his fault. She owed him her life, essentially. But for him, she'd have been married to that dirt-bag Kimball when she was barely fifteen. That would have killed her. One way or another.

'No' had not been an option at GodsAcre. What Jeremiah said was law.

She'd tried to run away several times. They'd dragged her back. The last time, Kimball had her publicly flogged. She didn't remember much about the actual event, having blocked it out. But in her nightmares, she remembered Kimball's glittering eyes as he watched. How he'd licked his lips. Liking it.

After that, Paley's three stepsons, Anton and Eric and Mace, had taken matters into their own hands. They stole money from the treasury to buy a bus ticket to her aunt in California. Anton had led her through the woods himself, on steep, tortuous paths where they wouldn't get seen or caught.

They zig-zagged over the ridge, down Garrett Creek Canyon and eventually down into Shaw's Crossing.

Anton had practically carried her at the end, her back hurt so badly. But he got her to the bus station.

And there, to her utter surprise, he'd kissed her goodbye.

Every last tiny detail of that kiss was burned into her memory.

She still remembered his long, dark blond hair blowing back in the wind as the bus pulled away. Those beautiful, muscular bare arms, tanned to gold. Those intense dark eyes, locked onto hers through the glass. Willing her to be strong and tough. Like him.

She'd been in love with him since forever. He was so gorgeous. Tall, strong, whip-smart. When kids hiked down to the swimming holes below the upper falls, she'd stared helplessly at his powerful body when it was wet and gleaming. His sharp cheekbones and full lips. That long, shaggy hair, all different shades of blond, from dark to light.

The bouncer was pushing open a heavy door. The time for frantic second-guessing was done.

Fiona walked into a large, wood-paneled room. It had sleek, essential furniture in black leather and steel. Banks of monitors and electronic equipment were smoothly incorporated into the walls, like the bridge of a luxury intergalactic space yacht.

"Ms. Garrett?"

She jerked around, startled, but the guy who had spoken wasn't Anton. He was tall and striking in his own right, his big, heavily muscled body dressed in a tailored white shirt and black dress pants. Black hair. A hooked nose, a strong jaw, dark beard scruff. His deep-set eyes were keen and curious as he looked her over.

"Nate Murphy," he said, extending his hand. "Anton's head of security."

She shook his hand politely. "I see. Did Anton ask you to check me out for deadly weapons? I often inspire terror in the hearts of men."

"Not exactly." His eyes flicked over her body. "I don't know where you'd keep deadly weapons if you had them. I won't search you. Anton said you guys go way back?"

"That's right." She just waited, offering no more details.

"So do we," Murphy offered. "I met him in Vegas a long time ago. He got me a job as a bouncer at a club he worked at on the Strip after I got out of the Marines. I can't imagine Trask as a kid."

She made a noncommittal sound. Of course he couldn't. Anton had never been a kid. Neither had she. But that was nobody's business.

When she provided no further comment, Murphy opened the door behind him and beckoned her in. "He's waiting," he said. "Go on in."

Fiona took a long, deep breath and jacked up her attitude-o-meter to its maximum setting. Shoulders back. Tits out. Chin up. She strutted past Nate Murphy. A slow, hip-swaying, take-no-prisoners saunter.

The room was dim and long, a black leather living room set at the far end in front of a bar. Low black couches and armchairs, a wide, low wooden coffee table, a dimly geometrically designed hanging lamp that was a modern art piece in itself. A floor-to-ceiling window overlooking the dance club dominated the first half of the room. Pulsing lights from the club flickered against the far wall. She glimpsed the gyrating throng on the dance floor below as she walked in.

The pounding music was barely audible. It seemed a physical impossibility to insulate a room from music that loud and that close, but somehow, they'd done it.

"Fi." She froze at the sound of his voice. Even deeper and richer than she remembered. He'd been slow to talk and soft-spoken, but everyone had always leaned in and listened to every word. What Anton said had more weight than other people's bullshit.

She forced herself to turn. Her heart thudded heavily.

Anton sat at a huge desk set into a niche in the back of the room. The dim light from the hanging lamp painted his starkly sculpted face with shadows. His shadowed eyes gleamed, unreadable. She tried to speak, but he beat her to it.

"It really is you," he said.

You doubted it? Who else even knows I ever existed? They're all dead. Words whirled in her head, but she couldn't pick out what to say and what to discard.

Keep it simple, like Patti had said. Keep it light. *Hi, Anton. Long time no see. Looking good. How's life treating you. Nice place you got here.*

But no. She had fuck-all to say to him. The cupboard was bare.

She coughed to shake her voice loose. "Hey," she croaked. "Anton."

She'd been afraid of this. That she'd freeze, tongue-tied, empty-headed. Just her frantically beating heart deafening her from the inside. She'd hoped adulthood would help.

No such luck.

He was crazy gorgeous. Even more so than she remembered. She missed the long hair, but the thick brush of dark blond stubble cast his chiseled male beauty in sharp relief. She'd been following the buzz on him, ever since he burst on the scene some years back as an up and coming DJ. His rise to fame had been swift. The cover of Billboard, BPM, URB, the article in Vogue, the interview in GQ. The guy was freaking everywhere.

Not that she was complaining. She owned every scrap of info printed on paper.

He'd gotten even more infamous last summer after a steamy, highly publicized fling with a Hollywood starlet, a red-haired It Girl. The affair ended badly. The starlet had complained bitterly. He was emotionally unavailable, the starlet bitched. Elusive. Remote. She'd felt used. Boohoo. *Bad Boyfriend*, the tabloids blared.

And there were all the videos online. Shows, festival clips, interviews. Commercials for athletic shoes, whiskey, champagne, luxury cars, men's cologne, high-end sports watches. She watched them obsessively, sucked into his hypnotic, complex rhythms of his dance mixes. She had her many favorites saved on the desktop of her computer for quick and easy reference. Her secret addiction.

Anton leaned back in the chair, his gaze inscrutable. As was his custom, according to all the magazine articles, he was bare-chested beneath his jacket. His chest was densely covered with tattoos. The black satin jacket was cut perfectly for his broad shoulders.

Jeremiah Paley had hated tattoo art with a fiery passion.

Anton opened a desk drawer and took out a remote, pointing it at the glass viewing area overlooking the club. She heard the muted hum of a motor, and hanging vertical blinds marched across the window, sliding into place to cover it completely.

The colored flickering light vanished. The room felt

suddenly smaller. Breathlessly intimate. Another gesture with the remote, and a pool of light flicked into being, all around her. A recessed bulb in the ceiling, right above her head.

Like a spotlight. As if she was the floor show, performing for an audience of one.

Patti's advice flashed through her head again. How to talk naturally to men. How to combat being shy and tongue-tied.

Just pretend he's naked.

Oh, man. In this case, Patti's classic advice was a terrible idea. Once she thought it, she couldn't unthink it. And her brain just went apeshit.

"What's with the outfit, Fi?" he asked. "It's a little much."

Fiona glanced down at her ensemble. He was right, but she would die before she could admit it. "It's a dance club," she said. "Jeans and a tee-shirt would've stuck out. I wanted to blend in."

He laughed under his breath. "It's not working," he said drily. "Sorry."

"I don't consider other people's opinions when I choose my clothes," she said. "I got enough of that back at GodsAcre."

"So this is rebellion? A fuck-you to the Prophet's tight-ass memory?"

She gazed at him without speaking for a moment. "I don't make decisions based on the past," she said. "I wear whatever I want. My life is not a reaction to my past. That gives them power over me even after they're dead."

He inclined his head slowly in acknowledgement. "True enough," he said. "But you're not comfortable in it."

She couldn't in all conscience deny it, but goddamn

him for noticing. She resisted the urge to tug the skirt further down over her thighs. Since there was nothing to tug.

"It doesn't matter," she said. "I'm never comfortable anyway."

His eyes turned her inside out. No one looked at her that way. She was used to being checked out, but guys mostly looked at her ass, her lips, her chest. She had a force field for that. Shields up. Their gazes bounced right off her.

Not Anton. Her shields didn't work on him. His eyes sliced right through her defenses as if they weren't even there and penetrated, straight into her soul.

"I'm sorry," Anton said.

"About what?"

His eyebrow tilted up. "That you can't be comfortable."

Crap. She didn't want him feeling sorry for her. She wanted to have this interchange from a position of strength. And standing in front of him under the spotlight like merchandise on sale at a brothel did not help. "Could we go sit down?"

"I'm good here."

Hmm. So much for common courtesy. "Well, I'm not." She threw her shoulders back and refreshed the attitude, ratcheting it back up a few notches as she strolled toward his desk. She circled his desk with her best in-your-face swagger. "I'll just sit down right here, then." She perched her butt on the desk in front of him.

Anton shifted back, one leg crossed over the other. Black leather lace-up boots. Faded jeans clung to his thickly muscled legs. He was so strong. Muscles rippling as he moved in the chair.

Oh, boy. At this range, the effect was overwhelming. Now she could smell his cologne. Feel his body heat right on her skin. The subtle field of male energy about him enveloped her completely, making her short hairs prickle up all over her.

Anton exuded an aura of things about to happen. Danger barely averted. Total combat readiness. Raw, seething sexual energy. It beat against her senses like a high wind.

She was spellbound by the sharp angle of his jaw, the sensual shape of his unsmiling lips. His beard scruff glinted dark gold. Those wary eyes never wavered, constantly assessing, re-evaluating. Dark, thick slashing brows. He was everything she remembered, just bigger, stronger, hotter. More of everything he'd always been. Too much to process. He made her dizzy.

"Hello, you," he murmured.

His silky tone made her shiver. She braced her hands on the edge of his desk, fishing desperately for something to say that wasn't *please just take me now.*

"I was hoping to catch one of your sets tonight," she said. "They say you do at least one set at one of your own clubs every week. I read that in Billboard."

"Not this week. I took time for personal business."

She didn't say a word, just waited. To her surprise, he actually answered the unspoken question. "I was in Shaw's Crossing for a couple days with Mace and Eric."

That startled her. "For real? God, why?"

"A funeral. My foster father, Otis Trask. He's the one who took me and Mace and Eric in after the fire. He died last week. A stroke."

Her gaze dropped. "Oh. I'm so sorry to hear that. My condolences."

He nodded in acknowledgement. "In any case, I'm scaling down the performances. I do a set once or twice a week at my own clubs. Some festivals. Hand-picked. I prefer to focus production work now. I'm sick of all the traveling, the crowds. The bullshit."

"Clubs in Portland, Seattle and San Francisco," she said. "Plus the production company. And all the advertising work. It's really something, what you've built."

"Yeah, I'm diversifying these days. Opening up in Vegas and Chicago next year."

"I saw you at Coachella once," she told him.

"Really?" His eyes widened. "Why didn't you come backstage to see me?"

She laughed out loud. "My ass. Do you have any idea the quantity of screaming, desperate girls who were waiting to come see you after that set? The whole world wanted a piece of you that night."

"You would have jumped right to the head of the line if you said the word."

"That's gratifying," she murmured. "Thanks for deigning to receive me tonight."

He narrowed his eyes at her. "You follow this kind of music? I wouldn't have thought electronic music would be your thing. You don't strike me as the clubbing type."

If you're the one making the music, then hell yeah I follow it. "I'm a big fan," she said. "I don't like crowds, so I don't do clubs or dance floors much, but I listen to some of your sets all the time. I listened to last year's Tomorrowland set all last summer whenever I went jogging on the beach. It was awesome."

His lips curved briefly. "Thanks." He gestured toward the hidden viewing window. "You heard that kid downstairs. The one doing the opening set. What do you think?"

She considered the question for moment. "Not bad. He's high energy, and he's got them dancing, but there's room for the sound to grow when the headliner comes on. The crowd will be primed for the peak set. It's good work. Disciplined. He's got brains."

He nodded. "My conclusion exactly. He's playing his cards well."

"You're giving him his first break?"

"Yeah. I like to giving space to new talent," he said. "Let them struggle and sweat now. It's their turn. I've already paid my dues."

"That's good of you," she said.

"Good business. An investment in the future."

"Of course. Excuse me for implying that you have a heart."

He rolled his eyes with a noncommittal grunt and declined to answer that.

Fiona ran her finger up the gleaming length of a fountain pen that adorned his desk. "Pretty," she said. "Very fancy. Solid gold, I assume."

"Of course."

"Ever written anything with this? A love note, a contract?"

"No."

"Just for show, then." Her eyes landed on a bronze statue in the corner, lit with its own dedicated beam of carefully angled light. Some tormented looking nude. "That, too, I expect. Looks expensive."

"It was," he agreed.

"So you're into art appreciation? Classy. Goes with your image."

A perplexed line appeared between his dark brows. "Which is what?"

"Inscrutable bad boy genius. Pop stars and Hollywood

A-list actresses love to fling themselves against you and smash themselves to pieces."

"I'm an artist, businessman and producer," he growled. "The rumors are bullshit."

"Hmm. Remember all of Jeremiah's sermons? His favorite theme? Vanity, vanity, all is vanity. Then I read in GQ about your fleet of luxury cars—"

"It's not a fleet. You actually believe that gossipy shit?"

Hmmm, she'd scored one. Gotten under his skin. "Where there's smoke…"

"There's always smoke," he said. "All those people do is blow smoke. Stop sniping at me and make your point, Fi."

She would if she could, but she was still working up to it. Next to the fountain pen there was a perfect, palm-sized pink rock with veins of green, tumbled to a smooth matte sheen. She hefted it. It felt good in her hand. "What's this? Kryptonite?"

"Just a river rock. It's from Garrett Creek, right below the upper falls."

She froze for a moment, then set the rock down carefully. "Why do you keep that?"

He lifted his shoulders. "To remember where I came from."

"Really? You need a reminder?"

"Not really. But it serves a dual purpose. I could cave in somebody's head with it if I needed to."

"Ah. Now you're talking my language." She looked around at every detail of the luxurious room. "Fancy art. Gold pens, fancy lighting, sleek black leather…what does this man cave represent? You're too young for a mid-life crisis. Not thirty-three yet, right?"

"In a few months. Mid-life crises are for people who

spend their whole lives not getting what they want. Then they wake up to it, and they panic. Not me. I take exactly what I want, whenever I want it. There's no delay of gratification. No panic buildup."

"Wow," she murmured, impressed. "Sweet."

A lazy smile curved his lips. "If you say so."

"But you're rebelling," she told him. "Jeremiah hated, oh, let's count the line items. Ostentatious wealth, loud music, alcohol, drugs, dancing, sexy outfits, frivolous use of vital resources such as energy. Tattoos. Even that designer jacket. What is that, Armani? You would have caught a thundering load of scorn from him. I can already hear the rant about the decline of modern manhood into decadent irrelevance."

"It's Armani. Good eye. Glad you like it. Good thing he's dead. We don't have to listen."

"Damn right," she said.

There was a brief, charged silence before he spoke again. "How about you?"

Fiona looked at him blankly. "What about me?"

"Do you get what you want, Fi? Do you even know what you want?"

She bristled. "What the hell kind of question is that?"

He took so long to reply, she started to fidget. "I haven't seen you since you were a teenager," he said finally. "Then, out of nowhere, you show up wearing a cock-teasing costume that makes you nervous as a cat in a bathtub. You're all up in my face. Something is bugging you. Which doesn't surprise me. Anyone who survived GodsAcre is fucked up by definition. But you're not here for your health, Fi. You're not here for fun. What do you want from me?"

So much for the smooth-lead-in. Fiona clutched the edge of the desk, trying to remember her carefully scripted speech. Gone from her head, poof.

"This is going to sound crazy," she said.

"I'm fine with crazy," Anton said. "Lived around it all my life. Out with it."

"OK." She cleared her throat. "It's about Redd Kimball."

Anton's eyes narrowed. "What about him? The bastard is dead. And I'm glad."

"Well, that's the thing," she said. "He didn't die in the GodsAcre fire. He's still out there. And now he's trying to kill me."

<hr />

Available for preorder now!
https://shannonmckenna.com/books/hellbent/

The saga of the Trask Brothers continues in Heedless, The Hellbound Brotherhood Book Four, coming soon!

Turn the page for a peek...

HEEDLESS
THE HELLBOUND BROTHERHOOD
BOOK FOUR

Whatever it takes to protect her...

Security expert **Nate Murphy** came to Shaw's Crossing to kick ass. He has his hands full helping the Trask brothers with their murderous enemies, but he's knocked off his feet by the elusive Elisa, the mysterious woman who works in Demi's restaurant. She's way out of his league, and he can tell she's holding something back...something big. Nate's an ex-soldier and ex-bouncer whose specialty is breaking heads...but the fear in Elisa's eyes makes him want to crush whoever put it there. If only she would tell him the truth...

Secrets and lies...

Elisa Rinaldi is hiding from a killer. Her ex-fiancé Gil is a dangerous sociopath, but she can't prove it. Hiding in the small town of Shaw's Crossing had seemed like a good idea at the time, but getting attached to the people there was not, much less to Nate Murphy, the hard-eyed, hard-bodied security expert. Then violence engulfs her new friends, and the press is everywhere. If facial recog flags her, Gil will find her and kill her. She has to leave Shaw's Crossing—after a parting gift to herself. One night with Nate. Then she'd do the right thing…even if it breaks her.

Nate can hardly believe his luck when Elisa leads him up to her little apartment. The night that follows leaves him gasping for breath. Then she vanishes—but Nate can't rest until he finds her and claims her for his own.

Elisa will risk everything to get her life back and be with the man she loves. But her mortal enemy is playing a game of cat and mouse

And now the stakes are both their lives…

Available soon!
https://shannonmckenna.com/books/heedless/

DID YOU MISS Demi and Eric's earlier story, in Hellion, The Hellbound Brotherhood Book One? Check out the scorching tale of how Eric and Demi's romance began…
Available now!
https://shannonmckenna.com/books/hellion/

HELLION

THE HELLBOUND BROTHERHOOD

BOOK ONE

He's a ticking bomb...

Eric Trask is counting the days before he blasts out of Shaw's Crossing forever. He and his brothers were raised at GodsAcre, a mysterious doomsday cult deep in the mountains, and are the only survivors of the deadly fire that destroyed it. The townspeople see them as time bombs just waiting to blow, but Eric's going to prove those bastards wrong. He's an ex-Marine, fresh off a tour in Afghanistan, working three jobs and barely sleeping. Utterly unprepared for Demi Vaughan's dazzling green eyes, lush pink lips and sexy curves. She's the town princess...he's a dangerous outcast. It was a sure recipe for disaster.

But the closer he gets to Demi, the more impossible it is to resist...

Forbidden fruit is the sweetest...

Demi Vaughan has big plans for life post- college, and Eric Trask, notorious bad boy with a complicated past, is not part of them. So when he saunters into the sandwich shop where she works she tells herself he's just tall, ripped, smoldering eye candy, nothing more. Eric was damaged. Marked by violence and tragedy. He'd be the ultimate bad boyfriend, and right now she was too busy even to shop for a good one. But his hot eyes and hard body, his sensual smile and that rough, sexy voice of his shook her resolve. After all, she was leaving this place forever. A little taste of heaven...what could it hurt?

But Shaw's Crossing has deeper, darker secrets than Eric or Demi could guess. The evil that destroyed GodsAcre is lying in wait...**and it will stop at nothing to keep Eric and Demi apart...**

Available now!
https://shannonmckenna.com/books/hellion/

If you are enjoying The Hellbound Brotherhood, you should check out Right Through Me, Book One of The Obsidian Files! Available now!

Turn the page for a tantalizing peek...

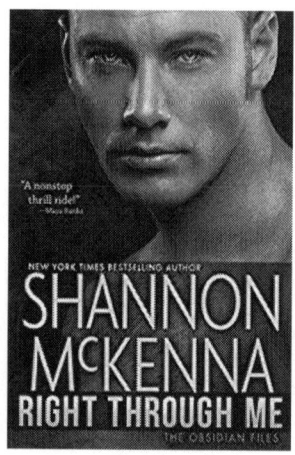

RIGHT THROUGH ME
THE OBSIDIAN FILES

Stranger, speak softly...

Biotech tycoon Noah Gallagher has a deadly secret: his clandestine training as a super-soldier gives him abilities that go far beyond human. Yet he's very much a man. When Caro Bishop shows up at his Seattle headquarters with a dangerous secret agenda, his ordered life is thrown into chaos. Caro is a woman like no other—and her luminously sensual beauty cloaks a mystery he must solve.

Caro's lying low, evading a false charge of murder. She means to clear her name, and she'll do whatever it takes to survive—but seducing a man like Noah is more than she bargained for. His amber eyes have the strangest glow when he looks at her—she could swear he sees the secrets of her heart. The desire smoldering in Noah's eyes awakens her own secret hunger, but Caro has to resist his magnetic pull. Anyone close to her becomes a target. The only right thing to do is run, far and fast, but Caro can't outrun Noah's ferocious intensity — or deny the searing passion that explodes between them.

Nothing else matters — until a vicious enemy bent on the ultimate revenge puts his murderous plan into play. Noah and Caro must battle for their lives...and their love...

Turn the page for a taste of Right Through Me...

RIGHT THROUGH ME

1

Someone just cut the lights. What the hell?

Noah Gallagher put down his pen and looked around, startled, as drums began to thump from the hidden sound system of the penthouse conference room. Some exotic instrument joined in, throbbing and wailing.

The door to the conference room opened to a shimmery jingling sound, then a flash of fluttering purple. Everyone at the table was staring and murmuring.

Oh, Christ. Not possible. Noah rose to his feet, but the belly dancer was already halfway through the door, her hands weaving in a hypnotic pattern. Wide, light-catching green eyes laughed at him brazenly as she shimmied straight toward him, leading with one pulsing hip.

Her eyes caught him . . . and held him.

The world narrowed down. Whatever he was going to say or do stopped. Words were gone. Air was gone. Air didn't matter. Nothing moved while she moved.

She had commandeered all movement. With that smile.

Those eyes.

He was sitting again, with no memory of deciding to do so. His mind had gone blank. The woman was like a walking, breathing stun code, personally keyed to him. He'd always wondered how it would feel to be one of the unlucky chosen few at Midlands who'd gotten stun and kill codes embedded in their minds. His own brain implants had been bad enough. Stun and kill codes were worse.

But this dancer wasn't a goddamn stun code. She was just a random woman, shaking her stuff. When her act was done, he'd pull it together. Exert the fucking authority he was entitled to as the CEO of Angel Enterprises.

He had exactly until the music stopped to get control of himself.

Simple enough to figure out who'd dreamed up this unwanted birthday present. His younger sister Hannah lurked by the door. The wide-angle enhancement of his sight made it possible to see the gleam in Hannah's eyes without looking away from the belly dancer for a single second.

Not that he could have looked away.

He saw his fiancée Simone's face with his peripheral vision. She'd chosen to sit at his side for this important meeting. It was painfully obvious from her tight, expectant smile that she was waiting for him to turn to her, to smile and laugh and make light of this stupid situation. Not just for her. For everyone in the room.

He couldn't do it.

Try. Do an analog dive. Grab a hook. Concentrate.

A spotlight from somewhere gilded the dancer's body, highlighting every perfect detail. Silver anklets that jingled over her small, bare feet. Golden toenails. Shapely legs flashed between purple veils that floated from a low-slung, glittering belt. The belt and top were swagged with shining chains and dangling beadwork. Still more chains, draped from an ornate headdress, dangled over her forehead and under her chin, creating a constant soft shimmer of sound.

High, full breasts quivered, lovingly presented in the spangle-studded velvet bra. She arched back, floating a purple veil edged with spangles high in the air above herself and swishing her thick fall of of glossy black hair around. Had to be fake hair, falling to well below her ass. It brushed the curve of her hips. Fanned out as she twirled.

Everything he'd monitored in his peripheral vision was gone now. He no longer saw Hannah, or Simone, or anything else. His inner vision was too busy with the vivid fantasy of that woman straddling him. Imagining her bold, sensual smile as she swayed over him, teased him. Running her fingers through her hair, lifting it, tossing it. Coiling it around her waist like a slave rope.

He wanted to rip away all the filmy veils and all the goddamn beads and chains. See her bare-assed. Bare-breasted. Yeah.

The deep curve of her waist was perfectly shaped for his fingers to grip. The curves and hollows of her belly and her hips looked so soft. Touchable.

His hands shook with the urge to reach, stroke. Seize.

The rush of erotic images ramped up his advanced visual processor into screaming overdrive. Even with eyes shielded from eighty percent of the ambient light, even using a double layer of custom-designed shield specs, his AVP combat program was off and running, scrolling a thick column of data analysis past his inner eye.

And even that couldn't distract him from her show. Not for one instant.

His heightened senses reached out, so greedy for more that he found himself actually taking off the back-up shield specs. He'd have popped out the contacts, too, but his AVP was already going nuts at the lower protection level. Combine that with adrenaline, and a huge blast of sexual arousal—*fuck*.

The light level in this room could zap him into a stress flashback if he didn't protect his eyes. Not only that. The dark shield strength contact lenses hid the animal flash of amber luminosity caused by his visual implants. Outsiders couldn't be allowed to see that. The room was packed with outsiders. He wanted them gone.

Especially Simone. Which made him a total asshole. He tried hard, really hard, to feel guilty. Not so much as a twinge. His conscious mind had been almost totally hijacked by the dancer.

He wanted to throw everyone else out and lock the door. Study that woman with his naked eyes, dancing under the spotlight. But only for him. He wanted to gulp in the whole data flow. It was being filtered out in real time and lost to him forever, and it drove him . . . fucking . . . *nuts*.

And he couldn't do a thing. Not with an audience. His fists clenched in fury.

Heart racing, temperature spiking. Sweating profusely. No way to hide it. It was an AVP stress dump. A massive dose of fight-and-conquer energy, channeling straight into his dick, which strained desperately against his pants.

He struggled to grab onto the analog hooks that he'd established. His hooks were emergency mental shortcuts, activating an instant, deep withdrawal into the ice caves of his subconscious mind when the AVP got out of control. Best way he could devise to calm his stress reactions and stay on top of himself.

Not a hook to be had. Couldn't find them, couldn't feel them. Couldn't use his highly developed power of visualization at all, after years of grueling practice. All gone.

He was fully occupied imagining that woman naked and writhing beneath him.

His intense reaction to this spectacle made no sense. He'd seen belly dancing before and been unmoved. He did not have complicated fantasies or fetishes. He didn't even get the fun factor. He wasn't known for his sense of humor. In fact, he had no imagination at all, unless you counted biotech engineering designs, or plotting ways to grow his business, or scheming to keep his chosen family alive, secret, and safe.

That demanding enterprise left no bandwidth for fun and games.

He wasn't playful about sex, either. He was tireless, focused. Relentless in making sure that his partners were satisfied. To the point of exhaustion, even. Theirs, not his. They would tell him he was the hottest lover ever and then call him cold.

So? Noah didn't do emotions. Cold was safer for everyone concerned.

Not that he could explain that to whoever happened to be in bed with him.

He couldn't change his nature. He saw to it that his lovers had many orgasms to his one, to compensate for those mysterious intangibles. Whatever the fuck else they wanted from him, it just wasn't there. He didn't even know where to look for it.

The dancer's arms lifted, swayed. He inhaled the scent of her dewy skin as she spun closer. Fresh, sweet, hot. Sun on the flowers. Rain on the grass. His mouth watered.

Since what happened at Midlands, his senses were

sharper than normal by many orders of magnitude. He had ways to blunt the overload, but not this time. He was catching a full data load now, shields and all. Tripping out on her undulating hand movements.

He was reading her energy signature, right through the shield lenses. A cloud of hot, brilliant colors surrounded her. Her floating purple veils blended with trailing clouds of her body's energy, to which his AVP overstimulated brain assigned all the colors of the spectrum and more besides. Colors not visible to anyone but him.

Along with it a strange sensation was growing. Tension, anticipation. Dread.

He was used to being alone in an insulated bubble. Other people's drama raged outside that protective barrier and left him completely untouched. He needed it that way to stay in control. Maintaining isolation required constant effort and vigilance.

Now, suddenly, he wasn't alone. The girl had danced through his force field. Invaded his inner space. It was messy and crowded in there now.

She took up room. Confused him with her colors, her scents. Her smile was so unforced and sensual. She was bonelessly flexible, yet still regal in her diaphanous veils.

It made him jittery to have someone so close. The intimacy felt awkward. Ticklish.

He felt hot, red. No control over his face. Stuck here, sitting among colleagues and family, right next to his fiancée. Any one of them could watch him watch her. At least the massive conference table concealed his colossal hard-on.

He had not felt this helpless since Midlands.

Her luminous green eyes met his and then flicked away, but the electric buzz of that split instant of intimacy jolted him to depths he'd never felt before.

He knew he'd never seen this woman before, and yet he recognized her.

Caro narrowly missed slamming her hip into the table. For the third time.

Look away from the guy, for God's sake. Get a grip. It's just a dance.

But her gaze kept getting sucked back to Noah Gallagher, the birthday boy. Ultra-powerful CEO of the oh-so-mysterious Angel Enterprises, cutting-edge biotech firm.

The man was gorgeous. Barrel chested. A dense slab of muscle. Short hair showed off the sharp planes and angles of his face, a wide, strong jaw. He wore shaded glasses, but he'd taken them off a few seconds into her dance. It was incredibly hard to stay focused on the music and remember her moves while being examined with such blazing intensity. It wiped her mind blank. Made her lose the thread.

To say nothing of her physical balance.

Holy flipping *wow*. They said he was turning thirty-two today, but he seemed older, or maybe it was just his expression. Each time she twirled, she snagged a new yummy detail. The shape of his ears. Thick, straight dark brows. Sexy grooves framing a stern but still sensual mouth. Sharp cheekbones. His face was a taut mask of tension, as if he were suppressing strong emotion. But it was his eyes that really got to her.

His scorching laser focus made her temperature rise. She'd always been sensitive to the quality of a person's energy. Noah Gallagher's energy dominated the room. He looked like he'd tear you to pieces if you gave him any trouble, despite the elegant suit that sat just right on his huge shoulders. He didn't laugh or look embarrassed like most men did when surprised by a belly dancer. He just sat there, with the charged stillness of a predator poised to spring. Radiating danger.

Her smile faltered as she shimmied and spun. Suddenly, she was hyper-conscious of the erotic allure of the dance. His silent, very male sexual energy made it feel deadly serious. As if they were alone, and she'd been summoned for a private, uninhibited performance designed to drive him crazy.

Oh my. What a stimulating scenario.

She was actually getting aroused. For the love of God. Rising panic began to shred the sensation. Enough of this ridiculous crap. She had to get out of here, and fast.

Finish the dance. You need the cash. He's only a hot guy, not a celestial being. You're freaking yourself out. Chill. Usually she spread the wealth, bestowing flirtatious smiles on everyone. Not tonight. They weren't feeling it. Young men were usually always enthusiastic, and there were several of them here, but no one made a sound. Tension was thick in the air. No laughter, no snickering, no whistles.

Who cared. Her mind was fully occupied with the task of not gaping at Noah Gallagher's godlike hotness. Being aware of every inch of skin she displayed to him.

Her gaze bounced across the blond woman who sat next to him. A little younger, but not a colleague or an assistant. They sat too close together for that. The woman's mouth looked tight and miserable. Next to her sat a flushed, heavy older man who stared fixedly at Caro's beaded bra, nostrils flared.

Rise up, cupcake. Take back the power. This was a tough crowd, maybe, but everything was relative. The people in this room weren't trying to frame her for murder, kidnap her or kill her. And she certainly had the birthday boy's full attention.

So she'd play with it. What the fucking hell. That man needed to be humbled. To worship at the feet of her divine awesomeness. She'd dance like she'd never danced before, blow his mind, and melt away, forever nameless. Leaving him to ache and writhe.

That's right, big boy. Prepare to suffer.

But Noah Gallagher's fierce, unwavering gaze was having a strange effect on her. Ever since she'd gone into hiding, she'd had a sick, heavy lump in her belly. For months it had been sitting there, like a chunk of dirty ice that would not melt. But when she looked at him, that pinched coldness eased. It turned soft and warm and alive.

It felt amazingly good. Dancing for him, she could actually breathe again.

For as long it lasted.

The dance was ending. Caro sank to her knees, arching back in a pose of abandoned sensual ecstasy as the music reached its climax, luxurious fake hair brushing the ground in her grand finale. Dancing had never made her feel so naked before. She was stretched before him like a sacrificial virgin on an altar.

Take me.

The pose felt obscene, but only because there were other people in the room. If there hadn't been, it would have felt right. It would have felt . . . *hot.*

The sound of one person frantically clapping broke the silence. Hannah Gallagher, the girl who had hired her. Noah Gallagher's younger sister, from the looks of her. Caro rose slowly to her feet. Noah Gallagher didn't applaud. He just stared at her, as if he wanted to leap over that table and pin her down.

Tension built like an electrical charge. The other people in the room looked up, down, anywhere but at her. Caro smiled brightly. Held her head as high as possible.

Not fair, to throw a paid performer into the middle of someone else's big fat faux pas and make her swim in it. Bastards.

"That was fabulous!" Hannah's voice was a little too high. "Thanks for a gorgeous dance, Shamira! Happy birthday, Noah! Wasn't she awesome, everyone?"

Not one yes. There was only dead silence, downcast eyes, awkward looks exchanged all around. And still, Noah Gallagher's devouring eyes.

So what. She'd stay dignified. While running for her life, fighting the powers of darkness, scrambling for money. Even if it involved putting on a scanty costume and shaking her booty for rude or indifferent strangers.

Or, in this case, one single intense, lustful, smoldering stranger.

She took a slow, deliberate bow, as if she were in front of an adoring crowd. Taking her own sweet time. Rubbing their faces in it.

Take that, you rude shitheads. Like it would kill you to clap.

She didn't need any validation from these self-important bio-tech-nerd idiots. Just her fee, which she would get whether they liked her performance or not.

Fuck 'em. She had things to do. Important things. After one more hungry peek at the mouthwatering godking. Lord, he was fine.

She flash-memorized him in one breathless instant, whipping her gaze away from his face before eye contact could start the inevitable sexual mind-melt reaction. Then she swept out of the room, chin up, shoulders back. A regal sweep of purple veils.

That was it. She would never see him again. She wasn't going to feel that hot rush of opening in her chest, ever again.

Suck it up. Ignore the lust buzz. Sport sex is reserved for normal people. Fugitives do without. And don't whine.

Hannah followed her out of the room, and slammed the door harder than was necessary. "You were gorgeous," she said fervently. "You're so talented. I'm so sorry they didn't clap or anything. I'm going to tell them all off. Noah will kill me, but I'm used to it."

"I'll rather not watch that," Caro said hastily. "I'll just be on my way."

"Oh no! Stay just a minute! You have to at least say hi to Noah. No matter what he says to me, he certainly enjoyed your dance. I'm the villain here. You're just an innocent bystander. Noah's very fair that way. And I'm sure he'll want to meet you!"

In your dreams, honey. "Let me, ah, change first," Caro said, backing away.

"You remember the way to the office? Come back after. I'll introduce you."

The door flew open. A man strode out, not the birthday boy. This one was tall, blue eyed and very built, his thick dark blond hair hanging down to his shoulders. His eyes flicked over her with controlled curiosity and then turned back to Hannah.

"What the *hell* were you thinking?" he asked.

Definitely her cue. Caro took off, hurrying back toward the nondescript office that'd served as a dressing room. She didn't even want to know what Hannah's answer might be.

Not her family, not her fight.

Once inside the empty office, she could still hear them arguing from behind the door. Other people had gotten into the mix. Voices were being raised. Her heart pounded as she peeled off her costume and packed it up. She pulled on her shapeless street clothing, trying not to overhear. She had her own problems. Big nasty ones. Time to cruise discreetly away and let them get on with theirs.

Makeup pads got most of the paint off. She rolled the expensive dancing wig into its carrying bag, and put on her street wig, a thick brown bob with heavy bangs and wisps curling in around her face to conceal its shape. When she arrived, she hadn't worn the mouth prosthesis, which puffed out her cheeks and distorted her jawline. She'd figured that the coat and hat were enough weirdness for the client to swallow. But the job was done, and she hoped to God she could slink out unnoticed, so in went the mouth thing. Big tinted glasses finished the look, topped off by her hat with LED lights in the brim, ordered off the Internet to foil facial recognition software her pursuers might use to find her on social media.

Who knew if it really worked. At least the wide brim kept the Seattle drizzle off.

Her hands still shook as she pulled on her oversized black wool coat. The foam lining she'd sewn in bulked up her shoulders and hips. She looked sixty pounds heavier, and slightly humped.

At first, she'd tried changing the way she moved as part of her disguise, but after all the bodywork she'd done in college, she decided that the psychological toll of slumping and shuffling was dangerous to her soul. Inside her frumpy cocoon of foam and wool, she still had her pride and attitude.

Hidden, maybe, but structurally intact.

When she exited the office, she looked like a sketch that had been blurred on purpose. Noah Gallagher would stare right through her even if she were inches away.

That thought was so depressing, she could barely stand to think it.

Chin up. She'd had her fun, turning him on. Time for the disappearing act. Eat your heart out, Laser Eyes.

But disappearing didn't feel powerful to her. It just felt flat. Empty and sad.

The route back to the elevators took her right past the conference room.

Hannah Gallagher and several others were still arguing outside it. If she kept her head down, turned the corner and cut swiftly across the open space, she'd only be in their line of vision for a few seconds. Then it was a straight shot to the elevator.

One, two . . . *go.*

When she was squarely in the danger spot, Noah Gallagher came out the door.

That was her undoing. She slowed down. Not consciously, but simply unable to resist the temptation to steal one last look at him before fleeing.

His gaze snapped onto her, like a powerful magnet coupling.

Oh, God. Oh, no. He strode through the center of the group, scattering them, and followed her. Even with her back to him, his eyes burned through her layered, ugly disguise, a focused point of heat against her concealed skin. She stabbed the elevator button. He was twenty yards away. Fifteen, and closing. Picking up speed.

He couldn't have recognized her. In this dreary get-up,

she couldn't be more different from Shamira the sexy dancing girl. She barely recognized herself dressed like this. The door slid open. She lunged inside. No other riders, thank God.

"Hold the door!" Gallagher called, loping for the elevator.

Asfuckingif. She punched the close button, and the mechanism engaged.

Their eyes locked, as the doors shut in his face.

Her heart was thudding, as if she'd done something wrong and had almost gotten caught. Maybe he was just wondering who the scruffy stranger was. Dressed like that, she stuck out like a sore thumb in the muted corporate elegance of Angel Enterprises.

She hurried through the lavish front lobby. Outside, a cab was letting a passenger out. She bolted for it, waving it down.

Noah Gallagher emerged from the entrance just as her cab pulled away. His eyes locked onto hers again instantly. Even shadowed by the hat, obscured by the dark glasses, through the back window of a cab that was already a half a block away.

He started running after her. Right out onto the street. Eyes still locked. The contact felt like a wire, pulling tighter and tighter. Then the taxi turned a corner and he was lost to sight. It hurt. As if something vital had been snipped with bolt-cutters.

Her fizz of excitement died away. The cold lump of fear was back in place.

She was so sick of feeling this way. She wanted to yell at the driver to circle the block, just on the off chance of catching one last glimpse of Noah Gallagher. To feel something different than that cold, heavy ache in her core. Just for a second or two.

But she could not have this. Not even a stolen taste of it. She could not let lust trash her good judgment. She had to stay murderously sharp. Constantly on the defensive. Without rest.

Sexual frustration wouldn't kill her.

But there were other things out there that definitely could.

Available now!
https://shannonmckenna.com/books/right-through-me/

Join Shannon's newsletter mailing list to never miss a new book or a fabulous promo, and look for your free gift book when you join!

http://shannonmckenna.com/connect.php.

Follow her on Bookbub to receive new release and discount alerts!

https://www.bookbub.com/authors/shannon-mckenna

ABOUT THE AUTHOR

Shannon McKenna is the NYT and USA TODAY bestselling author of over twenty action packed, turbocharged romantic thrillers, among them the wildly popular McCloud Brothers & Friends Series, along with two new scorching romantic suspense series, The Hellbound Brotherhood and The Obsidian Files. She loves tough and heroic alpha males, heroines with the brains and guts to match them, terrifying villains who challenge them to their utmost, adventure, blazing sensuality, and most of all, the redemptive power of true love. Since she was small she has loved abandoning herself to the magic of a good book, and her fond childhood fantasy was that writing would be just like that but with the added benefit of being able to take credit for the story at the end. The alchemy of writing turned out to be messier than she'd ever dreamed, but what the hell, she loves it anyway and hopes that readers enjoy the results of her experiments. She loves to hear from her readers. Contact her at her website, http://shannonmckenna.com, find her on Facebook at https://www.facebook.com/AuthorShannonMckenna/ to keep up with all her news! Follow her on Bookbub to get new release and discount alerts!

https://www.bookbub.com/authors/shannon-mckenna

If you'd like to know when the new installments of The Hellbound Brotherhood will come out, and hear about my new releases and promos, join my newsletter at http://shannonmckenna.com/connect.php.

I'll give you an Obsidian Files novel as a welcome gift! See you on the other side!

Made in the USA
Middletown, DE
15 March 2020